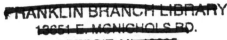
FOUR SHADOUGH

P U B L I S H I N G

PRESENTS:
A BROOKLYN STORY

This Game
Has
No Loyalty IV

NO More Games

by:

JUNE

JUL 2017

FR

No More Games

Editor: FourShadough Publishing Editing Services

Printed in the United States of America

First Edition

ISBN#:   13-digit: 978-1-4961-5424-8
          10-digit: 1-4961-5424-x

Published by: FourShadough Publishing, LLC

FOUR  SHADOUGH
PUBLISHING

This Game
Has
No Loyalty IV

NO More Games

by:
JUNE

Acknowledgments

There are so many people I want to acknowledge and I'm sure they know who they are even if their name isn't mentioned. This project was in the making years ago but I wanted to wait before releasing it, writing other stories so I was sure that being an author was really my calling. I have written a total of ten books and have a bunch to go but what keeps me writing is my fans, supporters, friends, family and well wishers. So I'm going to thank some of you guys since it's you who have been an integral part of my writing journey.

Stacey Nelson from the BX, Shawanda Hamilton, LaTonya Garrett (Thickness), Sandy Peoples, Janelle LaBorde, Tiffany Smith, you guys were the first to support this project and helped promote so thank you for believing in my work for your support.

I want to thank all the Angels in my book club, June's Book Haven. We are a small club but we family. Shout out to Jewel - Jew...els Horace my staunchest supporter, Colisa Songbird Garrett, Gwennie MzCreative Williams, Kitty Galore - meow, Mary Denise Allen-Gibbs, my girl Jessyca Patryce, Sandy Peoples, Mariell Edwards, our new Angel Kenya Guy, Athena and the rest of the angels, thank you guy for your undying support and for believing in my writing skills.

Shout out to OBIBB Book Club, My Urban Book Club and all the Facebook book clubs I post in on a daily basis.

I want to give a special shout out to the Book Club that I truly love and respect - Not Just Books. I want to thank each member for taking a chance with my first book and given me the opportunity to tell you guys my story. I have a new family in

you guys and I cherish that sincerely. Charaine, Mom, Brenda, Jeff and the rest of you guys are my family...love you guys.
I want to thank all my family and close friends, you know who you are. Without your support I don't think I could have written so many books lol!

My children Sha-Juan Harmony Miller, Shaaid Miller, Shadiya Miller and Shamel Miller, you are the reason for FourShadough Publishing. Special Shout to Harmony Miller who just penned her first story under FourShadough - she writes for the company she owns!

I want to thank God because without him none of this would be possible.

No More Games

Chapter 1

The low humming noise coming from the fluorescent lights hanging above the four people sounded like a revving motorbike in the ominously quiet barbershop that minutes ago erupted in earsplitting gunfire.

After the gunshots stopped and the smoke cleared, lying on the floor were two bodies both being cradled in the laps of two women who were quietly whimpering while rocking back and forth with streams of tears raining from their eyes. They were enemies but their immediate focus was the welfare of the two men who lay still in their lap suffering from gunshot wounds.

The door of the barbershop flung open and the usually quiet ding sounded like clashing cymbals as Junior's cousin Bo ran inside with his eyes wide gripping a black magnum. He stopped and looked down at the brick red blood that pooled where his cousin lay in Muffin's lap. He scowled then quickly turned his attention to Gloria who instantly screamed when she saw him pointing his gun in her direction.

"NO! NO! Please don't!" She cried out ducking her head down while still holding KB's head in her lap.

"Shoot that bitch Bo!" Muffin screamed. "Kill her!"

"God no! Please don't kill me…"

Sirens could be heard in the distance and Bo looked back to Junior laying on the ground then back at KB.

"Kill her Bo! Fuck you waiting on! Go 'head and body that bitch! Let them both die together!" She gazed down at Junior sorrowfully. "Look what he did to my baaaaby!" Muffin wailed as the pain she felt oozed out in each syllable.

"I know. I see him but the law on they way here." The noise from the sirens were getting louder and Bo's attention was drawn to the guns on the floor. "I gotta to get them guns outta here first!"

The .357 Junior dropped and KB's nine millimeter automatic were picked up from where they were laying then Bo walked over to Muffin.

"Listen here. I'm gonna get rid of these then I'll meet you up at the hospital. Just be sure not to say anything to the law about what happened in here." Bo turned and stared at Gloria menacingly, pointing the huge magnum in her direction. "That goes for you too bitch! Down here we handles our own so keep your fuckin' mouth shut or I'm gonna shut it permanently!"

Gloria stared at Bo and saw fire dancing in his pupils then slowly nodded her head in agreement.

Bo turned and left the barbershop then glanced over his shoulder. "You don't know what happened. You hear me! That's what you tell the law!" His statement was directed to Gloria.

A crowd had grown outside the barbershop after the shootout but no one ventured inside they just watched from the street. Minutes later an ambulance pulled up in front of the barbershop. Two paramedics quickly ran inside and upon seeing the two bleeding men lying in the laps of the women, they immediately radioed for another ambulance.

"Please help him!" Muffin cried out when they entered.

"Help me, please!" Gloria pleaded too.

"Has he been shot?" The paramedic asked Muffin smelling the strong smell of cordite in the air.

"Yes! Help him!"

The paramedic immediately ripped open Junior's shirt and cut his pants leg then began to administer medical attention while his partner went over to KB to inspect his wounds. While the paramedics worked on the fallen men two police detectives walked into the barbershop. One of the detectives, a stout double chinned Caucasian man wearing a tight blazer with an

equally tight shirt and tie that had the fat around his neck swallowing his collar, approached Muffin with a cup in his hand.

"'Scuse me ma'am. Can you tell me what happened in here?"

Muffin looked at him and squinted her eyes. "I don't know."

He cocked his head to the side and mumbled then spit something dark into his cup; it was so disgusting.

He walked over to where Junior was being worked on then knelt down and inspected his wound.

"Gunshot huh?" He asked the paramedic.

"Yes sir." The EMT replied as he focused on stopping the bleeding.

"Hmmm." He rose to his feet then walked over to where KB was being worked on.

His partner, a tall thin Caucasian man wearing Oakley sport shades with sandy brown hair and a sun burnt face was talking with the other paramedic about KB's wounds.

"Gun shot wound too?" The stout detective asked his partner.

"Yep. Shoulder wound, doesn't look too serious." He guessed.

The stout detective looked at Gloria. "You know what happened in here?"

Muffin looked at Gloria when she heard the detective ask the question and her eyes lowered into slits and her lips got tight.

"Yea, he was shot."

"By whom?"

Muffin stared daggers at Gloria as two more paramedics entered the barbershop.

Gloria matched Muffin's stare and pursed her lips. "Junior. Junior the one that shot him!" She said defiantly.

"Who is Junior?" The stout detective asked as he pulled out a pad and scribbled the name down.

The other paramedics rushed in to assist in transporting both men to the hospital, interrupting Gloria before she could answer the detective's question.

"I know you're concerned about your friend here so I'll come down to the hospital to finish getting your statement once he's gotten the medical attention he needs." The stout detective told Gloria as the paramedics carefully hoisted KB onto the gurney.

"Let's secure this crime scene and see if we can gather some evidence in here." The sun burnt detective said to his partner.

Muffin was already outside standing by the ambulance waiting for Junior to be put into the back when she saw Gloria come out following the paramedics wheeling KB to the other ambulance.

"You a real stupid bitch! You don't believe shit huh!" She started walking up to her.

"Fuck you! Suck my pussy you dirty bitch!" Gloria screamed back.

The sun burnt detective stepped out the barbershop and put a cigarette in his mouth and looked over in Muffin and Gloria's direction then lit it. Muffin backed up but her face and mouth was twisted in hatred.

"Ok bitch! Don't let your mouth write a check yo' ass can't cash! We gonna see if you keep runnin' yo' fuckin' mouth once I get my hands on that ass!"

"Whateva bitch! This my fuckin' mouth!"

Gloria stepped into the ambulance and the paramedic slammed the door. KB opened his eyes and moaned.

"Aaah!"

"Shh baby. Don't try to talk. We on our way to the hospital."

"Glo?" He mumbled. "This shit burning like a muhfucka, I'm in so much pain!"

"Hey there buddy." The paramedic looked down at him. "You've been shot in the shoulder but it looks like it went straight through. You're going to be all right. Just try to relax until we getcha to the hospital." He put an oxygen mask over KB's mouth and nose; KB's eyes closed slowly as he continued to moan.

Muffin held Junior's hand tightly in hers as the sirens in the ambulance screamed. She looked at the paramedic who was sitting on the opposite side of her preparing an IV.

"How bad is it? Is he gonna make it?"

"It's a gunshot wound, those are never good. I can't tell you anything right now because I'm not a doctor but I know he's been hit in a bad place and has lost a lot of blood."

Muffin breathed out and looked down at Junior and squeezed his hand tighter but there was no response from him. Her heart swelled as her eye sockets filled with tears.

"Can you hear me baby?" She leaned in and whispered in his ear. "I'm going to make sure both them fuckers pay for this shit, I promise you!"

Her eyebrows lowered and evil protruded from every orifice in her body and stunk up the interior of the ambulance as her mouth tightened and eyes twinkled sinisterly while she looked out the square back window of the ambulance thinking of a way to make both Gloria and KB pay for what happened to Junior.

Chapter 2

"The surgery was a success. He's very lucky, considering it was a groin wound. What made his injury so much more dangerous is the bullet severed an artery and he lost a significant amount of blood. He's weak so his recovery will not be quick but should be progressive." The doctor explained to Muffin.

"Groin, that's near his dick. Will he be able to walk?" Muffin's tactless description didn't throw the doctor off.

"Sure, he may have a limp but he should be fine after therapy."

"Thank you doctor. I was so worried."

"You're welcome. He's going to need a lot of bed rest right now, that will help with his recovery. No strenuous activities until he has fully healed."

"I got you doc. No fucking." Muffin continued in her tasteless use of descriptive words.

"Right." He responded then turned and left.

Muffin walked back into the room where Junior was resting. There were tubes coming out of his body attached to a machine that was beeping every couple of seconds. Although the doctor told her he was going to be all right, she couldn't help the rage she was feeling seeing him so helpless. She said a silent prayer as she stood over him. She wanted Gloria so bad she could taste her blood in her mouth and when she caught her she was going to beat her to within an inch of her life if she didn't kill her.

"How he doin'?"

Muffin turned around to see Bo entering the room.

"The doctor said he's gonna be fine." Muffin looked back at Junior. "But I'm scared because I never seen him like this before."

"Don't worry too much, he a bull. Did the police ask any questions?"

Muffin quickly ran and closed the door then turned to Bo. "That bitch told them Junior the one that shot her man!"

"She did what?" Bo's mouth was agape.

"She ain't even hesitate when they asked then talked shit to me right after like she ain't give a fuck. I was going to bust that bitch head to the white meat but that fucking D came outside. I was waiting for you to come so you could hold me down. I can't risk Junior going to jail behind this bitch running her mouth. You got any country bitches down with you that can send this bitch a message after I whip her ass then apply pressure on her to keep her mouth shut?"

Bo walked over to the window and looked down into the parking lot, he turned and stared at Junior laying in the bed then his eyes focused on Muffin.

"Yea, I know just what you need, don't worry." He nodded his head slowly.

"Ok cool. Come with me so you can watch my back while I check this hoe."

"Ok." His voice held an unsure tone.

Muffin heard his hesitation and stopped at the door and stared at him trying to gauge what he was feeling.

"How far you willing to go Bo?" She questioned. "I need to know you ain't gon' fold up on me 'cause you looking suspect right now!" Muffin was always wild but she had to step her game up now that her man was laying in a bed with a serious injury.

"I'll go as far as I have to for my cuz, believe that." He spoke with confidence.

"Just checkin', I gotta be sure, you feel me?" She pointed behind him. "I'll kill a muhfucka for that man laying in that bed."

"I know." Bo swallowed hard. "He said you a thoroughbred."

"And he ain't never lie. I need to take care of this now before them police come back here to listen to that bitch sing. I don't want her to have a voice when I'm done! Let's go!"

Bo followed behind her slowly, unsure of her plans when she got to the room. She was so erratic compared to how she was when he first met her and he wasn't used to her new attitude or aggressive behavior.

Gloria was sitting in a chair next to KB's bed when the door flew open and Muffin and Bo entered the room.

"Get the fuck outta here!" Gloria yelled when she saw Muffin.

"Shut the fucking door and lock it!" Muffin directed Bo as she ran to Gloria and grabbed her by her throat with so much force Gloria's eyes bulged.

Muffin used her free hand to smash Gloria in her left ear while she tried to steal her breath with her death grip.

"Mmph!" Gloria squealed as she pawed at Muffin's hands.

"You like talking huh bitch! Told you I was gonna get that fucking mouth." Her fist crashed into Gloria's lips, bursting the bottom one on impact. "Now I'ma choke the last breath outta your black ass so you'll never utter another muhfuckin' syallable again!"

Gloria surrendered to one knee as she began to feel lightheaded. Her eyes were blood shot red and were silently pleading with the devil in front of her to ease up on the pressure around her windpipe.

Bo went over to them then pried Muffin's hand from around Gloria's throat. Muffin looked at him and scowled then used the same hand to slap him viciously.

"Don't fuckin' touch me!" She was breathing like a charging rhino.

Bo backed up rubbing his cheek in shock as Muffin dived on top of Gloria and threw three stiff blows to her face then jumped to her feet. Gloria let out a scream but Muffin silenced her with a brutal stomp to her mid section, producing a deep groan out of Gloria's mouth.

Muffin turned to face Bo. "If you woulda bodied this bitch in the barbershop I wouldn't have to be going through none of this shit!" Her eyes were cold. "And don't ever touch me when I'm handling my business muhfucka!"

Bo was speechless, he didn't know what to say or how to respond to the crazed woman in front of him. His mind was telling him that she was only acting that way to scare Gloria because if she wasn't, there would be no way he would take that from her.

Muffin turned her attention back to Gloria as she gagged and held her neck while rolling around on the floor. Muffin walked over to KB's bed and looked at the machine monitoring him and grabbed the cord to try and disconnect it. Seeing that, Bo knew she was going too far. He ran over to her and grabbed her arm as she turned and swung on him again. He ducked the blow then pulled her to him tightly.

"Ay listen, you gon' get us sent to prison if you pull that plug out and he die gurl."

"I don't give a fuck. I shoulda killed his ass the first time!" Muffin's eyes were black and nothing but death permeated from them.

Gloria crawled towards KB's bed and was stomped in her back and her chin crashed against the tiled floor as Muffin spewed hate filled words. "You and your man betta not open y'all fuckin' mouths! You hear me bitch! Now you've been warned properly!" She turned and looked at Bo then back to Gloria. "You betta be glad this muhfucka was wit' me 'cause both y'all woulda checked out today!" Muffin turned to Bo with

death emitting from her pupils and he moved out of her way as she unlocked the door and disappeared into the hallway.

"I strongly advise you listen to what she said and keep your mouth shut to the law. That bitch dere is shell bell, I can see it in her eyes. Looks like she done had it wit' you and ain't playin' no more games." Bo eyed Gloria then turned and left the room.

***

"Damn Muffin, I didn't know you was gon' do all that." Bo said as he stepped in Junior's room.

"What you mean?" She replied rubbing the side of Junior's face with the back of her hand.

"The way you was beating on that gurl and shit, that was kinda crazy."

Muffin showcased a creepy half smile. "I ain't have no choice, I had to do that. That bullshit threat you threw out in the barbershop didn't scare the bitch. I don't know how they do shit down here but in Brooklyn, talk is cheap, action speaks louder than words! I bet that bitch won't say another muhfuckin' thing now. I just put the fear of God in her!"

"After all that shit you just did, I reckon she won't. I'ma put something else in play just to be sure 'cause I don't want my kinfolk locked away in prison either." Bo looked over at Junior. "I kinda feel responsible 'cause I'm the one that told him to come down here."

"Well don't. He got a shit load of other problems back home so he was lucky to have this place to come to until he can clear that shit up."

"What you talkin' 'bout?" Bo asked.

Muffin looked at him sideways. "He ain't tell you?"

"He ain't neva say he had any problems up top." Bo responded.

"Oh it ain't nothin' serious like that." Muffin wasn't about to tell him anything if he didn't already know.

"Oh ok. I'ma get goin' to handle some business. If you need me call down on the block. I'll be out there 'til late."

"Ok, I will. And by the way, I was serious 'bout what I said."

Bo turned to her before opening the door. "What?"

"Don't ever touch me when I'm handling my business." A flash of seriousness washed across her face.

"Yea, ok." He replied as he walked out the door shaking his head.

When Bo was gone, Muffin looked at Junior. "I don't know why you got him on your team 'cause he act like he scared to make shit pop on the spot. You really don't need nobody like that, all you need is me." She kissed him on his cheek and took a seat and laid her head back, staring up at the ceiling, deep in thought hoping what she did was enough to scare Gloria into not talking to the police.

***

A nurse walked into the room while Gloria was crying. "What's wrong sugah?"

Gloria wiped her tears quickly and responded weakly. "Nothing." She sniffled.

"Hmm. Don't seem like nothing by dem red eyes of yours." The nurse said as she prepared to change the IV bag KB was hooked up to.

"How much longer is he gonna be in here." Gloria asked.

"That depends." The nurse replied.

"Depends on what? Is something else wrong with him?" Her forehead wrinkled in worry.

The nurse turned and looked Gloria in her eyes. "That depends on you."

Gloria's eyebrows raised. "What you mean?"

"Look baby. This is a small town and word 'round hear travels really fast." Her hand rested on her hip as she spoke. "It's really in your best interest to watch what you say and who you say it to. You understand what I'm saying?"

"You wit' that dude that just came in here threatening me?"

"Baby, I just work here and I'm not down with anyone or anything. All I'm doing is giving advice. It's up to you to take it." She turned to finish hooking up the IV then turned her head and spoke over her back. "But like I said, it would be in your best interest to listen to what I'm saying and hush."

"Oh my God! I need to get him the fuck outta here! All y'all muhfuckas is together!" Gloria was in a panic.

"You need to calm down sweety. Ain't no need to upset yourself anymore than you already are. You can make things better if you just do what you're asked and I'm sure everything will be fine." She said calmly.

"Get the fuck out!" Gloria screamed and pointed to the door.

"I'm going sugah but not before I takes care of your friend here." She walked over to look at KB bandages.

"Don't you fucking touch him!" Gloria blocked her from getting to KB.

"Wait a second honey, this is my job. I have to do my rounds on this floor and he's one of my patients. You don't have the medical experience to care for him in his condition so please let me do my job." She tried to go around Gloria but she sidestepped her.

"No! I want another nurse to tend to him I don't want you to do shit bitch!" Gloria's arms were spread out so she couldn't get near KB.

"Ok honey. I don't have a problem with that." She turned around and started walking to the door then stopped and looked at Gloria. "But what makes you think that whoever comes won't

tell you the same thing? I told you, this is a small town and word travels fast 'round here. You take care sweety and just remember. Be careful what you say and who you're saying it to." She pulled the door open and sucked her teeth as she walked out and closed the door behind her softly.

Gloria looked at KB and shook her head left to right slowly. She was alone in this small town with no one to turn to. The only person she could trust was laying in the bed heavily sedated. She didn't know what to do, it seemed that Junior really had the town on lock. She was scared shitless and needed to get KB out that hospital then leave town immediately. She already fucked up when she spoke to the police and told them Junior's name. Muffin and the nurse's visit proved to her that it was the wrong move and that she was way out of her league. She was sure the police was going to come back to take her statement but she wasn't sure what she was going to tell them, she couldn't lie because they already had his name. She was lost with no friends, it was just her and KB. A fleeting thought flashed through her mind, she missed her friend Shondra but that bitch tried to set her man up too so there was no need for her dwell on her at all. Muffin's head lowered into the palms of her hand. Tears seeped through her fingers as the turmoil she was going through suffocated her. If she made the mistake of giving up any information to the police when they came, it would mean the end of her and KB.

Chapter 3

The sun invaded the serene darkness in the room and breathed warm rays onto KB's face. His eyes opened slowly and his lashes blinked quickly as he turned his head away from the bright sunrays. When he was able to focus, he saw Gloria sleeping in an armchair next to his bed. He winced as he sat up in the bed then grabbed his watch off the food tray. It was 7:30 in the morning but he didn't have a clue of how many days passed. He felt a dull pain in his shoulder as he got up from the bed and walked to the bathroom pulling the IV stand with him.

"Aaah!" He moaned as he relieved himself in the bathroom then washed his hands quickly.

When he came out of the bathroom heading towards his bed he heard someone say, "knock, knock" and tap his room door lightly. He turned around and almost gagged when he saw Patricia peeling her head in the door.

"Hey Keith. Is it ok for me to come in?" Patricia asked before walking in.

"Sure, come in." He said looking behind him quickly.

"I'm so glad to see you're ok. Everyone has been so worried about you." She purred looking into his eyes.

"Yea, I'm lucky 'cause it coulda been worse. I'm grateful I was just hit in my shoulder." He lightly rubbed the shoulder covered with the gauze pad. "Thanks for coming by to check on me."

"Oh you shoulda known I was gon' come by to make sure you were all right. Now you won't have to worry about nobody saying they heard your legs were amputated or you're

paralyzed." She smiled and the dimples in her cheeks became prominent. "I told you how they talk down here."

"The story would change that much, huh? Damn, that's fucked up. Well you make sure them muhfuckas know I'm good money." KB replied with a faint smile.

"I sure will honey 'cause ain't no telling what's being said right now since nobody really knows." She smoothed out her hair then asked. "Well, when they gonna let you on outta here, seeing how you up and running around?"

"I'm not sure." KB rubbed the top of his head with his hand. "I'ma speak with a doctor today and find out."

"I know you ain't worrying about the barbershop right now but do you want me to open it for business or keep it closed until you get outta here? I went by there and the police took down all that yellow tape and mess. I locked it up for you and told the barbers I'll let them know something after I speak wit' you or your other half."

KB looked back at Gloria, her breathing was light.

"Well if it's not fucked up in there behind all that bullshit that went down, you can open it but just be careful."

"Ok Keith, then I'll open it for business today. I'm so glad you're ok. I was really worried." She walked up to him and kissed him softly on his lips as she peered over his shoulder at Gloria who was still asleep. KB closed his eyes and when he opened them all he saw were the deep dimples in her cheeks from her wide smile. "That's to quicken the healing process."

She winked and turned around and walked slowly out the door, her round ass shaking like jell-o in the loose fitting sweatpants she was wearing.

KB stood in the middle of the room gazing at the door in disbelief. He rubbed his fingers over his lip slowly and took short steps towards the door. He poked his head out the doorway and watched Patricia's apple ass sashay down the hallway. She looked back at him when she pressed the button for the elevator and blew him an airborne kiss that he literally

caught in his hand then watched as she boarded the elevator gracefully.

He leaned back in the room, his mind dancing with thoughts of the unexpected kiss from Patricia. He jumped when Gloria grabbed him from behind, placing her arms around his waist.

"What's wrong baby?" She asked. "Who you out there peeking at?"

"Nobody. I was checking to see if a nurse or doctor was around so I can find out when I can get the fuck outta here." He recovered smoothly.

"I spoke with the doctor last night. He said you should be released today." She confirmed.

"Good." He walked over to the closet and pulled it open. "Where my clothes?"

"They was ruined baby. The paramedics had to rip your shirt to get to where you was shot and your pants was stained with dried up blood. I ain't been home to get you anything to wear because I couldn't leave you here alone."

"Aiight. Well I need some clothes to wear outta here." He stated pulling the strap on the gown he was wearing.

"I know baby and I'm gonna get you some." There was a solemn look on her face. "Before I leave to get them I need to talk to you." She walked over to the door and locked it.

"What's up?" KB asked still looking through the closet.

"Look at me K." She touched his elbow.

He turned around and focused in on her face and just realized she was badly bruised.

"What the fuck...?" Surging anger wouldn't let him complete his sentence.

"K, the bitch that shot you came in here and jumped on me." Her eyes were bloodshot.

"In here?" KB squinted his eyes, his finger pointing down to the floor in a rapid motion.

The temperature in the room seemed to increase twenty degrees as he slowly stepped to Gloria and inspected her wounds more closely. He grabbed her by her chin gently and moved her head left to right slowly and his eyes welled but rage was the reason, his fingers balled into a fist as he blinked slowly.

"I don't have a choice." He spoke into the atmosphere unconsciously,."I'm gon' have to kill both them muhfuckas! Nobody 'pose to touch a fucking hair on my girl's head. No fucking body!" His fist balled up tighter.

"Calm down baby, please." Gloria implored.

"For what!" He screamed turning his back to her and dragging the IV stand to the door with him. "Why the fuck would that bitch come in here and violate like that! You rocked out with her then me and Junior took it to the steel hammers!" He unlocked the door and stepped into the hallway.

"Where you going KB?" Gloria rushed out to get him fearing he was going to Junior's room.

"I'm going to straighten that bitch!" He looked up and down the corridor. "Which room that faggot in!"

"No KB. Please baby, let's go back in the room." She grabbed him by the wrist and pulled him gently back towards the room.

"Why? This is bullshit!" He pointed to her bruised face.

"I know baby and this shit has gotten outta hand; it's serious. It's like Junior has..."

"Fuck that muhfucka Glo!" KB boomed punching the air.

"Stop it K! Don't act like that! I don't want to relive what happened to you back in Brooklyn. That bitch shot you and now Junior shoots you too? I don't want there to be a next time baby, I just don't!" Gloria was shaking.

KB paced the floor. "I hear what you saying Glo and I don't really want no beef with that dude 'cause it's not that serious to me no more. The shit that happened in Brooklyn is

old news to me, you know what I'm saying. Stump got murked, so as far as I'm concerned, the beef I had with Junior suppose to have died wit' him."

"It should but from what just happened I don't think that's the case." She wiped her eyes and focused on KB. "You know who killed Stump K." She posed it more as a statement instead of a question as her lips frowned.

"I don't really know Glo 'cause I was in the hospital, remember? I know who you said you think did it but I can't be sure 'cause homicide police ain't never pick nobody up for it." He wiped the length of his face with the palm of his hand. "Shit, Stump had mad enemies gunning for him so it coulda been anybody. You know what I'm saying?"

"I hear what you're saying but you and I both know who did it." She picked up a tissue off his food tray and wiped her nose. "I don't think Junior wants to squash shit between you and him. When y'all bumped heads in the barbershop that shit wasn't supposed to jump off and that just proves he still want it with you but..." Gloria stopped speaking.

"But what?" KB questioned.

"It's just scary because it seems like he has this whole fucking town behind him." Gloria breathed out and shook her head.

"Why you say that?" KB's head tilted to the side.

Gloria sat down on the armchair slowly.

"What else happened in here Glo?" He pushed.

"Right after everything happened in the barbershop the dude that gave Junior the gun came in and threatened to hurt me if..."

"He did what!" KB's eyes grew wide. "That muhfucka put his hands on you too? Fuck this shit! I'm going to the kill them now before..."

"Let me finish K." Gloria interrupted his outburst. "In the barbershop he said he would kill me if I told the police anything about what happened and he took your gun and the

gun Junior dropped. Then while you was under all that medication the bitch came in here with him and beat on me." Gloria lowered her head. "The reason they came in here is because I told the police Junior was the one that shot you when they asked me in the barbershop."

KB looked at her and his lips got tight. "Why would you tell them that Glo? You know I ain't with that shit, I handle my own beef. I hold court in the street!" He was defiant.

"I know K but I didn't know how bad you were hurt and had a flashback of what happened in the club in New York and panicked. I'm sorry." Her eyes glistened with tears.

KB grabbed her gently and held her. "Nah ma, you did the right thing. Shit happened so fast you probably didn't have time to think. Don't worry 'bout it, I'ma straighten all this shit out. Just don't say anything else to the police, I don't want or need their help."

She looked up at him. "This ain't what we planned when we left Brooklyn KB. We was trying to get away from all of this, remember baby? We was supposed to leave all this bullshit behind us."

"I know Glo but what I'm 'posed to do now that it's right in front of me? I don't have no choice but to deal with it!" He shrugged his good shoulder.

"This a small town K and Junior has a lot of pull down here. Even the nurse that was taking care of you was telling me to keep quiet about what happened, or else. This is too much, I don't think…"

"You don't think what!" KB looked at her, his eyebrows lowered. "You don't think I'm built for this shit, huh?" He sucked his teeth. "Even if that muhfucka was mayor of this town, what you want me to do, tuck my tail between my legs and run?"

"No baby that's not what I think. I know you can handle yourself. I know your background. I just thought we was pass this shit. All I'm trying to tell you is that I've been beaten and

threatened about this shit and now I'm scared. There's no doubt in my mind about you handling this shit but down here I feel like we're outnumbered. We don't have nobody on our side K. We're in this alone! It's like us against a whole town!"

He held her at arm's length. "I hear you Glo but we came down here alone and I kept my promise to you; we have a business, we purchased our first home and we have a good life going for us. I never planned on seeing that punk way down here and I definitely didn't plan on getting shot again but the shit happened. Now I have no choice but to handle it." He stared into her eyes steadily and with confidence said, "I'm not gonna get ran outta this town. I already left BK, I'm not letting that muhfucka make me relocate again. That shit is outta the fucking question!"

Gloria buried her head in her hands. "I'm not saying leave town and I'm not suggesting we give up the barbershop and all of what we've built so far but what are we going to do K? This the second time you been shot! All this ain't worth your life!" She bawled.

"I'm sorry Glo." KB rubbed her back. "I'm just tight right now. The last thing I thought I would have to worry about was running into this dude down here but now that I did I gotta do something. I won't be able to sleep at night knowing he out here trying to murk me. He want me dead and I want the same fate for him. Straight like that." KB blinked slowly.

Gloria looked up. "Why can't I just tell the police and let them send his ass to jail? We can move to another town or stay in the house and let someone else run the shop until this blows over."

"That's not me Glo and you know it. I can't go out like a sucker running for cover in the hills." He stuck his chest out despite the pain he felt in his shoulder.

"Right, you rather get shot or killed before you ask the police for help." She shook her head left to right and blew out a burst of air. "Come on K, you're a businessman now, you

should be thinking differently. Leave all that gun slinging shit to Junior, he the one still in the streets!"

"So what you want me to do, snitch? How the fuck people gon' view me after eating cheese? How they gonna respect me when they know I let five o handle my shit?"

Gloria shook her head again. "I will never understand how guys think. Y'all rather lay down and die for some fake ass honor or code that doesn't even exist. KB, I don't know much but I'm certain there are a lot of muhfuckas that snitch, as you call it, to save their own lives."

"You're right Glo but I ain't one of 'em. When I was running wild, I didn't want a muhfucka telling on me so why should I rat now that I'm on the other side?" KB tried to make his point.

"Ok KB." Gloria relented. "How about finding a different way to handle this then. A way that won't get you hurt or killed."

KB walked over to the window and gazed out at the manicured lawn below.

"That's just it, there's only one way to handle this. I gotta kill him...or die."

Chapter 4

"What's happening! Why is his body jerking around like that?" Muffin asked the nurse, a worried look plastered on her face.

"I can't answer that right now sweety. Wait until the doctor finishes up and I'm sure he'll let you know." The nurse replied rushing back to assist the doctor working on Junior.

Muffin peeked over the shoulder of the doctor and could see Junior's eyes fluttering and rolling up in his head. She was pulled out of the room by a male nurse so the doctor could work in private and when she got in the hallway she burst into tears. She snatched away from the male nurse and banged her fist against the wall while tears streamed down her face in buckets. She turned her back and stood against the wall then slid to the floor and pulled her knees to her chest and leaned her forehead forward. She cried openly and after about five minutes, the doctor came out of the room wiping sweat from his brow. He looked down at her as she looked up at him with swollen eyes and struggled to her feet.

"He's stable now. Seems like he had an allergic reaction to the pain medication we were giving him." He said to her as he placed his hand on her shoulder.

"Will that happen again?" She sniffled.

"I can't really say because we have no way of knowing what, if any, medication he is allergic to. We've just given him a new generic medication that will hopefully work effectively but once he wakes up he'll be able to give us some background on his medical history so we can be sure something like this doesn't ever happen again."

"Ok doc. Thank you so much." She breathed out and wiped her eyes.

"No problem ma'am, it's my job." He smiled and walked down the hall.

Muffin walked off staring ahead blankly thinking about Junior's condition. She was a bundle of nerves and was having a difficult time dealing with all that was happening. Her rage was piquing but she had to get it under control because Junior was in such an unstable state and needed her full attention. She was about to go back into the room when Bo came up behind her.

"What's goin' on?" He asked noticing the faraway look in her eyes.

"He was just shaking and shit a minute ago. The doctor said he had an allergic reaction to the pain medicine. I can't take this shit, it's fucking my nerves up and driving me crazy." She admitted openly to Bo.

"Don't worry, he gon' come outta this fine." Bo shuffled his feet. "Ay, I need to holla at you about something. Let's go downstairs for a minute."

Muffin followed Bo to the elevators and when the doors opened, two detectives got off. The stout one looked at Muffin briefly then continued down the hallway.

"Ah shit, you think they going to my room or Gloria's room?" Muffin asked Bo as she watched where they were going.

"Ain't no tellin' but they gon' to one of 'em that's for sho'."

"I should follow them to see if she tells them about what happened and if she do, go right in that fuckin' room and crack her fuckin' skull so she know I ain't playin' no fuckin' games!" Rage suddenly replaced sorrow.

Bo looked at her with unbelieving eyes. "You is really crazy gurl."

"Fuck that Bo! My man laying up in that hospital bed going through convulsions and shit and it's that muhfucka's

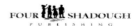
fault! This here is for real. I gotta make sure he gets outta here
without handcuffs and healthy; that's a lot of pressure on me. I
don't need that bitch throwing a monkey wrench in this to
prevent it from happening either!" Muffin remarked.

"I hear you but you can get yourself in trouble too if..."

Muffin cut him off. "I don't give a fuck about that shit
you sayin' Bo! Me and my man down here together so we in
this shit together, bottomline!"

"Awright." Bo showcased a nervous smile and shook his
head. "Let's get downstairs so I can rap wit' you real quick, it's
real important."

"More important than me handling this shit up here?"
Muffin's head retracted and tilted to the side.

"I wouldn't say more important than this but it's just as
important and it won't take long." He corrected himself.

Muffin agreed so she could see what was not so
important and boarded the elevator warily. When they reached
the lobby she followed him outside to a car. He turned around
and leaned up against the hood then pulled out a cigarette and lit
it.

"I'm not sure how much longer Junior gon' be up in there
but I'm running low on product. He was supposed to give me
some more work right before all this happened." Bo blew out
smoke as he continued. "I'm a need some more work soon."

At first Muffin got angry when Bo started talking about
running low on drugs because it sounded like he was only
concerned with making money instead of his cousin's current
state in the hospital. None of that shit mattered to her at the
moment but then she thought it out clearly and realized that
Junior was supplying the town with drugs and if he was no
longer able to someone else would eventually try and claim his
spot as boss and she couldn't let that happen. Although he was
laid up in the hospital trying to recover from a terrible gunshot
wound, his business couldn't suffer. He needed someone to look
out for his best interest and since she was his girl, she was going

to appoint herself, acting boss until he was able to run his operation again. From what she detected of Bo, his demeanor did not match what was necessary if someone violated. How he handled the situation with Muffin was not how Junior would have or any other boss so him even being a prospect was ruled out.

"Ok, so what you need me for?" Muffin questioned looking him directly in his eyes.

"I need you to tell me where the rest of it is so I can get what I need to keep things rollin', just 'til he get outta here." Bo answered smoothly.

Muffin looked at Bo sideways then fixed her hair.

"That's it? Just tell you where the rest of it is? Ok, no problem. I can get you what you need but um, don't you have some bread you need to give me first?" She squinted her eyes.

"Yea, I was gon' give that to him when he come out the hospital." He replied blowing smoke out his mouth and nose simultaneously.

Muffin snickered. "Nah player, it don't work like that. Get me that bread first then I'll give you the work, aiight?"

"Yea, but I don't want no mix up with the money you know whatta mean?"

"Yea ok. I think I know what you mean." She nodded her head slowly. "Look Bo, let me set you straight right quick since you think I'm a crash test dummy. Junior's my man and I'm the one that fucks him so believe me boo boo, there'll never be a mix up when it comes to OUR money." She raised her hand in the air. "Matter of fact, you know what, why don't you just wait until he gets outta here so there won't be no mix up with the work either, ok?"

Bo shook his head in disagreement. "Hol' on a minute Muffin. I need the work now, I got people waiting on me." Seeing he wasn't going to get what he wanted without giving her what she asked for, he conceded. "I don't have a problem

giving you the money but I need to take care of this now awright?"

"Now that you understand me, I see I gotta handle you different. If you want to do business with me then you gon' have to do it my way or not at all from now on player. Got it?" She gave him a one sided smile.

"Awright." Bo smiled weakly and shook his head. "Boy my cuz wasn't lying about you." He said under his breath.

"You don't know the half muhfucka." Muffin read his lips. "I ain't your average bitch Bo! Believe that!"

"I hear you, can we go take care of this now?" He was rushing her.

"Wait a second, let me go back upstairs to make sure Junior's fine." She answered aggressively. "That's my first priority!"

"Awright, I'll wait down here for you." Bo threw the cigarette down and stomped it out with his Jordans.

Muffin rushed back upstairs; she was going to check on Junior but she also wanted to check to see if Gloria sang to the detectives about the shooting. She was prepared to kill her this time if she did. When she entered Junior's room the stout detective was standing at the foot of his bed looking at his medical chart.

"Excuse me, can I help you?" She asked with hidden attitude.

"Oh yes." He turned to face Muffin. "I was looking for Junior. Is this him?" He was pointing over to the bed.

"No, his name ain't Junior." Muffin countered.

"I can see that from this chart. Could it be his nickname?"

"Nope, his nickname is daddy." She answered smugly. "Anything else I can help you with?" She couldn't hide her annoyance and poked out her lips.

"I came by to see if I could get a statement from the victim but it seems like he's under a lot of medication." The detective replied looking at his chart.

"Yea, the doctor said he's gonna be out of it for a while and he just had a bad reaction to some medication they gave him so maybe you should come back another time." Her words were polite but her tone was dismissive.

"Sure, sure. I'll come back in a couple days then. He should still be here right?" He put the chart back down.

"Yea he should be." She was hoping like hell he wouldn't.

" What about you? Weren't you there when the shooting occurred?" The fat under his neck jiggled every time he talked.

"No, I came after everything was over. I already told you that at the barbershop." She answered with a tinge of annoyance in her voice.

"Right, right. Ok uh, if he comes around before I come back have him give me a call. Here's my card." The stout detective handed her the card then turned to leave.

"I'll give it to him." She took the card and read the name, Richard James. She laughed to herself because he had two first names. "Hey? Did you speak to the other guy that was shot?" She looked up from the card to look into his beady eyes.

"Yes I did but he says he doesn't know who shot him." He looked at Muffin with a raised eyebrow. "You know what I don't understand? We have two males with gunshot wounds, no weapons, no witnesses who seen anything and no motive. We're batting 0 with all these no's. Guess we'll just have to wait to see what your friend can tell us when he wakes up."

"I guess. Ok Mr. James, thanks." She chuckled under her breath.

"No problem ma'am. Enjoy the rest of your day."

When the detective was gone, Muffin walked over to Junior's bed and grabbed his hand in her own. She stared at his closed eyes and leaned in and kissed him gently on his cheek.

"Daddy, when we started fucking around again I made you a promise that I would be there for you when you needed me most and that's a promise I'm gonna keep. You need me now Junior and I'm prepared to keep that promise." She wiped a tear running down her cheek. "You ain't got to worry about shit but getting better for me so we can spend the rest of our days together, just like I planned in the beginning. I'm not going to let you down and I damn sure ain't gon' let you lose all you've built. I put that on our unborn son! I love you so much." Muffin kissed him on his cheek softly then rushed out the door.

***

"Let me get that." Muffin said to Bo holding her hand out.

Bo handed her a stack of money and she looked at him squinting one eye then counted it out carefully. When she was done she looked up at him again with a frown on her face.

"Fuck this 'posed to be?"

"That's for the quarter key." Bo answered nonchalantly.

She threw the stack of money back in his lap. "It's short two gees." Her eyebrows had lowered.

"You sure?" Bo frowned, his forehead wrinkled.

"Now I don't know how to fucking count huh? You already tried to play me once Bo, stop trying to push your luck. Junior taught me well so I know prices and weight. Just by the dumb shit you doing you making me feel like you can't be trusted!" She clasped her hands together and faced him as she continued speaking. "This shit not gonna work because you think you can get over on me like I'm a slow leak. I know this shit better than you Bo, believe that! Playing me will back fire on you in the worst way and I put that on my own life!"

"I'm not trying to play you, I musta miscounted." He dug into his pocket and pulled out another stack of bills and gave all the money back to her, including the missing two thousand.

FOUR  SHADOUGH
PUBLISHING

Muffin huffed then counted the money again slowly. After confirming it was the right amount, she exited the vehicle. Bo got out and followed her up to the small colonial style house she and Junior rented.

"Hold on. Where the fuck you think you going?" She turned around and extended her hand, her palm in his face. "You ain't comin' in here with me. Stay your playing ass in the car, I'll be right back." She turned and put the key in the door and pushed it open.

"Why I gotta wait in the car?" He asked confused.

"The same reason you think I don't know how to count!" She shot back quickly.

Bo sucked his teeth, "Why you actin' like I'm not family. I ain't gon' steal from my kinfolk."

Muffin turned around briskly. "Look muhfucka, after that sheisty shit you just tried to pull, all that 'he your kinfolk' shit ain't gon' work on me." Muffin shook her head. "You must really think I'm slow." Her hands rested on her hips. "Answer this question for me Bo. Since y'all been doing this for so long, how come you don't know where the stash at yet?" She rolled her eyes and looked at his dumb expression. "Exactly!" She gritted her teeth. "Junior obviously ain't tell you everything about me. So before you keep embarrassing yourself trying to play me to the left, I'm gonna give you some time to re think how you gon' handle me going forward." Muffin slammed the door in his face.

She went to the bedroom and opened the closet door. She pulled some clothes off a safe in the corner, turned the knob and put in the combination of numbers then opened it. She put the money in but separated it from the money that was already neatly inside. She peeked out the window to see if Bo was in the car then opened the front door and waved for him to come to her.

"I don't know how you and Junior did y'all transactions and at this point I really don't give a fuck but at the end of the day, this is just business."

"Ok Muffin, whateva. You got the stuff for me?" Bo was showing signs of aggravation.

"I got it but it's not here. I'ma tell you where to pick it up."

"What kind of shit is this? This is crazy Muffin, you can't…"

"I can and I am! You're Junior's cousin not mine! I'm not taking any chances doing hand to hand wit' your shady ass." Muffin smiled devilishly. "Now if you have a problem with this then…"

Bo shook his head in disgust. "Awright man damn! Just tell me where I can get my mess. Time is wasting."

"It's gon' be in a black bag by the fence behind the rec center, close to the curb. The top of the bag will be sticking out in the dirt so you won't miss it." She instructed.

"Man, this is some real bullshit. I hope my cuz gets better soon. All this you got me doing just to get the work is just crazy." He sucked his teeth.

"Nah muhfucka, that shit you tried to pull is crazy and you better watch your muhfuckin' mouth talkin' slick to me!"

Bo's chest swelled and his teeth gritted. "You the one talkin' like I bleed once a month, I ain't no bitch Muffin and not gon' keep lettin' you sound off on me like I am one!"

Muffin blew out a burst of air. "You know something? You right. I can't wait 'til Junior gets better so I can tell him how you tried to play me for his money and work and if I know my man, he gon' second guess fucking with you!" Muffin's nose skinned up.

Muffin figured out what Bo was trying to do out the gate because he came to her speed balling about getting work. He was planning to keep the money he had, sell off all the work then use the money and re up himself and by the time Junior

came out the hospital he would give him back only the portion he sold, keeping the rest. His plans were to take over what Junior had built and make it his own. She wasn't going to allow that to happen; she couldn't let it happen.

"Why would you tell him some bullshit like that?" Bo asked in disbelief.

"Because it's the fucking truth, that's why!" She barked.

"I'm not trying to play you for his money!" Bo defended.

"Then stop trying to be slick! Anyway, the pack will be where I told you in a half hour." Muffin said slamming the door again in his face.

Bo turned and left in a huff while she watched him through the window smiling wickedly. *"Bet that muhfucka got the message this time. I ain't gotta worry 'bout him trying to play me no more!"*

She turned around and went out the back door to get the work from under the doghouse where Junior's brindle, man biting pit bull was laying in the dirt. When she brought the work inside the house she noticed there was only a half of a kilo left. She poked out her lip and looked up at the ceiling deep in thought.

"I gotta keep this shit flowing. I can't let him run out of work or Bo's slick ass might try and move in." She thought out loud.

She hurriedly bagged up the work for Bo, secured it in a thick plastic bag then grabbed the cordless phone as she searched through Junior's papers in the nightstand drawer in their bedroom. When she found the number she was looking for she dialed the number.

***

"Hello?"

"Hi. You probably don't remember me but I'm Junior's girl."

"This Shondra?"

Muffin sucked her teeth loud into the phone receiver. "Hell no! I said I'm his girl, this Muffin."

"Oh my bad, whaddup shorty?"

"I'm calling to tell you that something happened to your cousin. He got shot…"

The telephone fell out of Craig's hand when he heard what she said.

"… was telling me he gonna be ok though." Muffin had no idea he dropped his phone and never stopped talking.

"Hold on! I didn't hear what you said, my phone dropped. What happened to my cousin?" Craig's voice had raised.

"I said he got shot and is in the hospital down here. He was hit near his groin and lost a lot of blood but the doctor was telling me he's gonna be ok though." She repeated.

"Whaaaat! Who the fuck shot him!" Craig screamed out unconsciously.

"It was a dude named KB he had beef with back in Brooklyn." Muffin reported.

"What's his name?" Craig's eyebrows lowered.

"KB" She verified.

"That name sounds mad familiar, is it the same dude that got hit up in the club a while back?" Craig gazed up at the ceiling as he thought.

"Yup, that's him." Muffin confirmed nodding her head as if Craig could see her through the phone.

"Shit! How the fuck they bump heads way down there?" Craig rubbed his head with his hand slowly. "Where that muhfucka at now?"

"He in the hospital too. Him and Junior shot it out in the barbershop and he got hit with some slugs himself." Muffin was being animated.

"In a barbershop? That's some mafia shit!" Craig head nodded slowly. "Yo, I'm comin down there to check that muhfucka!"

"I hear you but I need to rap wit' you about something else if you don't mind."

"There's more shit to this?"

"Yea but it's not exactly about that, this is about business."

"I'm listening." Craig's ears sharpened.

"I'm sure you know what Junior does down here."

"Go 'head but be careful what you say over the horn." He warned her.

"Well it's drying up since he been in the hospital so I'm gonna be holding things down until he gets better. I was calling to see if you can help me do that when I come through." She was laying down her proposition and stating her position directly.

"When you coming?"

"Honestly I have to do this pronto so I plan to be there in a couple of days. I need to keep things wet, that's how he always kept it." She hoped Craig caught on to her code.

"Hmph. Well when you touch down get in contact with me and I'll take care of you." His voice turned monotone.

"Ok but make sure the numbers are right because I don't wanna waste your time."

"What?" His nose wrinkled and his top lip rose and trembled at the same time.

"I'm just saying, I don't want you to balloon the numbers, I'm good with that math."

"Ok Muffin, I don't know what you talking 'bout with all that number shit but don't talk that slick boss shit to me. I said I'll see you when you touch down end of conversation." Craig hung up the phone and rubbed his chin then said, "Cocky bitch!"

FOUR  SHADOUGH
PUBLISHING

Muffin held the phone in her hand then looked at it and said, "I hope I ain't fuck that up."

Chapter 5

Gloria walked out the entrance of the hospital headed to her car. KB had just received his discharge papers from the doctor so she was on her way home to get him fresh clothes to wear. She drove slowly, her mind swirling with thoughts of leaving the place she and KB accidentally chose as their home. It wasn't their plan to settle down in this town but it was so quiet and serene, a far cry from the noise and violence in Brooklyn. It became the perfect place to start a new and safe life but now it wasn't looking so safe and quiet anymore with him getting shot again. What were the odds of them choosing a town where Junior's family lived? She wanted a better life since all the drama in Brooklyn. The life KB was living in New York caused him to get hurt and almost killed but it also was costly to her, she lost an irreplaceable friend. She figured since she and KB didn't know anyone down there their relationship would strengthen and that would replace the empty space Shondra once filled.

While driving, she remembered she left her house keys on the office desk at the barbershop and made a detour to get them. She pulled up in the back because she wanted to avoid anyone who might wanted to question her about what happened. When she opened the back door she was shocked to see the lights on and could hear the sound of clippers humming. She ventured all the way inside and saw Patricia and two of the barbers with clients in their chairs.

"Excuse me Rome. How the hell did y'all get in here?" Gloria asked the barber, purposely ignoring Patricia.

"Pat opened up this morning." He replied.

Gloria looked around the barbershop and noticed all the mess from the day before was cleaned up as if nothing ever happened. Thoughts of her fighting Muffin that day surfaced and she became angry and wanted to tear Patricia a new ass hole.

"Who the fuck told you to open the shop bitch and where the hell you get keys from!" Gloria shouted at Patricia.

"Keith told me to open up." Patricia stated calmly, not looking up from the girl's hair she was braiding.

Gloria placed her hands on her hips. "Oh really? And when the fuck he tell you this!"

"Oh, he told me early this morning when I went to visit him at the hospital. You was sleep." Patricia remained composed and never looked at Muffin as she continued braiding her client's hair.

"You came up to the hospital to visit my man bitch! You must really think I won't fuck your ass up and..."

"Look now," Patricia interrupted Gloria, "I'm not gon' be too many more of your bitches. I have a client here and it's very disrespectful for me to start yelling in her ear and carrying on with you. If you have a problem with the shop being open, you need to take that up with Keith." Patricia eyed her dangerously.

"You fucking bitch!" Gloria took menacing steps towards Patricia.

Patricia stopped braiding her client's hair and put her comb down at her station and balled her fists up. "Keith not here so if we lock ass this time, no one is gon' pull me off you so be careful how you move honey."

Gloria stopped short and thoughts of the nurse coming into KB's room threatening her, resonated in her mind as she looked around at the barbers and then back to Patricia. She was up against a whole town and couldn't win. She knew she could beat Patricia's ass if she really paced herself but she was right, no one was there on her side and if was winning the fight, she was sure someone would come to her aid.

"I'm gonna talk to my man bitch and find out what the fuck is going on and if we do lock ass believe me, it would be me that would have to be pulled off your fat ass!" Gloria turned and went into the office and retrieved her house keys.

When Gloria was out of earshot Patricia chuckled and said to the barbers, "She sho' got up out of here quick when I told her nobody gon' pull me off that ass. Her face already look like somebody earth slammed her so she better pump her brakes 'fo she crash into this dump truck." Patricia slapped her ass with her open palm.

Gloria left out of the barbershop quickly and once inside the car held the steering wheel tightly. On top of everything happening that bitch Patricia had become a thorn in her side. She had to address the bullshit KB was allowing that bitch to do in front of everybody. His actions was making her look like she was weak and she didn't like that at all. Hot tears drained from her eyes as she flew out the parking area of the barbershop to get KB a change of clothes to come home in.

***

Muffin was sitting in Junior's room when the doctor walked in.

"Not up yet huh?" He asked as he checked Junior's chart.

"Nope not yet." Muffin said yawning.

"Well it's not unusual with the extent of his wounds and the amount of blood loss. We have to keep him heavily sedated." He checked Junior's pupils and pulse. "I'll monitor his progress every four hours and decrease the dosage as necessary."

"He's gonna be fine isn't he doctor?" Muffin eyes were steady.

"Oh sure. He's just gon' be under the weather for some time." He smiled warmly and grabbed her hand. "I can see

you're pretty worried about this gentleman. Hold his hand there for a second."

The doctor walked over to Junior and touched his shoulder gently.

"Hey buddy, I need you to do me a huge favor right now. I have this beautiful girl with this high distinct li'l voice standing here holding your hand. She's been by your side the entire time you've been here and has this worried look on her face. I need you to go on and squeeze her hand and let her know you're just resting fine buddy. Do that for me willya."

Muffin squealed when she felt slight pressure from Junior squeezing her hand. Then she looked at him with tear glistened eyes and saw half a smile on his face. She knew right then everything was going to be fine. She turned to the doctor who was smiling and about to walk out the door.

"Thank you so much. I feel so much better." She jumped up and stopped him before he left and hugged him tightly.

"Ah li'l lady, none needed. Told ya he was gon' be all right."

"I needed that to make me feel better, thanks again doc."

"No problem young lady. See ya later and remember, no extracurricular activities until he's fully recovered." The doctor chuckled as he closed the door behind him.

"Junior, can you hear me daddy?" Muffin squeezed his hand gently. "Well baby, I'm going to make sure you have nothing to worry about but your recovery. I'm gon' handle everything for you until you get better."

Junior squeezed her hand and his eyes flickered.

"I guess that means you all right with that huh?" She felt pressure again and smiled. "Yea, I know I was right."

Muffin pulled his hand to her face and rubbed it against her cheek lovingly. She realized she loved him more than she thought because now that he was unable to do anything for himself, she wanted to take care of all his affairs and make him proud of her, like a father is of his daughter. She kissed him on

his hand and placed it on her stomach then looked toward the floor with a strange sparkle in her eye.

FOUR  SHADOUGH PUBLISHING

Chapter 6

The Greyhound pulled into the Port Authority bus terminal and Muffin grabbed her carry on duffle bag from the top compartment then exited the bus. She took the escalator up to the street level and walked out onto 42nd Street. She stood on the corner of 8th Avenue and waited impatiently holding her bag tightly. It had been almost a year since she'd been back to NY and was feeling anxious. She watched as a man dressed in black slacks and white linen shirt with three buttons opened exposing his neck full of chains walked up to a girl who literally had her head in the sky. She was obviously amazed by all the tall buildings which was a dead giveaway that it was her first time in the rotten apple. The well dressed vulture swooped up on her and slid his arm around her shoulder and looked up at the tall buildings with her.

"Tell me which one you want to see and I'll take you on a personal tour." He sang into her ear.

She looked frightened at first but the more he serenaded her with witty words, eloquent speech and that New York lingo had her surrendering her will to him almost immediately. Muffin shook her head in disgust, she knew the pimp had scored another hooker for his stable. The young girl had no idea what she was in for but Muffin knew her innocence was about to be stolen and sold to the highest bidder.

"Ay yo!"

She turned around to Craig waving his hand in the air and she walked over to him quickly.

"What's up Craig?" She asked when she reached him.

"What's good? How was your bus ride?" He asked reaching for her bag.

"I got it." She held her bag close to her. "That was a long ass uncomfortable ride. I'm glad that shit is over."

"Yea." Craig looked at her with a raised eyebrow then opened the passenger door of his 190E Benz.

"Thanks." She took her seat and placed the bag on her lap.

When Craig got inside the driver's seat he looked at her and sucked his teeth. "Yo put that bag in the back seat."

"Nah, I'm good." She declined.

Craig shot her a mean look. "Aiight, I see I need to school you on some shit before you get yo' feelings hurt. There's rules to this shit and I'm gon' explain them to you so there won't be no misunderstandings before I pull off." Craig turned around in his seat facing Muffin. "Number one, don't ever discuss business over the phone with me, EVER! The second thing, don't come around me acting noid (paranoid) and shit because if I ever feel there's something suspect about you, it's a wrap...for you! Now the way you babysitting that bag in your lap there's one of two things going on. There might be some bread in there or it might be something else." Craig put his index finger over his lips in a motion to hush Muffin then ripped her shirt open.

"What tha fuck!" Muffin was shocked and gathered her shirt up to her bosom quickly.

"Gotta make sure you ain't wired. I don't gamble anymore so I don't take risks!" Craig felt around her waist, feeling for anything that would clear up his suspicions. "Now if you ever try or think about setting me up, I'll put a hole between your eyes before the feds can save you, no questions asked. You understand me?"

"I do and I'm sorry Craig. Believe me I'm not trying to set you up, I'm just a little nervous. I guess it's because I never did this alone before. Junior always told me money changes

everybody so always watch my back so that's why I'm so wound up." Muffin explained.

"Everything my cuz told you, he learned from me 'cause I'm a boss! Stop trying to impress me with all that boss talk and just fall back and play your hand. Now, you either put that bag in the back seat and ride with me to go take care of business or get the fuck outta my whip and go try your chances copping on your own from the Dominicans uptown. Make your choice."

Muffin put the duffle bag in the back seat immediately.

"Aiight smart choice. Now we can go handle some business." Craig said pulling off into traffic.

"Craig, can you drop me to my mom's crib first so I can freshen up? I feel so dirty and sticky being on that bus for 11 hours." Muffin asked as she pulled her hair into a ponytail.

"No problem. How long you gonna be there?" Craig turned his head to her. "If you let me know how much work you want I can have it ready for you after you finish getting cleaned up so we don't waste unnecessary time. Feel me?"

"That's cool. I want to get about 3 keys."

"About 3 or exactly 3? You gotta be specific."

"I want 3 keys." Muffin affirmed.

"Ok." Craig paused for a minute calculating numbers in his head. "You got fifty two thou on you?"

"No but Junior told me it's 15 thou a key so that's forty five for three, right?"

"That's what he said huh?" Craig shook his head and laughed deep in his throat. "Aiight forty seven and tell him it's Brooklyn prices and not uptown prices because this perico is fishscale. It comes back with two extra o's (ounces) after you cook each brick. You got forty seven?"

"I got it." Muffin inwardly smiled to herself. It was her first time negotiating and she think she played it out the way she was supposed to; she got the price she wanted.

"Aiight cool. Now what's up with my cousin? Was he up and talking when you left from down there?" Craig asked changing the subject from business to personal.

"Yea he was up but he wasn't talking 'cause he still doped up with a lot of pain meds. The doctor said he should be getting out after he takes some more tests." Muffin informed him.

"That's good 'cause I was on my way down there to body the muhfucka that hit him up. I still don't see how they bumped heads in that small ass town, that's like a one in a million chance of happening."

"I know. I was shocked to see his bitch Gloria when I went in the barbershop to get my hair flipped. She ain't have no idea I was the one that blasted her man in the club but when he saw me, he remembered, then I had to beat flames out her ass. Junior pulled me off the bitch and told me to leave and then a few minutes later I hear boom, boom, boom. I ran in there and him and KB was on the floor bleeding out and I freaked." Muffin relived the events as she told Craig.

"Damn! Did the police come through after all that shit jumped off?"

"Hell yea, but before they got there your cousin Bo busted up in there waving his hammer all around and that bitch started screaming and begging for her life." Muffin giggled wickedly. "She was scared to death and I tried my best to amp him into offing her greezy ass but he was 'bout his business. He took the guns that was on the floor then told the bitch not to tell the police shit. He specifically told her to tell them she didn't see nothing and nobody."

"I ain't know Bo got down like that." Craig smiled. "So what happened when the beast (police) came through?"

"Oh that bitch snitched like the rat she is! But it's all good 'cause I straightened her out at the hospital. I but the beats on her then Bo put the icing on the cake." Muffin smirked. "Bo got a lot of pull in that small ass town. He had the nurses in the

hospital threatening the bitch and the whole nine! I know that spooked the shit outta the bitch along with the thorough ass whooping I delivered, so I don't think she said nothin' else to the police." Muffin burst out in laughter.

"What about the dude Junior shot, KB. What's his status?"

"I think he got discharged because before I left, I checked and he wasn't in his room no more." She clarified.

"That's not good, I got to call down there to make sure Junior ok while this muhfucka out roaming around."

"I thought about that too and told Bo to find out for sure before I left and to have somebody with Junior at all times. KB got a li'l barbershop down there so I don't think he gone fake any moves right out the gate."

"The muhfucka got a barber shop down there? Damn then that shit coulda just happened on a humble but I still can't sleep on him. No matter what a muhfucka might be doin' now, he ain't never gon' forget the muhfucka that clapped him. Junior drew first blood."

The car pulled up in front of Muffin's house and she got out and grabbed her bag from the back seat and started making her way to the brownstone. She heard the horn beep and turned around.

"Ay yo, you gotta get that bread to me now." Craig said leaning over and speaking through the passenger side window.

"Oh shit, my bad Craig." She walked back to the car.

"We can't count that shit out here. We need to go in your crib or something."

"Ok give me a second. I need to make sure my mom's not home." She ran up the steps and disappeared inside.

Craig sat impatiently in the car while she went inside the house. She reappeared in the entrance and motioned for him to come in. He got out of the car and walked up the stairs to the front door of the brownstone.

"Come in." Muffin closed the door behind him. "My moms at work. You can have a seat right here, I'll be right back."

Craig took a seat on the couch and brushed his pants off. When Muffin returned, she had changed into a t-shirt and sweats carrying her duffle bag. She placed it on the center table in front of Craig and started emptying out stacks of money, placing them next to the bag.

"This is forty gees right here." She said pushing the four rubber-banded stacks of money toward him.

"Ok." Craig took a money stack in his hand, removed the rubber band and began counting the bills."

"What? You don't trust me?" Muffin smirked.

"This is business and nothing else, ya feel me? You my cousin peoples, not mine." His tone was serious.

"I hear you. Well I'm all business too so I'm good with that." She finished counting out the remainder of the money and placed it on the table.

"Well I'm gonna go clean up real quick..."

"Nah, nah. Just chill right here while I count this bread in front of you to make sure the count is right. After that I'll leave and take care of the work. I don't have time to wait on you to finish taking a bubble bath and shit."

"I ain't gonna take no bubble bath." Muffin chuckled. "I was just gonna wash up real quick, I wasn't gonna take that long. I feel sticky and shit."

"Take care of that when we done here aiight? Craig advised.

"All right." Muffin sat down across from him and watched as he counted the money. He counted it quickly but carefully and stacked the money in neat piles on the table.

"The count is right." Craig said after counting all the money. "Now tell me how you want to do this. You want me to drop it off here or you want to pick it up?"

"Since I'm not driving, I think it'll be better if you bring it here but can you call me first 'cause I want to make sure my moms ain't around when you come through. I don't need her asking me any questions."

"Cool. I'ma get outta here and go take care of this now."

"Here, take my number so you can call me when you're on your way." Muffin passed him a paper she wrote her number on.

"Aiight. I'm out. I should be done like two or three hours."

"Ok. See you then." Muffin said as she closed the door.

Muffin took off her clothes and jumped in the shower to cleanse herself from the long bus ride from North Carolina. She was feeling fresh when she got out of the shower then put on her robe and laid down on the bed staring up at the ceiling. Feelings of empowerment and independence filled her as she twirled her hair around her finger. She was on her way to proving she was capable of holding her spot as Junior's girl by taking care of his business, just like he would. She secured it by employing a no-nonsense, strictly business attitude from the beginning, just like Junior spoke about, so she would be taken serious and to gain respect. Bo was the first recipient of that tactic and his reaction proved it worked. She was sure he didn't like how she handled business but he definitely respected her. Now she was making deals and getting plays on copping weight just like Junior would. She smiled wide and spread her arms apart and flapped them in the queen size bed making a sheet angel then grabbed her cordless phone and dialed some numbers. The phone rang five times and she was about to hang up when someone picked up.

"Hello. Room 225."

"Who is this?" Muffin asked.

"I'm the nurse on duty."

"Where is Junior?"

Muffin could hear talking in the background as the nurse put the phone down. She heard Bo and Junior's voices faintly.

"Yea, I called my ex to tell her what happened and she cried like a fucking baby kid. She wanted to come down but I told her nah 'cause you know my shorty don't play, know what I mean?"

"Uh huh. And wit' the way I seen your ole lady carry on, I can just imagine what would happen." Bo replied.

"Tell me about it. Muff ain't no joke cuz." Junior cosigned.

"I know. I saw her in action wit' my own eyes when..."

"Excuse me, the phone is for you." The nurse said interrupting his and Bo's conversation.

"Pass it to me Bo." Junior said stretching his arm out for the phone receiver.

"Hello." Junior's voice sounded strained.

"Junior?"

"Muff? What's up baby?" His voice lightened up when he heard her voice.

"Nothing daddy. Just checking on you. You ok?"

"I'm aiight. Just in here talking with Bo and shit."

"Oh, ok. I'm glad you're finally up." She said sincerely.

"Me too but it's crazy, I can't remember shit about what happened that day, it's kinda of fuzzy. Like I know I shot out with that muhfucka KB but after that, I'm drawing a blank."

"The doctor said that might happen. When did you wake up?" She questioned.

"Um, like yesterday afternoon." He replied looking up at the hospital ceiling.

"Oh so it's been a whole day for you. I'm so glad you came up out of that shit 'cause I was so fucking scared." Muffin was being sincere. "After something like that I know you wanted to reach out and tell your family. Did you call any of your peoples to let them know what happened since you been up?"

"Nah, I ain't call nobody yet."

"Oh really. I was sure you woulda called somebody from Brooklyn to let them at least know what happened. You know how shit like this finds its way back to your people." Muffin rolled her eyes at the lie he told.

"I am but I wanna do that when I get outta here. I don't want them worrying and feeling like they need to come down here to see me and I'm laid up in this hospital. Where you at anyway?" Junior questioned.

Muffin decided to tell her own lie, one good lie deserves another.

"Oh, um that's another reason why I'm calling. I'm in Brooklyn and before you get upset baby, I made sure everything with you was ok before I broke out. I woulda never left if the doctor didn't say you were going to be fine and when I got the phone call from..."

Junior cut her off. "What! Hold on Muff, let me tell this nurse to get outta here 'cause I don't want her to hear my conversation." When the nurse was gone Junior continued. "What phone call you got? And what could be more important than me right now, especially after what just happened?"

"Baby you know I would never leave you unless I knew you was ok. Don't make me feel bad." Muffin's tone changed to a plea.

"Aiight, just tell me what was so important for you to leave me in the hospital and go to NY?"

"I'm here to take care of something for my moms." Muffin crossed her fingers.

"Take care of what?" He was anxious to find out what happened to her moms. He didn't have feelings for her like that but he was concerned.

"Well you know it had to be an emergency with my family daddy. My moms been going through some hard times and her bills are backed up. I offered to send her some money through Western Union but you know my moms is proud and

57

refused my help. Then I got a call from my aunt and she told me my mom's been out of work for months and the house is in foreclosure. She said she was gonna lose it unless the balance was paid up in full." Muffin sighed heavily into the receiver. "So I made this desperation move to pay her balance and the mortgage for 6 months until she finds another job. Baby I hope you're not mad at me." Muffin's fingers were still crossed. She surprised herself with how quickly she came up with her lie.

"Nah, I ain't mad. Damn! I didn't know your moms was about to lose her crib, that's serious. I'm sorry she gotta go through this." Junior was being genuine.

"That's ok baby. I was praying you would understand and not be mad with me." Muffin smirked and uncrossed her fingers. "So how are you feeling? I thought I was going to lose you."

"Yea, that was some real bullshit that popped off. I didn't even know that muhfucka was down here let alone owning that barbershop. I gotta make sure I take care of that clown 'cause this town is mad small and we gon' always bump heads. I gotta do fam quick fast in a hurry." He was serious.

"You know that bitch Gloria snitched on you right? She told the police you the one that shot KB." Muffin informed him.

"Get the fuck outta here!" He exclaimed. "Black bitch!"

"Yep but I don't think you have to worry about her telling nothin' else, me and Bo took care of that." Muffin laughed. "I'm just glad you ok 'cause I was so scared."

"Yea, that shit was pretty spooky huh? When you coming back down here?"

"I'll be back tomorrow." Muffin smiled to herself.

"Ok."

"Baby?"

"Yea ma, what is it?"

"I took some money out of the safe to pay for..."

"You don't have to explain, I figured that when you said you went to help her. Just take care of your business and come back soon as you're done."

"I will daddy. I promise."

"Ok, I'm gonna hang up now. Hopefully they gon' let me outta this fucking place today so I'll see you when you come in tomorrow. I love you baby."

"I love you too daddy. See you soon." Muffin hung up the phone then said to herself. "I can't believe that lying muhfucka! I don't see what the fuck he still sees in that broke down bitch! I'm the one here holdin' him down." She was extremely upset and paced the floor. "I'm tired of him lying to me 'bout this bitch all the time! He way the fuck down there shot the fuck up and when he wakes up he calls that bitch first? That's that bullshit!"

Muffin bowed her head and wiped a tear that escaped her eye and looked in the mirror. "Ugh! I'm tired of this shit. I'm here trying to make sure this muhfucka's money is still rolling in and he way down there with that bitch Shondra on his mind. What's wrong with this picture? I was gonna tell him the truth 'bout why I came here but why should I when he lied to me without even coughing. Shit, I can lie too! Maybe I should be thinking of myself instead of worrying about him 'cause he clearly ain't thinking 'bout me." Muffin was eyeing herself evilly in the mirror and a smirk emerged on her lips. "I love you Junior but I gotta make sure you not playing games with me so from now on, it's about me and what the fuck I want! Fuck that fake love shit!"

Chapter 7

Her stomach was round, full-bodied and firm to the touch. Her nose had gotten wider, her ankles swollen, her breasts full and tender and she had gained an additional 10 pounds since her pregnancy. She wobbled to the bathroom where she sat down and pissed like a racehorse. She was due to deliver in 8 weeks and the baby resting on her bladder had her running to the bathroom almost every 2 hours. When she was finished, she washed her hands and when she looked up in the mirror there was an unsure look in her eyes. She sat back down on the toilet and rubbed her belly in a circular motion looking down and whispering loving words to the life moving inside of her while tears of confusion, hurt, and fear danced down her cheeks.

Over the months of her pregnancy, although the love she had for Junior invaded her heart, she had buried those feelings away somewhere deep inside her heart and had gotten stronger in dealing with the reality of their break up. It had been over 7 months since she'd seen or spoken to him after he left for North Carolina but when she received a phone call from him today, anxiety filled her heart when she heard his voice but when he told her he had been shot and was in the hospital, fear and worry consumed her immediately. Her love for him instantly resurfaced and she trembled at the thought of him being hurt and desperately wanted to be there with him. It was a devastating blow to her when he politely declined her offer to come be by his bedside. His rejection only ignited feelings she had suppressed and disrupted the time it took her to get over it all. In all the confusion the one thing that was clear to her was

the reality of her situation, she was pregnant with another's man baby.

Shondra heard an unfamiliar sound echoing off the walls in the bathroom and soon realized it was her own cries of sorrow. She didn't understand why she was so emotional because she already knew her circumstances with him but the phone call seemed to bring back confusing feelings that were not realistic at this point. There was no chance of her and Junior ever getting back together because he would never accept her pregnancy and the fact her first baby was not seeded by him. She shuddered at the thought of him not being the father and cried even harder. Her heart ached so much and life seemed so unfair. The baby kicked, almost in protest, and she rubbed her belly softly.

"I hear you baby. No matter what, mommy is going to be there for you. Nothing will come before you. I'm gonna make sure you have all the love you need so don't worry."

***

"Can I ask you a question Craig?" Muffin looked at him as he wheeled his vehicle through traffic.

He looked up and nodded his head but continued driving.

"I know you don't know me like that but I want to ask you something and it doesn't really have anything to do with business…"

Craig cut her off. "Don't ask then."

"Wait, it kinda does but it's really about family, your cousin Junior."

Craig cut his eye at her. "What about him?"

"I'm gonna keep it real with you. He don't know I'm here getting this work from you…"

"I already know that, that's why you not getting shit until I speak with him." Craig interrupted. "You played yourself

when you got here acting all suspicious. I had a feeling you was doing something sheisty that's why I called down south to speak to him myself to find out what the real deal was wit' you. I ain't speak to him yet but when I do and he confirms you on the up and up, I'll give you the work." Craig said plainly.

"Hold on Craig, you can't do that! Let me explain myself. I'm trying to show Junior I can hold him down under any circumstances and won't fold under pressure when he needs me most. Please don't try to stop me from making that happen." Muffin protested.

"And who money you using to show him all this?" Craig's eyebrows lowered.

"It's his money but..."

"Yea, that's what I thought." He smirked.

"No wait! I'm not finished."

"Go 'head, I'm listening." Craig blinked slowly.

"This his money but I didn't steal it, I'm using it to cop. I don't steal from my man, I got access to all his bread and I never once stole shit from him to buy bags or heels. Junior takes care of me and I take care of him, that's why I'm out here now, to make sure he keep getting his money even though he in the hospital." Muffin explained.

"I hear all that fly shit but it still don't mean a fucking thing to me. What you know about this game?" His eyes rolled to the top of his eyes.

"I know Junior didn't usually cop from you..."

Craig laughed out loud, "How you figure? He told you that?" His head tilted to the side as he glared at her.

"He didn't tell me exactly but I know he copped uptown 'cause I used go with him to cop." Muffin was attempting to authenticate her position.

Muffin remembered the time Craig pulled a gun on Junior and how he cried and told her he wouldn't fuck with him anymore after that. She was hoping he still wasn't copping from him so that could at least give her some leverage, not to mention

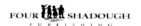

how much money she was spending. Craig was all she had right now, she hadn't come this far just to lose out.

"Really? Where he cop from?" Craig asked with interest.

"Amsterdam Avenue from some Dominican named Venezuela. I'm not bullshitting you Craig. What I'm trying to do is use you instead of him going uptown but I'm not sure how he feels about that. I know y'all had a falling out awhile back."

Craig was throwing her curve balls but she was hitting every pitch out the park. He still didn't believe she was authentic but his business sense was taking over. The fact that she was spending close to fifty thousand in one sale was not a drop in the bucket. To be able to get that monthly would be a good look for him.

"Aiight, I'll talk to my cousin and see what we can negotiate…"

"No! I want to quarterback this Craig. Let me talk to him myself. I want to show him I can make major decisions in his absence. I want to prove myself to him. I want him to know he can trust that I will always be able to hold him down...across the fucking board!" Muffin pressed.

"Why you feel like you can?" His look was disconcerting.

"You want me to keep it real?" Muffin's lips pursed. "A lot of his success down there is because of me. I did a lot of shit for him and been through mad shit with him. I played a key role in all this shit Craig." Muffin championed herself.

"So what? That still don't put you in position to make boss decisions about his business all of a sudden." Craig checked her hard.

"It does! I was the one that clapped that muhfucka KB in the club and I did it because I wanted to make sure he didn't wind up on the receiving end of a gun blast! I made sure of that shit!" Her emotions were high strung now.

"Yea, but that just proves my point. What makes you think you ready to quarterback this shit and you couldn't do that right?" Craig was hitting her low and hard.

Muffin looked at him sideways, "What you mean I ain't do that shit right? I shot that muhfucka!" She was miffed by how he acted as if what she did had no merit.

"Yea, you shot him but you ain't kill him! That's why Junior laying up in the hospital now!" Craig drilled his point home.

"You blaming that on me? That's some bullshit!" Muffin was visibly offended.

"Nah, you the one using that incident like it gives you leverage to run shit in his absence. You can't possibly think you qualified to do this shit if you couldn't complete that job. There's no room for mistakes in this game. You don't get a second chance to do it right!" Craig spoke from experience.

"Well I did because I ain't make that mistake when I killed Lakim!" Muffin played her hold card out of desperation.

"You the one that murked that muhfucka?" Craig chuckled deep in his throat.

"Yea. Junior set it up but I'm the one that bodied him!" Muffin was pushing hard to prove herself.

"Ok. Well now I'm impressed. I remember when that shit happened. I thought it had my cousin stamped all over it. I woulda never guessed it was a broad that put work in like that." Craig nod knowingly.

"Well I got blood on my hands for him and I'll do it again if I have to prove how much I love him, I'm down for Junior. I'm gonna kill that muhfucka KB and his bitch because I love Junior just that much Craig. I'm going to show him he can trust me if he don't trust nobody else in his camp! I'm on his team and I won't let him down, ever!" Her eyes rolled and showed extreme confidence.

"I can respect that but love and business don't mix because emotions will always force a bad decision." Craig schooled.

"I don't believe that." Muffin said in disagreement. "My love is what forced this decision and I know it's not a bad one. You know that yourself Craig."

"Ok, so what you asking me to do, not to tell him I'm the one that hit you with the three keys?"

"I'm asking you to let me tell him, let me broker this deal. I promise you'll get the numbers you want and I can promise it to you at least twice a month." Muffin was showing her business sense.

"That's a big call you making. That's almost a hun'ed gees a month you talkin' bout. How you so sure you can keep that number consistently every month?"

"Craig, I been down there with him almost a year now, that ain't shit for him to clear in a month. Just let me bake this bread and I promise you'll be our connect."

"Ok, starting next month I expect to see you a minimum of two times, but," Craig scratched his chin, "you better make sure he know everything before the next time you pick up. This is business but blood takes priority, ya feel me? At the end of the day Junior my family and I'm not going to do no kind of business behind his back. No excuses and no bullshit! We clear on that?"

"Yes and thank you Craig. Thank you so much."

***

"Can I speak to Bo?"

"Hold on! Ay Bo! Bo! Phone man!"

Bo stopped shooting pool and walked over to the dangling pay phone then picked it up. "Yea."

"What's up Bo?"

"Who 'dis?" He asked, unable to recognize the voice.

FOUR  SHADOUGH
PUBLISHING

"It's Muffin. I was hoping I'd catch you on the Block."

"Oh. What's goin' on?"

"Nuthin'. You know I'm in NY right?"

"Yea, I heard Junior sayin' something about that."

"Well, I'm here making some major power moves and if you off your bullshit then I think it'll be something you gonna like."

"Oh really? What is it?" Bo's interest piqued.

"Can't tell you over the horn but I'll talk to you soon as I get back. It's gonna put you way ahead of what you been doin', feel me?" Muffin was setting up the playing field.

"I don't really know what ya gettin' at but I reckon I'll find out once you get here right?" He said eagerly.

"Absolutely. So Junior's doing fine now huh?"

Muffin didn't have anyone else to count on so in the meantime she had no choice but to utilize Bo in her plan. She already banked on him being on board because he displayed his greed early on. She wasn't looking for his loyalty she just needed him to get the ball rolling and to unknowingly show her the ropes on how things down south operated until she was able to take things over herself.

"Yea. I told you he a bull, it's in our genes." He reaffirmed.

"Right, right. He told me soon as the meds wore off and he was able to talk that he called up here to his peoples and shit. I know that bitch Shondra flipped out when he told her what happened to him." Muffin half laughed knowing she caught him off guard. "Don't trip Bo, I already know. Junior don't hide stupid shit like that from me."

"Oh ok but I don't really know what you talkin' 'bout so I ain't gon' say nuffin'." Bo wasn't sure what Junior told her but he wasn't going to cosign anything.

"Don't worry, you don't have to say nothing I don't already know, trust me. Anyway, what I got planned is gon'

make shit run so much smoother and you more happier. I hope you ready."

"I'm ready." A small smile formed on his lips.

"Ok, I'll talk to you when I get there." Muffin hung up the phone.

"I know my mind wasn't playing tricks on me. I knew what the fuck I heard when I called up to that fucking hospital, Bo think he slick but his reaction only proves I'm right." Muffin thought to herself.

Anger and jealousy was building up in Muffin as her breathing quickened and her chest heaved. She held the phone in her hand trying to calm down then dialed some more numbers.

"I'm not gon' play no more games this time, just like Craig said! If I want to be treated like a boss I gotta make boss decisions and this time I'm gonna finish what I should have when I had the chance!"

***

"Yo come on with that bullshit. Take it and get the fuck outta here!"

"Nah man, this shit too small." The crack addict refused.

"Go 'head with that bullshit man!"

"Let me see another one." The crackhead wanted to negotiate.

"Look, it's hot out here, I ain't got time for this shit!"

"Aight, let me get my money back. I'll go to Bushwick then."

"Fuck outta here muhfucka. I ain't givin' you shit back. You better get ghost 'fore I start firing at yo ass!"

"Come on man, let me get my money back. I can get a jumbo instead of this little shit you trying to give me!" The druggie pleaded.

Chico turned around and walked out the building followed by the addict pressuring him for his money back.

"I swear if you don't get the fuck outta here, I'ma pop your ass." Chico reached into his pocket quickly like he was about to pull out a weapon.

The addict quickly turned in the other direction and ran off. Chico sauntered over to the benches and took a seat and pulled his hand out of his pocket; he didn't have a gun. He gripped the money in his hand tightly then counted out eighty dollars in small bills. He sighed heavily then recounted the money to be sure of the amount. He dug into his back pocket and pulled out the remaining capsules and counted out five. He shook his head then lowered it. He was in a fucked up situation because he was about to have a baby and didn't have any money. Since La's murder there was no work in the projects and his pockets was suffering because of it. When Chico hustled for La he was never taught anything about the game except the very basics, sell the shit and don't get caught. La never talked to him about his connects or how to cop so Chico was forced to buy work already bagged up in weight from local dealers and the product was sub par at best which contributed to the loss of his customer base. He wasn't making anywhere near what he used to make with La and his depression was surfacing. He walked to the front of the building and was approached by one of the neighborhood boosters named Lenny.

"Chico and the man! What's up playboy? I got sumptin' for ya!" Lenny pulled out a pack of pampers and some baby clothes from a black plastic bag. "One stop shopping! Come take all this off my hands for the deal of the century." He was shuffling his feet as he talked.

"How much you want for everything?" Chico asked inspecting the items.

"Gimme tweny, tweny, tweny, thirty bucks!" The booster danced and laughed.

"Here." Chico dug into his pocket and gave him two capsules and twenty dollars.

"Hol' up boss." Lenny said after looking at the weight in the small capsules. "I don't want the work, lemme get the bread."

"Then just take the twenty 'cause I don't have no more change on me." Chico said annoyed.

"Aiight. Then let me get four 'cause those joints you selling is on a diet and I'm a fat boy that like eating cake." The booster laughed as he continued to dance.

Chico shuffled his feet uncomfortably then dug into his pocket and gave him two more capsules then grabbed the bag from him.

"Thank you boss. See ya on the rebound. Yep! Yep!" Lenny bobbed his head then skipped off down the street.

Chico walked across the street and went into the lobby of the building and walked up three steps then knocked on the apartment door.

When Shondra looked through the peephole she slowly opened up the door, just enough for her eyes to be seen.

"What's up baby?" Chico's voice was animated.

"I keep telling you, I'm not your baby Chico. Now what you want?" Shondra answered dryly.

"I got some pampers and some clothes for the baby." Chico held his hand out with the bag.

Shondra opened the door a little wider to look at the black plastic bag he was holding in his hand.

"You got that from another crack head huh?" She took the bag from him and inspected the contents then sucked her teeth. "I told you stop buying dresses and shit until you find out what the baby is. What I'm gon' do with all the dresses and pink outfits you keep buying if it's a boy? You not thinking." Shondra shook her head.

"Damn, I'm trying to do the best I can before the baby get here. You always beefing about anything I do like it's never good enough." Chico hung his head down.

"Really Chico? Where the baby gonna sleep huh? I told you to concentrate on things the baby gon' need soon as it's born. A crib, a baby carriage, formula...shit like that. When you wanna get something, think eat, shit and sleep! That way the baby will have what it needs no matter if it's a girl or a boy. When you do buy things, you always get girly shit like you know it's a girl. You just wasting your money."

"You act like you know it's a boy, if it is then let me know and I'll stop getting girl shit. This shit is getting real old Shondra, why can't I come in and talk to you instead of standing in the hallway talking through the crack in a door?" Frustration could be heard in his tone.

"We not gon' keep going through this. You already know it's a wrap with us Chico, the only thing we got in common is this baby. That's it. I was wrong for fucking with you in the first place because I was trying to get over Junior. All that shit that happened between us shouldn't have happened, it was a learning experience for both of us and I'm not gon' fuck with you like that again 'cause you still got a lot to learn and I'm nobody's teacher. I don't got no beef with you but we don't have to be together for you to be in the baby's life and I'm not gonna block you from being in the baby's life. Comprende?"

"That's fucked up, sounds like you not even trying to give me and you a chance to work..."

Shondra cut him off. "No boo boo, I gave you a chance and you fucked that up. That's what I'm talking 'bout when I said you have a lot to learn. That stupid shit you did only proved to me that if I woulda went for it you woulda just got worse so I chose to be by my muhfuckin' self. Now is that all?" She huffed.

"No, that's not all. We having a baby Shondra. Why you can't let that shit go and let me be there?" He pleaded.

"I know we having a baby and I'm gonna let you be there…for the baby. Now good bye." Shondra closed the door slowly.

Chico stood in the hallway staring at the door. He turned around and walked out the front of the building feeling defeated. He wanted to make things work with Shondra and he figured once his money situation got better and the baby was born that things would change. He went back across the street to see if he could sell the last of the work. He stopped short on the sidewalk and dropped his head and palmed his forehead. He had no idea what he was doing, he was barely surviving and because he didn't have any leadership abilities, he was always a worker and never aspired to be a boss.

"Hey! Pull over right here and don't leave me!" Muffin said as she shoved some bills into the slot and jumped out the cab. "Ay!"

Chico lifted his head then turned around to the girl he recognized from a while back that came to Baptiste claiming to be Junior's girl then getting into a fight with Shondra.

"What's up?" His eyebrows furrowed.

"Hey you. You remember me?" Muffin smiled.

"Yea, you the one that came over here and jumped Shondra with that broad Gloria." He confirmed.

"She lucky that's all that happened. While you mentioning her, does she still live over here?"

"Why you wanna know? You wanna fight her again?" He quizzed.

"Maybe." Muffin giggled. "Nah, I just need to talk to her about something real important." Muffin showed a one sided smile.

"What you wanna talk to her about? Junior still your man?" He tilted his head to the side with a smirk on his face.

"He sure is boo boo. Now why don't you tell me what apartment she lives in?" Muffin asked directly.

"I can't do that." His reply was dry.

"What I have to tell her is so important that I'm willing to pay for the information. How's two hun'ed sound for an apartment number?" Muffin pulled out a small stack of money and peeled off a couple bills.

Chico eyed the stack in her hand and his hand twitched as greed crept into his mind. He moved closer to Muffin, inching near the hand holding the stack of money.

"Don't get no dumb ass ideas Rodriguez." Muffin took a step back pulling out a small snub-nosed .38 caliber revolver from her bag cocking the hammer back. "Don't make me leave you leaking on this pavement!"

Chico backed up and held his hands up with a crooked smile on his face.

"Nah ma, I wasn't thinking 'bout robbing you. I'm just shocked you holdin' like you out here slingin' rocks."

Muffin looked at the stack in her hand. "This? This ain't shit Pedro. I told you who my man is, you musta thought I was joking. I'll add another two on top of the first two, just for the floor she lives on." Muffin smirked. "I'll find the apartment myself."

"Nah, I can't do that." Chico rejected her offer.

Muffin sucked her teeth. "Why not? This is easy bread Ruiz, you can't use four hun'ed bucks?"

"Damn right I could use it but I was thinking that maybe you could help me out with something else." The wheels in his head were turning.

"Why would I help you and you won't help me? Who I look like to you, Boo Boo the fool?" She asked seriously.

"Nah, I just wanna know if you can you talk to Junior and ask him if he want to put some work out here because ain't nobody out here no more since La got murked."

Muffin's eyes got wide as she stared at Chico.

"You want me to talk to him to see if he'll give you some work because there's none out here right now?" She purposely repeated what he said to be sure she heard him right.

"Yea 'cause it's only me in Baptiste right now but I don't have enough work to keep shit clicking like when La or Junior had it. Na'mean?" He explained.

"Yea, yea. I think I can talk to him about it but let me ask you something. Did he ever give you work before?"

"I'ma keep it real wit' you. When my man Rock got bodied he came through and hit me with something small. But shit got fucked up when La came back around. You know him and Junior had beef and when he found out I had Junior's work he told me I couldn't sell his shit out here 'cause they was going to war. I ain't have no choice but to get down with La since I live here. When Junior came through he whipped me out when I ain't give him the rest of his gwap from the pack he hit me with. If I get the chance to tell him how the shit really went down then maybe he'll fuck with me again, you feel me?"

"That sounds like some real disloyal shit right there Julio. How you expect a muhfucka to fuck wit' you after you switch sides? It's like you can't handle the pressure when it comes, not a good look. Do you feel me?" Muffin preached like a certified boss.

"I hear you but that muhfucka La dead and gone now so…"

"So now you got heart." Muffin laughed. "Look, I'll talk to him for you but how soon you ready to get to work?"

"Shit! I'm ready right now!" He responded eagerly.

"Ok, I'ma see what I can make happen but in the meantime, I need to find that bitch Shondra." She said focusing back on her reason for coming to Baptiste in the first place.

"I really can't help you with that because she's my…"

Before Chico could finish his sentence, Muffin eyes were fixed on the entrance of the building across the street. She watched in surprise as Shondra waddled out the door and made her way down the block.

"No fucking way! That bitch pregnant? Oh shit!" Muffin was talking out loud unconsciously. "I ain't gotta kill this bitch,

that stomach will definitely be the deal breaker. I couldn't ask for anything better. I'm gonna make sure Junior finds out about this in the worst way I can bring it to him." Muffin turned to Chico.

"Aiight Pablo, I'm gonna go talk to him. Give me a number so I can call you in case he decides to fuck wit' you again." Muffin's attitude had turned jovial.

"You know my name is Chico right?" He asked her with a bewildered look on his face.

"Ok what that mean?" She answered, eyebrows raised.

"You keep calling me different names."

Muffin looked at him with a smirk then took the number and jumped into the waiting cab. When the cab pulled off, she rolled down the window and stuck her head out while the cab passed Shondra and yelled, "Stinkin' bitch! I hope you fall face first in a pool of shit!" She laughed loud and hard then pulled her head back in the cab.

Shondra recognized the high-pitched voice immediately and cringed when she saw Muffin whiz by in a cab with her middle finger up laughing.

Chico dipped behind the building after hearing Muffin scream out at Shondra. He hoped she didn't see him as he walked to the back and sat on the benches near the exit. He guessed Muffin wanted Shondra dead because of something involving Junior. He wasn't going to let that shit go down but he needed her at the moment, she was going to be the key to him getting back on his feet, that's if Junior was still willing to fuck with him. He pulled the last vial out of his pocket and rolled it between his index finger and thumb.

He didn't like Muffin because he knew she wanted to hurt Shondra and because she was his baby mother he felt disrespected. He was hoping when he saw her again she would have good news for him because if she didn't, him and Junior was going to have beef because he planned on robbing and fucking her up.

Chapter 8

Muffin stopped on Broadway and picked up some empty capsules then headed home. She got a plate and Ziploc bags from the kitchen then went to her room. She pulled out the bag of work Craig had given her and took out a kilo of cooked coke. She put it on the plate then broke it in half.

"I'm glad Junior taught me how to bag up." She laughed to herself. "All this shit is coming in handy."

She started cutting the work up and bagging it up in five hundred dollar bombs like she used to do for Junior when he was the boss in Baptiste. Two hours passed and she smiled at how quickly she bagged up the kilo and remembered how long it had took her when Junior first showed her, now she was a vet in her own right. She put all the bombs into one of her empty Gucci boot boxes she got out of her closet then placed it into an empty Gucci shopping bag. She sat on the bed and looked down at the floor and turned her head to the left toward her dresser. She breathed out heavily then leaned over and picked up the cordless phone and pulled out a paper from her purse and dialed the number.

"Hello?"

"Is this Chico?" She asked.

"Yea. What's goodie?" He couldn't prevent the smile that formed in anticipation of what he was hoping for.

"Look, I made the impossible possible and got the green light for you."

"Say word!"

"Calm down Carlito. I need to talk to you before anything happens, capiece (means understand in Italian)? Meet me in twenty minutes in front of that building where I saw you."

"I'll be there."

Muffin disconnected the call and placed the phone back on the base. *"I'm gonna have to play this shit out right. I can't risk fucking this up."*

She called a cab and grabbed the Gucci bag and headed out the door and waited on the stoop for her ride to arrive.

***

After speaking to Muffin, Chico was so anxious that he ran down stairs to the back of the building although she said she would be there in twenty minutes. He sat on the benches behind the building rubbing his hands together. Things were beginning to go in his favor and his excitement couldn't be hidden by the dumb smile he had plastered on his face. He looked down at his watch and jumped up from the benches to go meet Muffin in front of the building. As he walked through the back exit door and through the lobby, he was shocked to see Shondra standing in front of the building.

"Ummm…What's up baby?" His voice had a nervous overtone.

"Don't what's up baby me Chico! What was you doing talking to that bitch in the cab a couple of hours ago!" Her voice was grainy.

"What you talkin' 'bout Shondra? I wasn't talkin' to no bitch!" He denied the accusation.

"Stop your bullshit boy. I saw your coward ass duck back in the building when I turned around to see where that hoe was coming from. I just want to know what she was over here talking to you about!" She questioned seriously.

"She wasn't talkin' to me like that."

"So you WAS talking to that bitch you lyin' fuck! What you up to wit' your grimy ass Chico? You already know I got beef wit' that squeaky voice bitch and you over here talking to her?" Shondra was livid and was concerned with why she was in Baptiste. Junior was in North Carolina in the hospital and she was here, that could only mean that he wasn't with her like that because if they were, she would be there with him, wouldn't she?

"I ain't do shit Shondra. She was walking by and when she saw me she asked me a question, that's it. Then she broke out." He told her.

"Really Chico. Walking by? Ok, what was the question she asked you?"

Chico looked down at his watch then looked up the street at the oncoming cars. "She asked me something about La. I told her he got murked 'bout six or seven months ago."

Shondra rubbed her belly slowly from the baby's movement. "You really want me to believe that shit, huh? 'Specially when she ain't got no business over here at all and no peoples out here. Why the fuck would she want to know about La for?"

Chico's left eyebrow raised. "She said something about Junior wanting to know."

Shondra leaned forward and looked deep into Chico's eyes. "You're such a fucking liar Chico with your sneaky ass! You only saying that because you know what I went through with that bitch over him!" Shondra was disgusted.

"Damn Shondra, why you just can't believe what I tell you without blowin' shit outta proportion? You asked me what she asked me and when I tell you, you call me a liar. I didn't even remember who the fuck she was until after she said his name."

"Your breath stinks you lying fuck!" Shondra turned and wobbled across the street to her building. As soon as she

78

entered her building a cab pulled up and Muffin got out and walked over to Chico.

"You got a place we can talk?" Muffin asked immediately.

"Um, you want to go up to my crib?" Chico looked over Muffin's shoulder eyeing the front door of Shondra's building.

"Where you live?"

"Next building. Come on." Chico started to walk off.

"Hold on Raul, you moving too fast. Pump your brakes, you speeding. Something don't feel right. Who you running from?" Muffin looked around suspiciously.

"Nah, I'm just hype because it's been a minute since I had some work and I'm ready to hit the block."

"Ok then, let's go." Muffin said following him to his building.

When they got inside the building, Muffin pulled out her snub nosed .38 revolver and kept it by her side partially hidden by the purse she was carrying. Chico never noticed the gun when he opened his apartment door.

"Come in and go to the door on the right, that's my room." He directed.

"Not gon' happen, you lead the way Paco." Muffin stood in the living room and waited for Chico.

He locked the front door then went into his room followed by Muffin. When she got inside, she placed the Gucci bag on the floor next to her.

"Aiight, let me tell it to you straight 'cause I don't have a lot of time." She stared deep into Chico eyes. "Junior didn't want to fuck wit' you, point blank."

The excitement in Chico's eyes drained when he heard that and he sucked his teeth in protest. His forehead wrinkled a bit and his mind raced to robbing and beating Muffin's ass.

"But I talked to him and he said he would on the strength of me so you can't fuck up this chance you getting, ya feel me?"

Chico's smile reemerged and he breathed out in relief. "Yo, on my unborn seed, I ain't gon' fuck up again. It's bone dry out here right now. The dudes in Bushwick got the whole hood on lock but that shit 'bout to change once I get back on the block." Chico was reenergized.

Muffin wasn't sure how Chico did when Junior gave him work but the spark he had in his eye told her he was ready to take things more seriously.

"Aiight Diego before I give you this work, I gotta tell you something really important and I want you to listen carefully." Muffin paused to make sure she had his full attention. "Once I hand this shit over to you, the split is 60/40, no shorts! Junior wants all his with no excuses. If you fuck up some bread, be a man about your shit and let me know. Don't run 'cause if you do, your people will suffer." Muffin's stare was deadly.

"You threatening me?" Chico took a slow step towards her in the small bedroom.

Muffin backed out with the .38 snub nose revolver and cocked the hammer back and aimed at his chest. "No muhfucka, I'm promising you! Let this be the last time you walk up on me like that or the next time will be your last time!" She chided seriously.

"Yo, hold on!" Chico backed up with his palms in the air.

"Nah Javier, keep coming so I can turn your chest cavity into a donut! You all in yo' feelings over what I said, maybe Junior was right and I was wrong..."

"Nah, nah Muffin. It's just that I was thinking about my unborn and my fam getting hurt. I wasn't gonna do nothing."

Muffin laughed wickedly. "You think I was worried? Negative Pasquale, never that. Now I'm wondering if I can trust your emotional ass with this work." The gun was still pointed at Chico's chest.

"I give you my word, I'm down with this shit all the way. I ain't gon' fuck up so I don't have to worry about nothing happening to my fam. So please, let's do this. I need to get back on the block and get right. My seed 'bout to drop and I need bread to take care of my responsibility." Chico confessed.

"Keep your emotions in check then Martinez, shit can bring a whole lot of problems to your life that you don't need, ya feel me?" Muffin waved the revolver then put it down by her waist. "Now let me finish before I was so rudely interrupted. You getting packs in five hundred dollar bombs. When you knock off five bombs you're gonna call the number I give you and say "done" and you'll be told where to drop off the bread. You have 30 days to have all the money for the work, not 31. You got it?"

"Ok. No problem. I got it." Chico confirmed his understanding.

"No shorts or excuses once you take this." Muffin said picking up the Gucci bag and handing it to Chico. "You got a whole brick bagged up in here so this your life, act like it depends on it Chachi."

Chico took the bag and the phone number Muffin passed to him. He opened the box and gasped at the amount of neatly bagged up packages of drugs.

"Damn!" His eyes bulged.

"What's the problem? Too much for you to handle at one time Papito? Let me know before I walk out that door 'cause once I'm gone it's yours and everything that comes with it." Muffin stated seriously.

"It's just I never seen this much work at one time before. I'm gonna have to get some help to move all this shit in a month but I ain't worried 'cause I know it can be done. As long as it's good, I'm not gon' have no problems moving it." Chico said inspecting the product in the bag.

"You pay them out of your pc. You got anymore questions for me? If not, I'm out. I got shit to do Ricardo. Talk wit' you real soon."

Muffin waited for him to lead the way to the door and stepped out into the hallway and once she boarded the elevator, she put the revolver back in her purse.

"*Whew! I thought I was gonna have to put a bullet in shorty. He was walking up on me all slow and shit.*" She smirked. "*I hope his ass can handle all that work I gave him and don't fuck up that money 'cause I just put all my eggs in one basket depending on that fool!*" When the elevator stopped she walked out the building and hailed a cab. A green and white colored cab pulled up and she got into the backseat. She gave the driver her address and then looked to her left at Shondra's building then scratched her head.

"*That muhfucka kept saying his unborn seed.*" A smile formed on her face. "*This is too good to be true. That bitch pregnant by the fucking help! That bitch might as well stick a fork up her ass 'cause she done!*"

Chapter 9

Junior winced when he bent down to open the safe. He knew he was running low on product before the shootout at the barbershop and was sure Bo was running low on work. Although he was just released his mind was focused on his business, it was important he took care of it so he didn't lose the stronghold he had on the town. The doctor told him to stay in bed and rest but handling his business was his main priority. He pulled the lever on the safe and opened it and was about to grab some stacks of money but a lot seemed to be missing.

"Muff musta took a lot of bread to help her mom's out, shit. I'm gonna have to find out how much she took when she gets back today." He said to himself because he was too weak to count it all.

He was beginning to feel light headed so he closed the safe and limped back to his bed on unsteady legs, holding the wall for support. When he got to the bed he sat down slowly and pulled his sweats down from off his waist. The bandage was soaked in burgundy and he suddenly began to feel the room spinning.

"Shit, I'm bleeding again. Damn!" He grabbed the cordless telephone and dialed 911 and leaned back as his eyes got heavy.

"911. What's your emergency?" The operator said in a rehearsed voice.

Silence.

"911. What's your emergency?" The operator asked again.

"*Mmmmm.*" The phone slipped out of Junior's hand as his hands dropped to his waist.

***

Everything Muffin was doing was working out better than she could have hoped. She was personally impressed with how she made boss decisions and handled business in the wake of all that was happening with Junior. As she grabbed her bag from the top compartment on the bus thoughts of Junior's betrayal invaded her mind. That was the only thing that wasn't going her way but the information she found out while she was in Brooklyn would change all that. She was planning to tell him as soon as she saw him since he was so quick to call Shondra to tell her he was in the hospital instead of trying to contact her first especially since she was the one by his fucking bedside the whole time. She knew once she told him Shondra was pregnant that it would hurt him but when she told him it was by Chico, a little nobody ass muhfucka he had to whip out because he owed him money, that would break his spirit. That news would severe whatever love connection was lingering in his heart for Shondra. Muffin knew Junior's pride and ego was enormous so there was no way he would allow himself to ever deal with her again. Muffin jumped into an awaiting cab at the bus station and headed home with renewed vigor.

When the cab pulled up in front of the house, Muffin grabbed her bags and jumped out running up the steps as quickly as she could. An ambulance and single police cruiser were sitting in the front with flashing lights on. The front door was open as she rushed through screaming, "Junior! Junior!" She dashed to the bedroom and was met by two paramedics lifting Junior onto a gurney.

"What the fuck happened!" She ran over to where Junior was being strapped down.

"We got a call from 911 to come to this address." The paramedic said as he secured Junior and pulled the gurney out of the room. "The police had to break the door down because no one answered."

"Oh my God! Junior baby, wake up!" Muffin wailed as she walked beside the gurney holding his hand. "Can he hear me?"

"He wasn't responsive when we got here, he was bleeding profusely from a wound…"

"Yea, he was shot. He was released yesterday evening. How could they release him and this shit happen?" She was looking for answers.

"I don't know ma'am. We stopped the bleeding temporarily but he did lose a lot of blood."

"Please don't let him die, please!" Her voice cracked as she relived the day in the barbershop over again.

"We'll do everything we can ma'am." The paramedic loaded Junior into the back of the ambulance and his partner jumped into the driver seat and activated the siren and they pulled off headed to the hospital.

Muffin stood in the middle of the street staring at the vehicle as it made a turn then she dropped to her knees. She felt guilty for wanting to hurt Junior with the news about Shondra's pregnancy: she felt bad for being selfish and only worrying about her feelings.

"*Not again Lord, please not again!*" Her grief seeped out in her words.

She stood up slowly then went back into the house. She grabbed her bag off the floor and went into the bedroom and was in awe with all the blood on the bed.

"*I gotta get to the hospital. I need to make sure my baby gonna be all right.*" She was speaking unconsciously.

She put her bags in the closet, retrieved the keys to Junior's Jeep and headed out the front door. She pulled it shut behind her but it didn't close because the locks were broken.

"*I can't leave this door open with all that work in the house.*" She deduced correctly.

She walked around to the back of the house and went to the doghouse and took their pit bull off the leash and brought him around to the front of the house. She looked for somewhere to tie him up then decided him being tied up outside wouldn't secure the room so she took him inside the house. She opened the bedroom door and let him go then shut the door behind her.

"*Hmph. That should keep the money and drugs safe for now. Drama will kill anything that comes to that door!*" She said to herself confidently.

Muffin left the house and jumped into the Jeep then sped off to the hospital. When she got there she ran into the small emergency room and was told Junior was having emergency surgery.

"Is he going to be all right?" Her lips were quivering.

"Ma'am, I'm sorry but we can't tell you anything right now until he's stabilized." A nurse informed her.

"Get me two hundred cc's of type O blood Stat!" Muffin heard a doctor scream out as nurses scrambled around pushing stainless steel carts full of silver operating tools.

Hearing that put Muffin's emotions in disarray and she immediately began fearing the worse once again.

"*Oh my God! I shouldn't have left him down here alone, I shoulda waited! I thought I was helping by going to take care of his business but I shoulda been here taking care of him! I'll never forgive myself for leaving if something happens to him! I failed, Oh God please, I don't want to lose him!*" She prayed.

Muffin began to hyperventilate and it soon became hard for her to breathe. She grabbed a chair in front of her and bent over trying to catch her breath. A nurse rushed over to her and passed her a cup of water.

"Calm down honey and drink this. I know you're upset but you have to try and relax or you will make yourself sick." She coached.

86

Muffin grabbed the cup in her shaking hands and sipped some of the water as her chest heaved.

"I know but I can't help it. I wasn't here for him. I shoulda been here with him!" Muffin held onto the nurse and slid down to the floor as her painful cries echoed off the walls in the emergency room. "Please help him! I love him so much!"

The nurse kneeled down and held Muffin in her arms and rocked back and forth, she could feel her shaking in her arms and tried her best to comfort her. They stayed on the floor for five minutes then Muffin struggled to her feet.

"I need some air." She mumbled.

She walked out the emergency room holding the walls as she made her way to the exit then over to the Jeep where she sat in the driver's seat and continued to wail and shake uncontrollably.

"*Why!*" She banged the steering wheel.

After an hour of non-stop crying Muffin ventured back into the emergency room on shaky legs and asked about Junior's surgery.

"He's stable and in recovery. The doctor will be out to talk with you in a minute." A nurse said to her.

Muffin composed herself and waited for the doctor. After some minutes passed she saw a doctor emerge from the back and he walked over to her with a worried look on his face leading her to believe something wasn't right.

"Is he ok doc?" She didn't wait for him to speak first.

"He's stable ma'am. We cannot figure out what caused his hemorrhaging so we're going to transfer him to another hospital facility located in Greenville."

"Whyyyy?" The word dragged through her voice.

"Well, we believe the medical staff in Greenville would be able to determine what is causing this severe bleeding. He's lost quite a bit of blood and he's still unconscious. We cannot give a prognosis because we don't have the equipment to do the specific tests needed. Greenville has the proper equipment to

administer those tests to diagnose the problem." He explained professionally.

"When are you going to take him there?"

"We're preparing to have him air lifted in about an hour."

"Air lifted? Is it that serious? Is he doing that bad?" Muffin bowed her head and shook it left to right slowly. The doctor put his hand on her shoulder gently.

"He's going to be fine. Don't worry yourself too much ok?"

"I can't help it." She breathed out.

"If you have anything you need to take care of, you should take care of it now and be back within the hour and you'll be able to ride with him." He informed her.

Muffin suddenly remembered she did have business to handle and looked up that the doctor.

"Can I see him real quick first, please?"

"Sure."

Muffin walked to the back and went over to the gurney Junior was laying on in the recovery room. He looked eerily peaceful and tears immediately burst from her eyes. She grabbed his hand and held it firm in hers and moved close to him.

"Baby, I am so scared right now but I know I have to be strong for you, for us. I feel so bad for not making sure you were completely healed before leaving but I wanted to show you I could hold you down and now I'm thinking I might be moving too fast. I never thought I would see you in this condition again and I'm so sorry. Maybe if I got rid of KB that night in the club, like Craig said, you wouldn't be going through this shit." Muffin dried her tears as anger surfaced at the mention of the man responsible for his condition. "I'm not going to make that same mistake twice though, I promise you that baby." She took a labored breath. "They're gonna take you to another hospital so they can help you get better. I'm sure you're

going to be all right because you made it this far, this is just a minor setback. I have to be strong for both of us but this time I'm riding this out all the way with you until you're back on your good foot." She smiled weakly and kissed the back of his hand softly then turned and left the hospital.

***

Muffin went back home and immediately called a locksmith to get the front door lock fixed. She took Drama back outside and bagged up some work for Bo then called him when she was done.

"I'm back." She said when he answered the phone.

"Ok. I'm ready. You want me to meet you somewhere?"

"I need you to come over here and drop that bread off and I'll fill you in on some things." She answered as she looked at her watch.

"I'm on my way."

"Hurry up." She insisted.

Muffin went into the bathroom and took a quick wash up before Bo got there. When she came out the bathroom the locksmith was at the door and she instructed him to change the locks on the front and back doors. She went into her bedroom and dressed quickly then went back out to check on the locksmith while she waited on Bo. The young locksmith was looking out the back door at Drama.

"He's tied up so you don't have to worry about him." Muffin said noticing his concern.

"You sure? He won't stop staring at me like I'm his dinner." The locksmith said still hesitant about opening the door.

"Well he loves meat." Muffin chuckled. "Nah but for real, you good. He already ate."

The locksmith looked at Muffin and wasn't the least bit humored by her comment. She noticed he wasn't going to finish

installing the lock so she walked out into the back yard and closed the gate so if Drama did get loose he still wouldn't be able to get the locksmith.

"Thank you." The nervous locksmith said as he began working on replacing the cylinders on the back door.

"You said you'll be done in another fifteen minutes right?" She questioned as she looked at her watch again.

"Yes ma'am. I may be done 'fore that." He said pulling out a screwdriver from his tool belt.

Muffin heard Bo at the front door and went to meet him.

"What's up Muffin?" Bo asked as he walked through the open door.

"Hey Bo." She greeted him warmly.

"What's happenin'? Let's go sit in the kitchen so you can tell me what the big surprise is." He said anxiously.

"Nah, the locksmith putting a lock on the back door so let's talk here in the living room in private."

Bo took a seat on the couch.

"What's goin' on with the new locks on the doors?" He asked noticing the shiny brass cylinders.

"Junior's back in the hospital Bo." Muffin struggled to keep a straight face. "When I got here from the bus station this morning the paramedics was in here already strapping him to the gurney. Junior musta called them before he passed out and they broke the door down to get to him." She sniffled to prevent a tear from falling.

"He awright? What happened?" Concern could be heard in his voice.

"I just came back from the hospital and the doctor said he was bleeding out again. This shit is driving me crazy!"

"Damn. When I spoke to him earlier he was fine."

"Well they gonna take him to the hospital in Greenville 'cause they don't know why he keep bleeding out like that. So I need to take care of this business first so I can get back to the

hospital and ride over there with him." She said switching back to business.

"You want me to come wit' you?" Bo offered.

"No, I'll keep you updated on what's going on with him. It's best one of us stay out here and take care of this business."

"Awright." Bo dug into his pocket and pulled out a stack of money and placed it on the center table.

"Hold up!" Muffin pushed the money back to Bo who caught it as it fell in his lap. She stood up and stopped the locksmith right before he walked into the living room.

"You're done?" She asked blocking his view into the living room until Bo had recovered the money.

"Yes ma'am." The locksmith looked at Bo then handed her a receipt.

"Let's go back into the kitchen so I can pay you." She said walking out of the living room.

Muffin returned to the living room a short while later and lead the locksmith out the door then looked at Bo sternly.

"You gotta be more careful how you do shit Bo. You don't want nobody to know what you're doing." She shook her head. "Now give me the bread."

Bo took the stack from his lap and put it on the table. Muffin counted it, placed it inside a brown paper bag then looked at Bo.

"Aiight, this is the deal Bo. I'm going to give you twice the weight Junior used to give you with a raise. Instead of you giving me back 70% you give me 60%."

Bo smiled, he liked the money increase.

"The catch is, for you to keep that raise you gotta get rid of it in three weeks which really shouldn't be a problem 'cause you moved that half of brick in like four or five days." Muffin knew Bo's greed would take over any previous thoughts he may have had about taking over and going out on his own. She figured more work, more money and a quicker flip would keep

him happier longer until he was in the position to cancel his contract with her.

"You want me to get rid of twice as much as I already been moving in three weeks?" Bo scratched his head then nodded quickly. "I can do that 'cause I got a lot of guys that want to work but I never had enough to give out. Now I can put most of them to work without a problem and probably get rid of it even before three weeks." He was thinking out loud.

"That's cool but you gonna have to pay them out of your cut. One more thing, I need my money up front before you take your cut so I can re up before you run out." Muffin explained.

"Awright. Where the stuff at?"

"I'm gonna tell you where you can pick it up in a minute. I just wanna make sure we understand each other. You got three weeks to get rid of everything and you pay me first." Muffin reiterated for confirmation.

"I got it." He affirmed.

"Ok. Pick your package up in thirty minutes by the railroad tracks by Haven's Garden. It's gon' be in a brown paper bag."

"Ok, I'ma leave now so I can go set this up with my guys."

"Aiight. I'm leaving to go with Junior. When I get to the hospital, I'll call and give you the number."

"Ok, I'm gone." Bo got up and headed out the front door.

"*Whew! That's outta the way now I can concentrate on my baby!*"

Muffin grabbed her new house keys and ran out the door to the hospital.

***

"I'm going with you!"

"Come on Glo'. I'm just going to close up and get the cash receipts to take to the bank in the morning." KB forehead wrinkled in aggravation.

"So why I can't go, huh? All of a sudden you wanna bard me from something we built together!" Gloria challenged.

"Aww come on Glo', you know it ain't like that."

"Well how is it then? Why you don't want me to ride with you?" She questioned.

"It's not that I don't want you to ride. I'm just going to take care of the receipts and close up. I ain't been to the shop since I been outta the hospital." He argued.

"I know and you got that bitch running everything." Gloria sucked her teeth.

"Aah man, don't start that shit again." KB blew out air from his mouth.

"I'm not, I'm gonna finish it." Gloria's fists were resting on her hips.

"We talked about this even before I got shot. You know we both decided to keep her in there then find another shop over in Greenville for you to run so there wouldn't be no drama between y'all two at this shop. You still was gonna do the books for this shop so I don't really see the problem all of the sudden. This is business Glo' and you trying to turn it into something personal."

"Really K, I'm the one turning it into something personal? Is that why you ain't tell me the bitch came to visit you at the hospital, was that a business decision we made too?"

"Come on Glo' don't do that. I told you I was sorry for not telling you. You acting like I told her to come see me!" KB threw his hands in the air. "You see how you reacting to that? That's why I didn't say anything because I didn't want you to flip. I already know there's bad blood between y'all."

"So you rather lie to me, your girl huh? I told you how stupid I felt when I went to the shop and she told me she came to the hospital and you told her to keep the shop open."

"Glo' baby, I'm sorry. I don't want you to make this a issue…"

Gloria cut him off. "It is an issue, a big fucking issue! I don't know why you can't see it. It's like you taking her side over mine K. Why?" Her eyes turned soft.

"I ain't taking her side on shit. You acting like she fucked money up since we ain't been there. She doing a good job Glo', you can't deny that. Our bread ain't never been short, in fact, we been making more money." KB pointed out.

"Oh my God, now you acting like she the reason for that, like she's the only reason the shop is doing good."

"No I'm not but the money she brings in contributes to the success of the shop." He admitted.

"And so does the fucking barbers but I don't hear you talking 'bout what they money contribute to the shop!" Her lips got tight.

KB breathed out a burst of air. "Business Glo', that's all it is for me period! Stop your bullshit! You act like I'm fuckin' her!"

"Are you? Do you want to?" Gloria asked almost in a whisper.

"No." KB calmed down and grabbed her to him lovingly. "You the only girl I want, I love you Glo'."

"I love you too K, with all my heart." Gloria reached up and kissed him passionately.

"Alright, so now please let me go take care of this business real quick, I ain't gonna be long. I'll be back in a hour."

"Ok." Gloria gave in reluctantly. "Stay true to me K. That's all I ask, stay true." She turned around and walked into the bedroom and closed the door behind her softly.

KB stood silently for some seconds looking at the closed bedroom door then turned and left.

***

KB pulled up to the back of the barbershop and exited his Acura. It was dark outside but the automatic floodlights popped on when he reached the back door. He opened the door and entered the shop slowly. He breathed out heavily as his heartbeat quickened. He was uncomfortable being there without a weapon as he walked to the front of the shop.

Patricia was alone in the shop and turned around when she heard a noise behind her.

"Oh my God! You scared me Keith." She said holding her hand to her chest.

"My bad. How's everything going?" KB asked looking around the shop and getting chills.

"Everything is fine. I'm just cleaning up before I leave. I didn't know you were coming by."

"I shoulda called to let you know so I wouldn't spook you. I was feeling a li'l better so I just decided to come through and check on things."

"You came to check on me?" Patricia flashed a seductive smile.

KB felt warm. "Yea, I came to make sure you was good." He walked to the front door and checked to make sure it was closed. "You 'bout done here?"

"Yea, just about. How's your shoulder?" She asked placing the broom against the wall.

"It's a li'l stiff but it's healing aiight." He rotated his arm around to show the range of motion.

"I'm glad. I was worried."

KB was at the cash register about to open the drawer.

"You was huh? I really appreciate that. Thanks for holding things down while I was in the hospital."

"No problem. You're a good guy and I don't mind helping you out. How's your other half? I'm surprised she's not here with you. Hmmm." Patricia half smiled.

"She good." KB laughed nervously. "She a li'l pissed off I ain't tell her about you keeping the shop open while I was laying up."

"I figured that by how she acted when she came by here the same day I went to the hospital. She was real hot with me." Patricia chuckled. "But don't worry, I was nice to her. I told her to take up any problems she had with you. I didn't get you in any trouble by coming up to the hospital did I?" Patricia batted her lashes.

"Nah, it's all love. I shoulda just told her to avoid any bullshit."

"Why didn't you?" She asked, one eyebrow raised.

KB looked at her and her deep dimples appeared when she started smiling.

"I forgot." He mused.

Patricia shoved him lightly on his shoulder. "You forgot about seeing me? Stop lying."

"Owww!"

"Oh I'm sorry Keith. I didn't mean..."

"I'm just joking." He laughed. "It's my other shoulder."

"Stop playing like that Keith, I thought I hurt you." She said in an innocent pouty voice.

"You wouldn't hurt me, would you?" His eyes lowered.

"Not on purpose." She purred.

Their eyes locked and they stared at each other for some seconds then he held her by the arm gently.

"I hope not."

Patricia slowly pulled away from KB and grabbed the receipts from the register. "I'm gonna go put these on the desk in your office."

She walked towards the back of the shop and when she was in front of his office she grabbed the door knob, turned around and looked at him seductively then pushed open the door.

KB looked at her backside as she walked away from him in slow motion. His breathing increased along with his heart rate as she paused at the door and smiled showing her dimples before going inside the office. He could have sworn she winked at him as he slowly walked toward his office. He glanced behind him just to be sure no one was outside the barbershop looking though the door then proceeded to the back. When he got to the office he peeked in and saw Patricia bending over at his desk picking up the receipts that just happened to accidentally drop. He stopped short at the entrance and watched her ass wiggle and jiggle as she picked up the small slips of paper.

"Y-y-you need some help with that." He stuttered.

Patricia turned her head while bent over and smiled. "Sure if you don't mind getting down here with me."

KB stepped inside his office and slowly walked up behind her and was tempted to grab her by her hips but she stood up and turned around and faced him. Their bodies were so close her breasts brushed against him slightly and he could smell the fruity flavor of strawberry on her lips from the gloss she was wearing. She looked up into his eyes and he showcased a nervous smile. He placed his hands on her waist and leaned down to her as she closed her eyes and lifted her head upward to receive his kiss. She dropped the receipts she picked up and wrapped her arms around his waist. Their lips met and Patricia sucked his bottom lip then inserted her tongue into his mouth. KB sucked on her tongue softly as his hands began to trace the form of her hips and made its way to her soft ass. He grabbed her softness and pulled her to him gently as his hard on met her middle. She kissed him harder when she felt him against her and began grinding as his hands lifted her shirt up. She felt a tingle through her body when his warm fingers touched her flesh as he unbuckled the snaps on her bra. Her breathing increased as she anticipated him grabbing her breasts in his hands. The snaps were released and her breasts relaxed as she

FOUR SHADOUGH
PUBLISHING

felt the front of her bra lift up. Her nipples became hard instantly from the fondling but when his wet mouth latched onto her left nipple her legs almost gave out on her. She grabbed him by the back of his head and pulled him closer as she backed up to the office desk. When her ass pressed up against the edge of the desk KB pushed books, papers and pens onto the ground to make room for her to lay down. He pulled at the button of her jeans and she arched her back to allow his hand access inside her pants. He rubbed his finger against her wetness through the fabric of her panties and his passion was amplified. He sucked her neck while pulling her panty to the side and inserting his finger into her slippery snatch. He sucked her neck hard and she whimpered as he stuffed his finger deeper into her gooey hole while her pelvis gyrated to his movements.

"I want you!" KB whispered to her as he bit her earlobe softly.

"This is my first time Keith." She admitted.

Patricia didn't know exactly what it was about KB but she was ready to give herself to him. She was well aware of his girlfriend Gloria but that didn't seem to matter at the moment. Her hormones were raging, her lust was at an all time peak and her kitty was sticky with her wetness. She was going to go against her strict religious beliefs about having sex and give herself to KB; she was ready.

"I'll be gentle." KB said as he massaged her hardened clit with his thumb.

"Ummm. Keith, please don't do this to me, this is wrong." She whimpered unsure if she was doing the right thing.

"No it's right. Don't stop me, I want you so bad Pat." He pressed.

"I don't want to regret doing this later Keith. Promise me you won't change." She was becoming emotional.

"I'll never change on you Pat. Never." He sucked her neck softly.

"Oooh. Talk dirty to me Keith! Tell me how bad you want me!" Patricia purred as she pulled his shirt up and raked her nails across his back.

"I want to fuck you Pat. I want to feel your wet pussy on my dick!"

"Ummmm. I want to feel your dick in this tight virgin pussy! I want you to fuck my pussy good and hard!"

"I want to taste it, I want to suck on your sweet pussy baby!"

"Ooooh yea. I wanna feel your tongue on my clit Keith. Take me Keith. Fuck my pussy!" She begged.

KB backed up off her and unbuckled his belt then pulled his pants down and let them drop to his ankles while Patricia pulled her jeans down and took one leg out and spread her legs wide for him. KB panted heavily as he eyed her shaved cunt and his rock hard staff jerked up and down. He grabbed himself in his hand and made his way over to her and was about to insert the tip of his growing head inside her then...

BRRRING! BRRRING! BRRRING!

The ringing phone startled both Patricia and KB. Patricia immediately sat up and KB paused holding his member in his hand. Patricia looked down at his throbbing mass but the ringing phone interrupted her erotic thoughts and she snapped back to reality.

"I think you should answer that KB. We know who it is." She said bending down and putting her free leg into her panty and jeans.

"Wait Patricia!" KB begged holding his hand up like a traffic agent as the phone continued to ring. "I'm not gonna answer it."

"Why? Then what Keith? You want to risk getting caught with your pants down, literally? You know if you don't answer she'll be down here in a New York minute." Patricia jumped off the desk and pulled her panty and jeans up on her waist. The phone stopped ringing.

"Let's go somewhere else. I don't want this to end." He proposed standing with his pants at his ankles and his bulging dick in his hand pleading with his eyes.

"I don't know Keith. I don't want to be the one to break y'all up. I really like you but I know this ain't right and maybe that phone call was supposed to happen and this wasn't." She deduced.

"I like you too Patricia and I want to be with you. I'm not thinking of her right now."

"That's just it, if we went all the way it woulda only been for right now."

"Nah, I promise you it won't be just for right now. I'm really feeling you."

"Really? Then call and tell her you not coming in 'til late tonight." She challenged.

"I ain't gotta call her, we can just go…"

"That's what I thought." Patricia rolled her eyes.

The phone suddenly started ringing again and Patricia looked at KB and shook her head.

"You should pull up your clothes and answer that. She's not gonna stop calling."

KB ignored the ringing phone and reached out to grab Patricia's arm but she moved away and picked the phone up and passed it to him. He looked at the receiver like it was on fire and then looked at her. He didn't take it so she dropped it on the desk then bent down to pick up the receipts off the floor. A muffled noise could be heard coming from the receiver and KB reluctantly picked up the phone while he struggled to pull his pants up with his other hand.

"Hello! Hello!"

"Yea." KB finally answered resting the receiver on his shoulder while he buckled his pants. "What's up?"

"Fuck you mean what's up? What took you so long to answer?" Gloria asked suspicion and anger combined in her tone.

"I was in the bathroom." KB looked at Patricia.

Patricia shook her head slowly then placed the receipts on the desk and walked out the office still shaking her head. KB tried reaching out to her but she sucked her teeth then closed the door behind her.

"Really K? You was in the bathroom?" Gloria paused for some seconds. "That bitch in there with you? Answer me K!"

"Ain't nobody here with me now. She was here but left soon as I got here, I'm just getting the receipts and sweeping up a little." He fixed his clothes.

"Why don't I believe you K, huh? Why did it take you so long to put the phone to your ear, did somebody pass you the phone?"

"Nah ma! Ain't nobody in here with me. You know I'm not fuckin' with that bitch! You gotta stop being so insecure. Why you checking on me anyway? We just talked about this."

"'Cause I smell a fuckin' rat! A country rat!" Gloria bellowed through the receiver.

"Go 'head wit' that shit Glo'. You know I ain't thinking 'bout that shit. I'm 'bout to close up and I'll be on my way in a minute." KB replied trying to get her off the phone.

"OK, don't let the sun beat you home K, I'm not fuckin' playin' either!" The phone went dead and KB sat on the edge of the desk.

He looked down at all the things he threw onto the floor and bent down to pick them up. What just happened with Patricia was heavy on his mind. He was wrong for what almost happened and guilt assaulted his mind but he couldn't help the lust that burned inside him for Patricia. He never thought about cheating on Gloria before but his attraction to Patricia was more than just physical; his attraction was more emotional and he wanted her in his life. After straightening out his desk he grabbed the receipts and stuffed them in his pocket then opened

his office door. He was startled to see Patricia standing in front of the door with her arms folded over her bosom.

"So I'm a bitch now, huh Keith?" She said plainly but there was hurt in her eyes.

"N-n-nah Patricia, let me explain..." He started.

"You know something. I thought you was different and fooled myself into believing you were. I shoulda never let you touch me. I knew it was a bad idea and I'm so glad I didn't go all the way. I hope you enjoyed your free feel 'cause that's the last time you'll ever touch me you lying fuck!"

She turned and walked off and he tried to grab her but she pulled away violently.

"Fuck off me! I'm a bitch remember!" She spewed.

"No Patricia! I didn't mean it like that!"

Patricia stopped at the front entrance of the barbershop and turned around to face KB who stopped short.

"You know something? I can't stand your girlfriend because that bitch is insecure and disliked me from the jump for no other reason 'cept that she felt threatened by me. I didn't like the way she treated me and knew if I fucked you it would bust her jealous heart wide open but I would never do it because I'm better than that. I didn't plan on liking you the way I did but when you defended me against her I knew you were fair and honest. What almost happened tonight was because I really thought you was different Keith, I was about to lose my virtue to you but I'm so glad I didn't make that mistake because I would be nothing but a BITCH to you right after! Fuck you and goodbye!" She pulled the door open then slammed it close behind her, shaking the plate glass.

KB ran to the door and snatched it open and stepped outside but Patricia was already in her car. He stood on the porch of the barbershop and called her name but her engine roared to life and her headlights popped on and the car screeched off towards the block. He turned around and walked

back into the shop and closed the door behind him and turned off the lights.

***

Muffin pulled up in front of the store on the block. She was just getting back from the hospital and wanted to let Bo know about Junior's condition and to tell him she needed his help to take care of some other pressing business that couldn't wait; her revenge on KB and Gloria. Seeing Junior laid up in the hospital just prompted her thirst to make them both pay for what he was going through and it was now going to be a priority along with handling the business. She wasn't too sure if Bo was down with the murder game but she didn't need him to pull no triggers because she was very capable of handling it herself; she already shot KB and bodied Lakim.

She had never been down on the block alone this late before. Guys were standing outside the store when she walked up and asked if they saw Bo. One of the guys told her he was shooting pool inside the store so she went in to find him. The store was run by an old timer with "old" money who generally kept it open to provide shelter for the guys who hustled because there was no place for the young people in town to hang out after the recreation center closed. He transformed the back of the store into a small game room with a small pool table and two video games.

Muffin walked through the door and all eyes were fixed on her. She scanned the store looking for Bo and after not seeing him, turned to leave. A young guy standing next to the payphone asked, "Who ya lookin' for?"

"Bo. You seen him? They said he was in here playing pool." She replied still looking around before exiting the game room/store.

"He was just in here playing wit' Scooter." The guy turned and looked out the plate glass window then pointed. "Oh, he right o'er there talking to somebody in that car."

Muffin pushed the door and walked over to where Bo had his head inside the passenger side of a small hatchback.

"Bo?" She called out to him.

"What's up?" He said as he turned his head while still leaning on the car.

Muffin bent down and peeked into the car to see who he was talking to before telling him about Junior. She recognized the girl as the beautician who worked in the barbershop.

"'Scuse me, can I talk to you for a minute?" She asked politely.

"Sure, gimme a sec." He turned to Patricia and told her to wait for him until he finished talking to Muffin.

He turned his attention back to Muffin and they walked a couple feet away out of earshot from Patricia.

"Ain't that the girl that work in the barbershop?" She asked him.

"Yea."

Muffin sucked her bottom lip hard. "How close you with that broad?"

"We ok, why?"

The wheels in Muffin's head began to turn.

"You think you can get her to tell you where that muhfucka KB rest his head at?"

"I don't know but I can ask her." Bo was skeptical.

"Nah, I don't want it to be too obvious. I don't want her to suspect anything."

"What you plannin' on doin'?" Bo already had an idea but wanted to confirm his suspicions.

"Damn Bo, you can't be that fucking slow. What you think I wanna know where that muhfucka live at for?"

"To be honest, I don't know." He lied.

FOUR SHADOUGH
PUBLISHING

Muffin looked left to right to make sure no one was in listening distance. "I'm going to kill that muhfucka and his bitch!" Muffin hissed.

Bo stared at her stone faced. "I definitely wasn't thinking that."

"I know you wasn't." Muffin sucked her teeth. "Look man, I came down here to tell you that I need your help to get rid of this muhfucka because that bullet he put in my baby is fucking him up real bad. The doctors keeping him in the hospital in Greenville because they monitoring him to find out why he keep bleeding out. It's KB's fault Junior going through this shit and I'm gonna end his life for trying to fuck ours, point blank!" She stared at Bo with hate filled eyes. "Now what I need to know is if you gon' help me. He's your cousin Bo."

"I'll do anything for my cuz but I don't think you understand how things down here work. This town small and the shit you talkin' 'bout doin' don't happen here regularly. This ain't a big city like New Yawk." Bo explained with reason.

"You think I don't know that shit Bo? You think I'm stupid? Haven't I showed you that I'm far from a dumb bitch? Huh?" She sucked her teeth loudly. "See, what you don't understand is that I don't give a fuck about nothing but bodying that muhfucka. If I hada finished his ass the first time, I swear Junior wouldn't be laying up in some funky ass hospital." She pointed to Patricia's car. "And seeing her tonight after knowing what I was coming here to ask you is a sign I'm supposed to get rid of that muhfucka so trust me, it's gon' happen, with your help or not."

Muffin side stepped Bo and walked over to the driver's side of Patricia's car.

"Hey." She said bending down and speaking through the open passenger window.

"Hey girl." Patricia jumped and immediately recognized Muffin's voice and as Junior's girlfriend.

"Oh I'm sorry, I ain't mean to walk up on you like that. I just wanted to apologize to you about that shit that went down in the barbershop. Believe me, I had no idea all that was goin' to happen." She sounded sincere.

"Oh shoot gurl, that wasn't your fault."

"I know but I still want to apologize to you. Well, I know you was talking to Bo so I'm gon' let you get back to your conversation."

"Oh that's fine. We weren't talking 'bout nothing important."

Muffin stood up to leave, took two steps away from the vehicle then stopped and turned back around. "Oh, by the way. I never did get my hair done, as you can tell." She ran her hands through her tresses. "Do you think you can do my hair for me, but not at the barbershop, I'm really not comfortable going back there."

"No problem. You don't have to worry about going there 'cause I don't work there anymore no how." There was disappointment in her tone.

"Oh shit, I hope it wasn't because of what happened when I was there."

"Oh no, that's not the reason." Patricia shook her head.

"Oh ok." Muffin blew air out of her mouth and held her hand to her chest feigning relief. "In that case when can I get my hair done and where?"

"I kin do it at my house if you want. That's where I used to do most of my clients' hair before my gran'ma started fussin' 'bout the electric bill. I still have a hair dryer and hair products there."

"That'll be cool. Why don't you give me your number and I'll call you tomorrow and set up an appointment."

"That's fine." Patricia reached in her glove compartment and pulled out a pen and a piece of paper and wrote her number down then gave it to Muffin.

"Ok, I'll call you tomorrow." She read the name on the paper, "Patricia right?"

"Yep. I'll talk to you then. Good night."

"Ok thanks mama, lata."

Muffin walked up to the store where Bo was talking to some guys.

"I'm done Bo, you can go back and talk to her."

"You want me to see if I can get that information you asked for?"

"Nah, I'm gon' take care of all that myself." She showed Bo the paper with Patricia's phone number. "I got this."

Chapter 10

Junior eyes opened as he lay in the hospital bed. He didn't move because he felt a numbing pain. He turned his head and saw Muffin sitting in a chair asleep next to his bed. He looked back up to the ceiling and tears suddenly fell from his eyes. He didn't know why he was crying but he couldn't stop.

"I'm so sorry Shondra. I love you Mooka." He cried out in agony. Muffin eyes were closed but she wasn't asleep and hearing what Junior said was the straw that broke the camel's back.

***

"PUSH! PUSH! PUSH!"
"UUMMPH!"
The crown of the baby's head appeared and the doctor held it carefully as he waited for the next contraction. Shondra was sweating and grabbing the hand of the mid wife while she pushed. She couldn't identify the pain because she never felt anything like it before. She pushed when the pain and doctor prompted her to and each time she did, she prayed it would end. Beads of sweat were wiped off her forehead and brow as the mid wife whispered she was doing a wonderful job. She screamed obscenities at the Caribbean born midwife who ignored her and continued to hold her hand and wipe her down.

"FUCK! TAKE IT OUT ALREADY!"
Shondra suddenly heard a suction sound like a vacuum sucking up water then a few seconds later she heard the most beautiful sound in the world, life. The baby cried out for its

mother, grateful to be out of the watery womb that was its residence for eight and a half months. The doctor checked to make sure the child was healthy then the nurse cleaned the baby up.

"Is it over?" Shondra asked winded, mouth dry.

"Yes honey. You're a mommy now." The midwife replied with a radiant smile.

Shondra eyes filled with tears as the realization of her new title of mother was now official. The baby was brought over to her wrapped in a white receiving blanket and she burst out crying as she held her child for the first time in her arms.

"Oh my God! I can't believe you're finally here. I love you so much already!"

The nurse looked at her and said, "You're the first mother I've ever met that didn't ask if it was a boy or a girl."

Shondra looked at her and said, "I didn't have to ask because I already know. This is my King!"

Shondra's son's eyes were closed and his thumb was in his mouth. She looked at his pink skin color and his jet-black wavy hair and sighed heavily. This was Chico's son.

***

When Chico heard the news that Shondra had the baby he was nervous, excited and disappointed all at the same time. He found out she was in Brooklyn Hospital after Pam, a crack head, asked him what did he have. He couldn't believe Shondra didn't at least beep him when she went into labor. He flagged down a cab then hauled it to the hospital. His mind was flooded with thoughts of him actually becoming a father, he wondered if he would be a good father and if the birth of the child would finally soften Shondra up. When the cab pulled up in front of the hospital Chico ran inside and stopped at the front desk.

"Can I help you?" The middle aged desk clerk asked.

FOUR SHADOUGH
PUBLISHING

"My girl, she just had a baby." He replied not realizing how hard he was smiling.

"Congratulations. What's her name?"

"Shondra, Shondra Brown." He replied quickly.

"Room 352." The desk clerk handed Chico a visiting pass.

He grabbed it and headed towards the elevators but made a quick stop in a hospital store that sold balloons and cards. The ride on the elevator to the third floor was the longest of his life. When the doors opened he looked at the room numbers posted on the wall and followed the arrow in the direction of rooms 320-360. When he was in front of room 352 he straightened his clothes and walked in.

"What's up Shondra? How you feelin'?" He asked with expectations of seeing her holding their baby.

Shondra turned over and looked at Chico then turned back around. Chico let go of the balloons he was carrying that said, "CONGRATULATIONS ON YOUR NEW BUNDLE OF JOY". His eyes darted around the room searching for signs of his baby.

"I came to see my baby Shondra. Is it a boy or a girl?" He moved slowly his heart fighting to get through his chest.

"It's a boy." She responded with her back to him.

"Wow! I'm a father!" Chico looked down on the ground and rubbed his shaking fingers between his braids. "Where he at? I wanna see him!" He screamed excitedly.

"You can't see him right now." Shondra turned over slowly and the whites of her eyes were crimson from crying. "He's sick Chico. He was born severely anemic, his little body is not producing enough red blood cells."

"Fuck! Wha...what's gonna happen to him? Is he gonna be all right?" Chico blabbered nervously.

"I don't know. The doctors are monitoring him right now." Her voice was getting lower as she was forced to tell him.

Chico flopped down in the seat next to her bed and lay his head back slowly. This was his first child and instead of rejoicing in happiness he was overcome with grief and worry. He prayed his baby would be ok. He lift his head up and looked over to Shondra and was about to ask her another question but immediately changed what he was going to ask her when he saw the barren and distant look in her eyes.

Chico grabbed her hand in his instead. "I don't know what to say or do Shondra but I'm gonna be here with you through everything. This is our son and we'll get through this together." He professed.

"I know." Shondra moved her hand from his and turned back around and prayed her baby would be ok.

 FOUR SHADOUGH
PUBLISHING

Chapter 11

"Hey Patricia!" Muffin shouted as she opened the screen door. "I hope you don't mind me poppin' up without calling."

When Muffin spoke with Patricia on the phone, she never gave her an actual appointment but did tell her she usually was free early in the mornings so Muffin decided to arrive unannounced in the morning when she figured no one would be there so she would have Patricia's undivided attention without interruption.

Patricia was standing by the sink mixing something in a plastic pitcher when she saw Muffin at the screen door.

"Naw girl it ain't a problem. I don't have no appointments this morning so you'll be my first. You want a glass of this iced tea I just made?" She offered.

Muffin took a seat in a white plastic lawn chair and nodded her head as Patricia poured her a tall glass of the tea from an old fashioned glass pitcher with yellow dandelions on it.

"How you want your hair done?" Patricia asked as she played in Muffin's hair feeling the texture.

"I don't even know what I want done to it, I just know it needs to be done." Muffin snickered.

"That's a cute outfit you wearing. What kind of material is that?" Patricia asked as she looked down at the expensive outfit Muffin was wearing.

"Thanks. It's European silk. I got this last summer from Bloomingdales." Muffin took a sip of the tea and frowned her face.

"What's wrong?" Patricia asked when she saw Muffin's expression.

"What kind of tea is this?" She placed the glass down on the floor next to her wiping her lips.

"It's iced tea. You don't like it?"

"Uh uh. It tastes like you made it with tea bags." Muffin replied with a disgusted look on her face.

"I did girl." Patricia laughed. "I told you it was iced tea."

"Y'all make it with real tea bags?" Muffin looked shocked. "We use powder ice tea in NY, I thought that's how everybody made it."

"Not here, we make real ice tea." Patricia laughed. "That powdered mess is nasty, that's like Kool Aid Iced Tea or some mess. I can get you some lemonade instead and before you ask, it's made with real lemons."

"I think I'll like that better. I'm sorry…"

"Girl don't worry 'bout it. I know y'all not used to how things are done down here, coming from NY and all." She said dismissively.

"Tell me about it. I remember when I first came down here and I was standing in front of Bo's house one night and I asked him what kind of big ass bug was flying so close to me and when he told me it was a bat I freaked the fuck out!" Muffin burst out laughing.

"Hol' on now, I ain't been to NY before but I heard about dem jungle sized sewer rats that's as big as a two-year old." Patricia jabbed back.

Muffin laughed out loud. "I can't front, them suckas big as a muhfucka and they'll run you down if they hungry!" She slapped her knee.

Both women hollered and enjoyed a hearty laugh as they continued to crack jokes on each other's place of residence. The house phone rang, interrupting their laughter.

"Hello?" Patricia answered then tried to move out of earshot from Muffin.

Muffin smiled and leaned her head as far to the left as she could trying to ear hustle on Patricia's phone conversation but she politely stepped out of the room killing any of that from happening. Muffin sighed hoping she would be able to get the information she wanted about KB from Patricia without her getting suspicious about her intentions. She planned on befriending her then getting the address of KB's house and then she would be able to take care of him and his bitch once and for all. She knew she had to be real careful in how she did it because the town was so small and she didn't want to get caught.

Patricia walked back into the room with a different expression on her face and Muffin noticed immediately.

"What happened Patricia?" Muffin asked taking advantage of the opportunity to comfort her.

Patricia breathed out heavily then looked down to the ground. "I'm ok. It's just that people can be so fucking common."

"What?" Muffin was not understanding southern slang very well.

"My friend was over here yesterday getting her hair done and we was talking. I told her I no longer work at the barbershop and how it's fucked up because now I won't be making enough money to pay all these bills I done acquired since working there. She took all that information I told her and went right over to the barbershop and asked them did they need a new beautician and they hired her!"

"Damn. It don't sound like she's a friend but why would you be mad? Was you planning on going back there?" Muffin didn't really care but was trying to stay on Patricia's side.

"I wasn't planning on going back there but she shouldn't have went there." Patricia surmised.

"Why? It's a job and from what I see down here, jobs are kinda scarce. You know what I'm saying?" Muffin replied honestly.

114

"I understand that but she's my friend."

"Ummm. No she's not boo boo. Friends don't do friends like that but in any case what are you going to do?"

Patricia sucked her teeth and shook her head. "I don't know what the hell I'm gon' do. I shouldn't be mad but I was making good money there and it had the space for clients to wait but in here it's gon' be harder." She looked around at the cramped space she used as her shop.

Muffin cut in and asked. "How so?"

"For one, my gran'ma not gon' let me have none of my clients waiting in her living room and I have to do hair out here on the back porch."

Muffin looked around the porch then looked at Patricia, "Ain't nothin' wrong with doing hair out here. It's screened in so you ain't gotta worry about bats and shit flying up in here."

Patricia forced a smile. "Yea but the heat or rain gon' be a problem; depending on the hair style it'll frizz up in the heat or drop in the rain." She shook her head in disappointment.

Muffin sincerely sympathized with Patricia's dilemma but saw it as the perfect opportunity to get what she wanted on two accounts. Money was so scarce that any implications on making some would instantly create a bond and loyalty. She had to gain her trust and friendship first but she couldn't be too brash or she would come off as too pushy.

"When you put it like that, you really do have a small problem. The more I think about it, I think your friend is wrong but not for taking your job but for not at least asking you. It's like she went behind your back and shit and that's not a real friend." Muffin put her hand on her shoulder. "If you don't mind me asking, why aren't you working there anymore?"

"Gloria had a problem with me working there." Patricia stated flatly.

"What kind of problem? Wasn't she the one that hired you?" Muffin quizzed.

Patricia wrinkled her nose. "Keith the one that hired me and I think it became a problem when she found out I was the only girl working in there. I just think she was jealous of me."

"*Keith*?" Muffin thought to herself. "*This bitch was fucking KB, her boss*!" She mused. "*Oh I definitely like how this bitch gets down already!*"

"So you and her didn't get along because ain't but one queen bee in the hive huh?" Muffin chuckled.

"I wasn't studding him so I don't know why she was so jealous. I was there to make my money girl." Patricia clarified.

"I know that's right. So what was the straw that broke the camel's back?" Muffin continued to push.

Patricia looked down at the ground as she prepared to tell a story that sounded true.

"It was something real stupid. She was mad he told me to keep the shop open while he was in the hospital and didn't tell her and when she came by and saw it open she was furious."

"That's what did it? You opening the shop because your boss told you to? It sounds like she was threatened by you." Muffin looked at her body and smirked. "I can't front girl, I probably woulda did the same thing with all that junk you got in your fuckin' trunk!"

"I can't help I got more ass than she do!" Patricia retorted.

"Easy baby, I'm not your enemy." Muffin said easily. "Look Pat, I know you tight and it seems like shit all fucked up but things will get better, I'm sure of it."

"I'm sorry Muffin I ain't mean to jump at you like that." Patricia frowned and spoke unconsciously. "I feel like I deserved to be treated better than that. I didn't deserve to be thrown to the side like old tennis shoes."

"Huh? What you talkin' 'bout now Pat?" Muffin lowered her head and her eyes looked up. "I know you wasn't fucking with KB?"

116

Patricia was caught off guard by the blunt question and it gave her pause and Muffin jumped all over it.

"You ain't even gotta say nothing baby girl. Silence is golden."

"No, no, no. I didn't sleep with Keith." Patricia defended. "Nothing like that at all, please." She sucked her teeth. "I'm not like that he has a woman."

"*Yea right bitch*." Muffin thought to herself. "*Your ass wouldn't be acting all sentimental and hurt if you got fired from Bojangels or some shit. Save them lies for the police bitch!*"

"Ok, I wasn't trying to call you out of your name. Shit like that happens all the time up top so I'm not one to judge, trust me on that shit." Muffin responded with conviction.

"I didn't think that, I just wanted you to know. People down here be thinking that as soon as a new guy come from outta town we drop our panties and give up the goodies and lawd, don't let them be from New Yawk, then we doing them, their friend and their father." Patricia said with sarcasm.

"I gotta keep it real wit' you Pat. When me and Junior got down here, these bitches were all over my man like a cheap suit. I was thinking I was gonna have to stick my knife in a couple of 'em and that's because I ain't 'bout to fight none of them straight up and fuck around and get dragged or slammed!" Muffin burst out in laughter followed by Patricia.

Patricia was beginning to feel comfortable and relaxed around Muffin and began speaking freely.

"You ain't neva lied because I had to beat Keith's girl ass in the barbershop. She always treated me bad but that day I had enough and I tore into her like a bear that found a picnic basket." Patricia chortled.

"Shit, that's why your ass got fired!" Muffin guffawed. "You can't beat the boss' bitch and fuck him too!"

"I didn't fuck him but if I wanted to I coulda! That strumpet lucky I didn't either 'cause after some of this virgin

country pussy he would kick her ugly ass all the way back to New Yawk!" Patricia chided.

"I heard that I did!" Muffin screamed.

While they were talking and laughing, the wheels in Muffin's head were turning and she was formulating her plan.

"So do you have any idea on what you're going to do about money now?" Muffin turned serious.

"I have no idea. I may can find a job working in the cotton factory or shirt factory but I don't wanna work for nobody, I wanna be my own boss. That's why I do hair, I wanna open my own salon one day." Patricia said.

There was a twinkle in Muffin's eyes as she spoke. "I really like you Pat and I really sympathize with your problems. I don't want to step outta bounds with you but if you want help with some money I might know something you can do that will help you and I don't usually do this for anyone." Muffin paused and waited to see what reaction she would get from her offering. Patricia showed interest but not enough for Muffin so for emphasis she pulled out a stack of bills from her bag. "What I'm offering you is a rare opportunity Pat."

Patricia's eyes were wide with wonderment when she saw the neatly stacked green backs Muffin was holding in her hand.

"You gonna give me all that?" Patricia asked dumfounded.

"Hell naw!" Muffin laughed. "You think I'm crazy girl? But I can show you how you can have your own and that's what I'm offering you." Muffin finally had the attention she needed. "Like I said, it's a rare opportunity and I'm sure anybody in this town would kill for it, especially a dude."

"Only people I know that be having money like that is the boys on the block." Patricia kept eyeing the money then the light bulb went off. "You sell drugs Muffin?"

"I don't sell shit Pat!" Muffin shot back with a knowing smile. "And that's the beauty of it all." Muffin's head tilted to

the side like a suspicious canine. "Before I start telling you anything I need to know if you're down first. Ain't no need to explain how all this shit work if you not with the program first, you know what I mean?" Muffin paused and looked at Pat but couldn't gauge which way she was leaning. Her expression proved she would make a great partner because she had a serious poker face. It would be key for Muffin to start something aside from what she was doing with Bo because after hearing Junior calling that bitch Shondra's name, she needed to make sure she was all right financially. It wasn't about greed for Muffin at this point, it was about being self sufficient, having her own and writing her own fucking ticket. There was no doubt in her mind that when KB and Gloria were bodied in that small town that Junior would have to leave town so it was a smart move to establish a strong team across the board to keep the money coming in no matter what.

Pat weighed her odds and although she needed money she was raised differently, morals and values were instilled in her and selling drugs didn't fit into her lifestyle. It was nothing she ever considered doing and if her grandmother ever found out she turned drug dealer, selling poison to her own people it would disappoint her to no end.

Pat looked at Muffin. "I'll do it as long as I don't have to actually sell it to anyone. And with all that money you have I shouldn't have to do it that long anyway. That ain't something I want to do but I know the money will help me out and then I can get my own salon and buy me a nicer car, and get my gran..." Muffin interrupted her before she started rambling.

"Ok, pump your brakes girl." Muffin smiled heartily. "I'm glad you trust me enough to give it a try because when you blow up, you gonna thank me forever. This is how it works, I'm gonna give you the stuff in weight and you're going to distribute it to be sold then pick up the money when it's done."

Patricia waited for Muffin to finish telling her the rest of what she had to do but Muffin just stared at her with a weird look in her eyes.

"That's it?" Patricia finally asked.

"Yep." She answered matter of factly.

"You sure it'll be that easy? Suppose one of the guys don't give me all the money? I hear about them fighting and shooting out over their money. Are they gonna do the same thing to me?"

"No they won't." Muffin said with confidence.

"How can you be so sure Muffin?"

"Easy. Won't be no boys...you gonna get girls to sell it for you instead. Fuck the boys!" Muffin had a one sided smile. "You know the sweet thing about that? The police will never suspect females of selling anything and bypass them and by the time the boys realize how much money we really getting it'll be too late for them to stop what we doing. Money is power and with that comes fear so nobody gon' fuck with us, trust me."

"Where I'm gonna find girls that know how to sell drugs? None of my friends know anything about it, their boyfriends are the ones that sell drugs."

"Don't worry about that, I'll find you some girls. I have that all planned out but you ask some of your friends that you know are broke and need some of this cheddar here." Muffin said fanning the money.

"Ok when do I start?" Patricia asked anxiously.

"We'll start tomorrow but I'm gonna need you to come to my crib so I can show you how to bag up the weight, how much money you supposed to get back and how to stash it when you're moving on the street."

Patricia was about to go against all the Christian teachings from her 'nana', throw caution to the wind and become a drug dealer. She tried to convince herself she wasn't doing a grave injustice to her community because she wasn't going to be the one selling the highly addictive drug but her

120

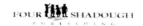
conscious mind wouldn't let her deny the fact that she was the one distributing the poison to be sold to the people in her community. She had friends whose parents were addicted to 'crack' and she remembered the horrendous heart breaking stories she was told about their mother sucking the dicks of young drug dealers just so they could get high or selling everything in the house that wasn't nailed down including food out of the refrigerator. It pained her to hear the stories of parents fighting in their bedroom when one of them smoked up the other's drug and it devastated her to hear about the death of one or both parents because they stole from one of the drug dealers then were brutally killed. Her heart was heavy and she sighed feeling an overwhelming amount of guilt but then the money Muffin still held in her hand was being waved in front of her.

"You ready?" Muffin asked.

"Let's go, I'm so fuckin' ready to do whatever I have to make that money!" Patricia answered following Muffin out the front door.

Muffin and Patricia walked down the street towards the block. Things in Li'l Washington was about to take a drastic turn, Muffin was going to be the new female boss.

Chapter 12

Junior sat up in his bed, his head felt light and the tubes in his arm were uncomfortable but he knew he needed them in order to recover from his wound. He looked out the hospital window from his bed and breathed out heavily. It had taken two days before he regained consciousness but when he opened his eyes Muffin was sitting in a chair next to his bed. He had been groggy so he wasn't able to talk at that moment but she rambled off to him about how she came home to him being put into an ambulance and for him not to worry because she was going to kill KB for putting him through all this shit. Then he remembered hearing her say something else that struck him as weird but he wasn't sure because he was under a lot of medication; she said for him not to worry about his business because she was going to handle everything for him until he was able to run things himself. He appreciated her for being there with him and holding him down but running his business was not something he wanted her to do. She was not trained on how to run his business, he only showed her how to bag up work, nothing else. If he did hear her right and she said that, he figured it was probably because she felt guilty about taking so much money out of the safe to help her mother. He didn't mind because he stacked plenty of money since hustling in the south and plus he did knock her mom's down once. He smiled at the thought of having slept with both mother and daughter. Those thoughts brought on feelings he had hidden far too long, he was still in love with Shondra and he needed her to know it. While he was drugged up he had a bad feeling something happened to her and he wanted to be there for her and then the thought of

getting out of the hospital shot to the front of his mind. He needed to take care of his business, he needed to get in contact with Bo and he definitely needed to re up. He never told Bo where the stash was because as a rule, you never give up too much information or you will no longer be needed.

The phone rang loudly in the empty hospital room and he reached over and picked up the receiver.

"Yo?" He answered.

"You finally up man?"

"Boy you gon' live a long time. I was just thinking 'bout calling you." Junior said recognizing his cousin's voice.

"Is that right? How you feelin' cuz? You was in a bad way for a couple of days."

"I'm still a little tired but I feel a hun'ed percent better. That's why I need to holla at you 'bout some things."

"I'm glad you feelin' better. What's on your mind cuz?"

"Did you run outta food yet? You need more groceries?"

"Um...nah mane. I have a cubbard full of food." Bo replied slowly.

Junior shook his head left to right slowly as his eyes rolled up in his head.

"I'm not talking 'bout the food in your cupboard man."

"Oh! My bad cuz. Yea I got some left, not alot though."

"You still got some left?" Junior was puzzled. "You ain't run out of food since I been layed up?"

"Oh yea but your ol' lady took care of that."

"Huh?" Now it was Junior's turn to be baffled. "How she do that?"

"You remember I was already running low before you getting shot and all so when I found out you was gon' be awright I asked your ol' lady did she know where you had the rest of the work..."

Junior interrupted him abruptly, "You mean food right?"

"Oh yea, food. Then she gave me the rest of the food and I gave her the money for the last groceries I got from you." Bo tried his best to speak in code but was doing a terrible job.

"You gave her all the money from what you had before?"

"Yea. No shorts." Bo answered.

"Ok. So I guess I need to make another trip to the grocery store. I'm gon' check to see how much longer they gon' hold me in this place."

"Ok, just let me know cuz."

"Kool. I'm gonna holla at you later."

"Ok, later on. Feel better."

"Hol' on cuz." Junior said before hanging up. "Why you called, everything aiight out there? You got something you need to tell me?"

Bo paused as he held the phone in his hand. "I was just checking on you cuz, making sure you was awright and e'erthing."

"Aiight then. Thanks cuzzo. I'll holla later. One." Junior hung up the receiver and reclined in the bed.

His door opened and a nurse peeked her head inside.

"Oh I see you're up. I just need to change your bandages and your IV." She said stepping into the room and walking over to Junior.

"Ay. Do you know when they gon' let me up outta here?" He asked as she unhooked his IV drip.

"I really don't know sugar but I can get the doctor in here for you when I'm done." She replied as she replaced his IV bag.

Junior laid down on the bed as she pulled his hospital gown up and removed the bandage over his groin. She cleaned around his wound carefully then pulled out fresh gauze and placed it over his injury and taped it down securely.

Junior didn't feel pain anymore in that area just slight discomfort. The wound was healing progressively but he still had a ways to go before fully recovering.

"Have you stood up anytime this morning?" She asked when she was done with changing his bandages.

"Nah, I was about to."

"See if you can get out of the bed and take a couple steps for me honey." Her voice was calming.

Junior swung his legs over the side of the bed slowly and sat in an upright position. He used both hands for leverage as he prepared to stand up. He breathed in deep and blew out a burst of air as he pushed himself to a standing position.

"Careful baby, take your time." The nurse coached.

He stood on shaky limbs for a second or so; his mind betraying him with thoughts of falling backwards onto the bed. He steadied himself and took one unsteady step, one hand still holding onto the bed for balance. He peeked over at the nurse who looked as if she were a mother watching a toddler trying to walk for the first time. He let go of the bed with his other hand and took another step, his leg wobbled slightly.

"Lift your head up baby, look ahead of you and don't concentrate on moving your legs, just do it naturally. Come to me." She urged him.

Junior's head lifted on cue and he slid his left leg then pulled his right leg in front of him and continued moving until he was near the nurse who was slowly taking steps backwards with her arms outstretched. Junior was drawn to her like a magnet and then determination kicked in and he lifted his leg and began walking straight to her. The nurse backed up to the door and Junior followed her and grabbed her hands when he was within reach. She smiled and he hugged her tightly and said, "I'm ready to go home."

Chapter 13

"Stop coming to me with these fucking shorts Pam!" Chico's voice boomed.

"I'm only a dollar short Chico, damn!" Her dirty hands held four wrinkled dollar bills.

"I told you no more shorts. Take that four dollars up the block to them muhfuckas in Williamsburg selling that baking soda."

Pam looked at him with pleading eyes and shifting her weight from one leg to the other. She looked down on the ground and bent down picking up something that was small and white then threw it back down when she realized it wasn't what she thought it was. She needed another hit and was getting desperate.

"Come on Chico baby. I'm going out tomorrow and I'll get something for your son."

"Fuck outta here Pam! You can't boost no more, look at you, you fell off." He said pointing at her with a disgusted look on his face.

Chico was right, Pam used to be the best booster in the hood but now she was completely strung out and looked terrible. She no longer dressed fly, lost all her natural weight and her skin had gotten darker; she even sported the infamous missing teeth. She was known in all the department stores now and all the security in the cheap stores in the hood already knew her, she was banned.

"Get the fuck outta here Pam, you making shit hot!" Chico shoved her almost knocking her to the ground.

"Aiight!" Pam turned around and walked off sucking her teeth.

Chico's anger was brought on by the current state of his newborn son. He had been to the hospital to see him and Shondra and today was the day he was supposed to be discharged. He told her he would come help her home with his son but she blew him off like she didn't want him around. She was being extra nasty to him since the birth of their son and he wondered if she blamed him for how the baby turned out being anemic. He had given her cab fare and told her he would be in the hood waiting for her and her response was so cold he felt like slapping her weave out her head. He understood she was upset because their son was sick but he was suffering too, he didn't expect nor want this to happen to his first born son.

Life was so funny, when he first started hustling it wasn't even for the money, at first he just wanted to be recognized in the hood with respect but when La, God bless the dead, came back, he made him realize he was in over his head. It wasn't all fun and games like he had thought when he worked for Rock, God bless the dead. Before La, everything was good but once he came into the game everything turned bleak. The money was the reward but the consequence was your life; the hustling game just wasn't all what it seemed unless you were on the bleachers or in the audience because when you became a player you experienced what playing the game was really like.

Now things changed for him again and it looked like for the better. Bumping into Muffin when he did was right on time, he was making more money than he was making with La and Rock put together and was now the official boss of Baptiste since there was no one left. He pulled out the brick of money in his pocket and stared at it for some seconds and nodded his head slowly, he was definitely a boss. He stuffed the money back into his pocket and waited for the money rush to start, it was the first of the month.

***

Shondra searched in her bag with her left hand for the money to pay the cab driver while she balanced her son in her right. She placed the money into the slot then tried to open the door but struggled to grab the latch. She switched arms with the baby then pushed on the door using her feet to swing it open. She scooted over awkwardly as she tried to exit the cab carefully. Her feet hit the ground and she stood up and turned around to grab the baby bag handle and pulled it to her. Her grip wasn't as firm as she thought and the bag fell onto the ground as she screamed out, "OH GOD!" startling her newborn. He sounded off with high pitch crying and she suddenly became overwhelmed. She bent down and picked up the bag and wrapped the straps around her hand and started for her building when Pam appeared out of nowhere.

"Let me help you with your bag Shondra." She held her grubby hands out to receive it.

"Nah, that's aiight Pam, I got it, thanks anyway." She looked so dirty she didn't want her to touch anything of hers.

"Aww, ain't he precious. Can I see him?" Pam tried to peek at the baby but his face was completely hidden under the receiving blanket.

"You can come see him later on once I get settled in." Shondra said it only to be polite.

"That's a nice baby bag right? It's the one I sold to Chico. I know he bought mad girl outfits but you know with onesies it don't really matter 'cause they babies." Pam said following Shondra and her crying baby into the hallway.

Shondra walked up the three steps that lead to her door as the baby's cries echoed off the walls in the building.

"You want me to get your keys out for you Shondra? They in your pocketbook or the baby bag?" Pam asked as she stood in front of her door.

"Yea if you don't mind. It's in my pocketbook."

Pam unzipped her bag and stuffed her hand inside and it came out jingling her house keys.

"It's the key with the green thing covering it." Shondra directed as she bounced the screaming baby in her arms.

Pam stuck the key in the lock and pushed the door open then passed Shondra her key back.

"Thanks Pam." She said as she stepped inside.

"You need me to help you do anything else?" Pam asked.

"Nah, I'm good. Thanks again." Shondra was about to close her door.

"Um, can you let me get a dollar Shondra? I'm so hungry and I ain't ate nothing all day."

It was too good to be true, she knew she wanted something. She placed the baby on the couch as he continued bawling his little lungs out then looked through her pocket book for a loose dollar or some change. While she looked Pam went over and looked at the screaming baby and made silly noises with her mouth trying to hush his crying fit.

"I don't have anything but a five Pam. I'm sorry." Shondra announced as she turned to grab her son.

"That's aiight. I got four dollars." Pam dug her hands insider her front pocket and produced four wrinkled bills and handed them to Shondra.

"Oh hell no! I thought you ain't have no money! I'm not paying for you to get high Pam, get the fuck outta here! You need to get your shit together and get off that shit, it's fucking you up!" Shondra screamed as she ushered her out the door.

Pam hurried out the door and turned to face Shondra then said. "Muhfuckas always wanna tell folks what to do with their lives when they should take they own advice. I can stop smoking crack Shondra but what about you, you gon' tell the truth to that precious baby?"

"Fuck you talkin' 'bout you crack head bitch!" Shondra was white with rage.

FOUR SHADOUGH
PUBLISHING

Pam turned and started walking to the entrance of the building.

"You keep on tellin' that boy he the father of that baby in your arms if you want when you know damn well he Junior's son." Pam let out a shrieking laugh that sent chills through Shondra as she looked down at her son who had suddenly stopped crying.

"Fuck you!" She yelled as she went back in her house and slammed the door behind her which initiated another sound off for the baby. She sat on the red velvet couch and gazed at her son closely while rocking him. She looked at his hair which was jet black, his complexion was light and pinkish and his eyes were round. There was no doubt he was Chico's baby. Her mind wandered and she thought back to the night in the hotel room before Junior left to go down south. She started counting the days and months and counted them again and again still coming to the same conclusion; she couldn't be one hundred percent sure which one of them was her son's father.

Chapter 14

The young Latin woman gagged, spit on the floor then wiped her mouth with the back of her hand. She enjoyed giving face and loved when guys flushed in her mouth. She got up off her knees and pulled a wet wipe from the container that was conveniently on the nightstand and wiped off the excess jizz from the dick that she sucked to orgasm moments ago. She was a sexual deviant, her fetish was sucking the cocks of black men and letting them cum in her mouth for money. She didn't enjoy physical sex with men but she wasn't a lesbian, she just preferred a stiff one in her mouth that made her gag while she played with her clit until she reached her orgasm.

Craig loved Spanish chicks almost as much as he loved money. He never got emotionally involved with women because he believed emotions was the downfall of any man in the business he was in but with Scarlet there was something different about her, maybe it was the fact she wouldn't have sex with him no matter how much money he offered her or it could be her calming character. He could only imagine how good her pussy was because her mouth was incredible. She had told him she didn't like him to cum in her mouth but he got lockjaw every time she sucked his insides out of him and couldn't warn her when he was going to explode. He believed she secretly liked it because after the first couple of times she should have been able to tell when he was going to bust off because his body locked up the same way each and every time. He was seriously thinking about making her his special girl, not willing to share her with any other dude. He laughed at the thought as he checked his vibrating pager.

"Yo Scarlet give me a sec aiight baby? I need to make a phone call right quick." He said as she nodded and lay on the king sized bed and turned off the porno movie that was playing on his Sony Vega television.

He liked how quiet and submissive she was almost like the African woman, Goonie Goo Goo, Eddie Murphy joked about in his comedy stand up Delirious. Craig laughed out loud to himself as he went into the living room to make his phone call.

"What's good?" He said into the cordless phone when his call was answered.

"What's up? I'm a week ahead of my schedule and I'm ready to get more pies."

Craig liked that Muffin paid attention to what he said about talking business over the phone but was more impressed with how fast she got rid of all the work he had given her. He was skeptical at first but remembered how he made the mistake with Junior when he first went down south, now he felt he was making a good decision by investing in her.

"What's happening? Your people ate all those pies already? Were they that good?" Craig was excited but didn't want her to detect it in his voice.

"Yep. They loving it! I need some more so I hope you'll already have them baked and bagged when I get there."

"As long as I have the dough, they'll be baked and ready. You want the same amount of pies you got last time?"

"Nah, I think I might need some extra."

"Aiight. Just let me know when you touching down and I'll have them ready for you."

"I'll be there this weekend." Muffin stated.

"Kool. I'll see you then." Craig put the phone on the base and a broad smile appeared on his face.

He went back into the bedroom where Scarlet was laying across the bed. He could see her chest lifting up and down slowly and could hear her breathing through her nose ever

so slightly. He stood over her and watched her and a funny feeling crept over him and he leaned over and kissed her lips gently. It was something he never did with any of the women he ever sexed and she moved away as she opened her eyes, taken by surprise by his show of physical affection.

"Easy ma. I just wanted to feel those soft lips of yours." He said smoothly.

"Mmmm." Scarlet moaned with a seductive look on her face.

She kissed him passionately, pulling him back down to the bed on top of her. Her hands traveled from his shoulders to his forearms then to his ass which she squeezed gently. Craig was enjoying her touch and lifted himself up and grabbed his pole with his right hand preparing to guide it into her. He traced her lips with the head of his piece and fished for the hole.

"No papi." She whimpered.

"Why baby?" He asked as he continued trying to penetrate her.

"Please Craig, I no wan' to lose my virgin 'til I marry. I will let you do anything else but please no take my virgin from me." She begged in a child's voice.

Craig stopped and his hard on went limp immediately, he felt like a rapist.

"My bad Scarlet. I ain't trying to violate you like that. I just wanted you that bad. I been fucking with you over a year and you never let me hit that."

"I tell you I will do anything for you Craig, just not that..." Scarlet began but was cut off by Craig placing his pointer finger on her lips.

"I feel different for you than I do for any other girl Scarlet." Craig said with sincerity.

"I no can believe that. You have many like me, some my friends. You say this only because they give you all sex and I no give you my virgin. I no like that Craig, I do this for the money you give me. I thank you any way you like but no give my

virgin. I like you Craig but I know you no serious man for woman, you like fun and it's ok. I like fun with you too but you have to know that money is only for me to feed my family. I no have no papers so I no can find good job to help my family. Before I do this, my mama tell me that no money is worth me giving my virgin away. She say money no can buy it back when I give it away. I sorry for make you mad Craig and I understand if you no wanna see me again." Scarlet shuffled to the side of the bed to get her clothes that was strewn all over the floor.

Craig never heard her talk so much in the year he been using her services. Everything she said touched him in a way he never felt before. He didn't know what he was feeling because he never felt it before. He had dealt with her over a year and never felt what he was feeling now. He couldn't describe it but he knew it was something he couldn't fight, it came out of nowhere and it was almost crippling. Everything Scarlet just told him drew him closer to wanting to be with her. It was time for him to stop all the womanizing he had been doing and time to settle. He grabbed Scarlet by her hand and looked into her eyes for what seemed like hours then got his voice to cooperate and began to speak.

"Scarlet, I'm gonna keep it real with you. Everything you just said moved me and I want you to know that I really respect you as a woman. You're only fucking with me because you need bread to take care of your peoples, I get it. You a virgin and you don't want your shit popped unless it's by a muhfucka who gonna make a honest woman outta you." Craig leaned in and kissed her on her lips softly. "I'm that muhfucka."

Scarlet looked at Craig and gave an awkward smile but didn't say anything. She hunched her shoulders and half tilted her head.

"You didn't understand shit I just said huh?" Craig questioned her after realizing she was a little confused. He cupped his hands under her chin and stared into her eyes. "I

want to be your man, I want you to be my girl. No more games. I want us to be a couple, me and you."

"You not only saying because you just wan' my virgin?" She had to be sure.

"Nah Scarlet. My word is bond, I don't just want to fuck you, I want me and you to be in a relationship. Just you, I'm not gon' fuck wit' no other bitches. I'll even wait until you ready to give up the puss. All you have to do is say you'll be my girl and we're exclusive." Craig clarified.

"Ok Craig. I want that if you are telling me true." Scarlet smiled as she lay her head on his chest.

Craig's heart suddenly went pitter patter and he wondered if Scarlet could feel it through his chest. He couldn't deny what he was feeling and smiled looking down at her, happy to be with a woman he genuinely cared about for the first time in a long time. He ran his fingers through her silky hair as he began making plans in his head about what their life was going to be like then he turned her so she faced him and his look turned stoic.

"Scarlet, if I find out you trying to game me, I'm going to kill you." His tone was even and serious. "I don't want to scare you baby, I just want you to know that from here going forward there are no more games."

Scarlet leaned in and kissed Craig slow and long.

"I have love you from first time you call on me. I was hope you would see I was different. I no play games with my heart or yours, I promise."

Craig melted and held her onto her as his eyes got moist.

The phone began ringing and he reached over to his night stand and pressed the talk button.

"Hello?" He spoke into the receiver.

"Done." The voice said and the phone went dead.

Craig dialed Muffin's pager number and put in the code to let her know he received the phone call. He was digging her

style more and more and smiled to himself as he lay down next to his girl friend.

Chapter 15

Junior was gathering his things and preparing to leave the hospital. He had tried to get in contact with Muffin but was unable so he called his cousin Bo to pick him up. He was a little bit upset with Muffin because she seemed to be putting him second to whatever the fuck she was doing when she wasn't making sure he was recovering fully. She hadn't been to check on his since he was up and moving around. He was feeling neglected and felt he was supposed to be first priority especially in his condition. He sat on the bed after packing all his belongings and let his mind drift to New York.

He was still in love with Shondra, there was no denying that. Muffin not being there with him made him question just how loyal she was to him. He was feeling that because he was injured and unable to move around like he used to that she forgot about him. He knew if Shondra had been there instead of Muffin that she would be sitting with him right now. When he called and told her he had gotten shot she sounded so worried and was ready to hop the first Trailways bus to come see him; that was true unadulterated love. He was sure Muffin loved him but for some reason he was getting disturbing vibes and didn't know where they were coming from. She was his ride or die not his true love amd she was displaying movements that seemed suspect to him and he couldn't put his finger on it.

"You ready cuz?" Bo asked coming through the door without knocking.

Junior rose to his feet and handed him his leather duffle bag. "Yea, I been ready."

"Cool. Let's be out." Bo took the bag and swung it over his shoulder effortlessly. "You need me to help you?"

"Nah." Junior replied confidently as he bent down and touched his toes with both hands. "I'm good my dude. Let's bounce."

They both exited the hospital and headed over to Bo's new Mazda Millenia. He opened the door and placed the bag in the back seat jumped inside the driver's side and cranked up the engine. Junior walked behind the car and looked down at the 30 day tags then walked on over to the passenger side and got in. Bo pulled off and Junior's mind started moving a mile a minute. He knew he couldn't jump to conclusions, he learned about that from when he faced Kendu and La's betrayal. He had to sit back and pay attention to all movements around him. It had been about three months since he been on the block so he was sure a lot had changed but he wasn't sure how much.

"Nice whip Bo." He said as the car drove down US 264 East.

"Thanks cuz. Just picked it up from Washington Motors 'bout a week back." Bo said changing the CD.

"Hmm." Junior looked out his window as the countryside whizzed by him in a blur. "How much it run you?"

"I put a down payment on it. $2,500 and put it in my lady's name." Bo announced proudly.

"Oh ok, you financed it. That's a good look. Just be careful, hope you and your lady stay together 'cause if not, this pretty ass whip is hers." Junior schooled.

"I ain't worried 'bout that, my ole' lady don't think like that."

"Yea, ok." Junior chuckled. "Money changes everything cuzzo, trust me on that."

Junior looked out the side window and thought how true his statement rang. He knew first hand that the introduction to a lot of money in a relationship that was void of it created disloyalty and dishonesty. His experience coupled with his

cousin's Craig jewels of wisdom about the love of money always ended up with him finding out the game he chose had no loyalty, whatsoever. He had yet to find anyone that was completely loyal to him without having any other motives. He lay back in the car and waited until he got home. He was going to get his business back on track but more importantly, he needed to make sure Muffin was still down with him the way he thought.

***

"That's eighty-five thou cash for the five pies." Muffin stated confidently as she finished counting out all the money on Craig's living room table.

Muffin was out of her element inside Craig's stash house with all that money. She was taking a big risk with this trip but it was all or nothing. Junior was still in the hospital when she called and checked on him before she left for New York. She hadn't been to see him the last couple of days because she had been so busy trying to show Patricia how to move the weight she had given her. She broke down everything to Patricia who proved to be an eager and willing learner. The problem they ran into was how to get rid of the work without the girls being detected. They brainstormed and Muffin came up with a fool proof way that would net them thousands in the matter of days. She had Patricia recruit the girlfriends or side bitches of some of the block boys. The girls would steal their boyfriend's clientele since they knew who their boyfriends were selling to and to sweeten the deal they would give them bigger rocks to keep them coming. In the first week of operation they moved one kilo which was why Muffin was back in New York.

The money came so fast she didn't have time to think. Even Bo was done and she was down to her last half of kilo. She had money coming from every direction and would be able

to replace the money she took out of the safe with the next shipment she was getting from Craig.

"How long you think it's gon' take you to get that to me?" She asked Craig as she leaned back in the couch. She was exhausted from the eight hour drive from North Carolina to Brooklyn.

Craig was still counting out the money coming out the machine as it made flapping noises. "I got you as soon as I finish counting the rest of this bread."

"Can I cut the shit down in here?" She asked looking at him carefully.

He stopped what he was doing and looked up at her, his eyebrows raised. "What you mean cut the shit down in here? This ain't no crack spot."

"I don't mean no disrespect but I'm on a tight schedule. I can't risk going to my mom's crib and bagging and breaking shit down there 'cause she gonna question why I'm back here so soon, you feel me?" She explained.

"I feel you but my best advice is you go get you one of them four hour jump offs and bag that shit up in the telly. You should be good 'cause ain't nobody gon' peep that shit."

Muffin didn't like the idea of going to a motel to bag up. Although she didn't know Craig all that well she felt safer around him with all that coke. Her nerves were getting the best of her because everything was happening so fast. The money scared her how fast it came and the amount of drugs she was about to take down there was fed status. She was a little spooked but not enough to stop what she was doing. The adrenaline rush she got from handling business was becoming addictive just as the coke were to the baseheads.

"Aiight fuck it, I'll go to the motel on Linden and bag the shit up then. Can I at least wait here until you come back from cooking and shit?" She asked in a dejected tone.

"Nah. This the stash house. You don't wanna be up in here with all this work. I'll take you to my crib and you can relax over there 'til my boys finish cooking this shit up for you."

"Thanks." She replied gratefully. "Can I use your horn to beep this dude to make sure he'll be around when you're done?"

Craig pointed to the cordless phone on the counter in the kitchen. "Help yourself."

Muffin got up and walked to the kitchen and picked up the beige phone and dialed Chico's beeper number. She hoped he was in Baptiste so she could drop off his work as soon as she finished bagging it up then jump on the highway and get back down south to Junior before he got out of the hospital.

***

When Bo pulled up in front of the house Junior didn't see his truck which meant Muffin wasn't home. He reached into the back seat and grabbed his duffle bag and pushed the car door open.

"Junior, hol' on. Here, take these." Bo said to him before he could exit the vehicle.

Junior turned his head and looked down at Bo's hand with a perplexed look. "What's those for?"

"These your new house keys. The police had to break down your door to get to you last time you were here." He passed Junior the keys.

Junior took the keys in his hands and tried his best to hide his confusion as to why Muffin would give the keys to his cousin instead of giving them to him herself; and where the fuck was she anyway? Junior was shaking his head as he jingled the keys in his hand as he walked up the stairs to the porch. He went to the door and with hands shaking from anger, he fumbled with sticking the key in the cylinder. He turned the key then pushed the door open. He stepped inside and blew out a

burst of air from his mouth out of frustration. He rubbed his head and tried his best to calm his anger. He dropped the duffle bag at the entrance then turned and through gritted teeth yelled out to Bo.

"Ay yo!" He waved his hand because he never exited the vehicle.

Bo looked through the windshield of his car then jumped out quickly.

"What's up Junior? You need some help in there?" He asked walking up to the porch and stopping at the top step.

"I wanted to know if you was straight. You need any more food?" Junior asked.

Bo hesitated then looked at the ground, a dead giveaway he was about to lie. "Nah man, I'm straight. It been really slow on the block lately so it's taking a longer time to get rid of it than it usually do."

"Yea ok." Junior smirked. "I'll get back up with you after I shower, shit and shave." Junior closed the door then locked it behind him. He looked around at the standard Heilig Meyers furniture, floral print sofas with wood arm rests and a single matching floral print recliner that doubled as a rocking chair. Junior took a seat in the chair and rocked back and forth. He grabbed the cordless phone and beeped Muffin then dropped the phone on the wooden center table.

There was something you were supposed to always go with and that was your gut feeling; Junior's gut was killing him. He didn't want to second guess himself but betrayal in this game was starting to become a regular thing and he was growing tired. He felt he could trust Muffin when it came to riding out for him but the allure of money, lots of money, could easily change the most loyal of people. Junior stood up and walked over to the window and Bo was just pulling out of his driveway.

"*I wonder if that muhfucka would cross me over money?*" Junior thought out loud to himself.

He grabbed his duffle bag off the floor and went to his bedroom. He threw the bag on the floor and plopped down on his bed and dropped his head, rubbing it with both hands. He lifted his head up and stared up at the ceiling.

"*Rule of thumb! Go with your first instinct!*" He spoke loudly into the atmosphere. There was no need for him to worry about something he wasn't sure about, that was the quickest way to stagnate yourself. Whatever the fucked up vibe he was feeling about Muffin, he couldn't let that shit slow down his movement. He had to make a trip to NY and re up then come back and flood the town again and this time he was going to make sure he stayed on top of his shit.

He got up from the bed feeling renewed and walked over to his closet. The door was partly opened and he grabbed the knob and pulled the door to him. His heart began beating fast as he dropped to his knee instantly and bent his head down and screamed out at the top of his lungs! "NO!" All the money in the safe was gone! There was close to half a million in there and it was all gone! He stuck his hand inside and felt around on each shelf like his eyes were playing a trick on him. He stood up slowly and rage overtook his body as tears of pain and frustration flushed from his eyes. He didn't know how loud he bellowed until he heard the echoes of his shrieks bouncing off the walls and vibrating in his ears, the noise was foreign and it pained him to no end. He backed away from the closet until his leg hit the bed and he welcomed the seat because his legs felt like they were about to give out on him. He stared at the open safe across from him in disbelief while his mind raced with thoughts of who could have been so fucking bold as to come into his home and rob him.

Biting his bottom lip, he got up and pulled the dresser out and grabbed the nine millimeter that was taped to the back of it. He released the clip and checked to make sure it was filled with sixteen rounds then slammed it back in then pulled the slide back, chambering a bullet in the pipe. He heard a grinding

143

noise and realized he was gritting his teeth as he stuffed the weapon inside the front of his pants. He grabbed the cordless phone off its base and dialed Muffin's beeper number repeatedly as he walked towards the back of the house. Before he got to the back door he dropped the phone on the kitchen counter then grabbed the knob of the back door; it was already open. He snatched the burner from his waist and flipped the safety off with his thumb then pulled the door towards him. His eyes scanned the backyard quickly through the screen door as the clicking noise could be heard as he slowly cocked the hammer back on his automatic weapon. He pushed the screen door open slowly with his foot and walked down the stairs cautiously; the burner in front of him now. His feet touched the grass and sank in as he moved sideways, his head and eyes darting back and forth. The fence on both sides of the property were over zoning code regulation size by one and a half feet so his neighbors couldn't see anything. The backyard was huge with a big tree in the middle of it with lawn chairs surrounding it in a circle to ward of the sun rays. Junior crept slowly and quietly until he was by Drama's kennel. It was unusual for him not to come greet his master with his tongue hanging out his mouth and tail wagging so hard his back legs rocked back and forth. Junior bent down and looked inside his dog house and was horrified to find Drama keeled over with his tongue hanging out of his mouth. He dropped his gun in the dirt and got on his knees and grabbed his canine, man's best friend, and with all the strength he could muster, pulled him out from the place Drama called home. Tears exploded from Junior's eyes as all his emotions were on full display. He rocked back and forth and couldn't stop them from flowing. Drama's oversized head lay in his lap right atop his gun wound but he didn't feel any discomfort, he only felt anger; anger because someone deliberately came into his home, killed his pit and robbed him blind. He continued rocking Drama until his eyes were completely drained and his crying quieted down to sobs. Drama's head was placed on the dirt

gently; Junior rose to his feet and brushed off his pants then picked up his gun. He checked to see if there was any work in the stash by the dog house and like he figured, it was empty. Looking at his dead canine as he passed Junior wanted revenge, he wanted to kill whoever was responsible for this; they didn't have to kill his dog.

He grabbed the cordless phone when he got back in the house and checked to see if there were any missed calls while he was in the backyard. Nothing. The phone was hurled at the wall and exploded into tiny pieces as Junior walked to the bathroom.

"That bitch betta call me 'fore I leave this muhfucka tonight!" The words squeezed though his clenched teeth as he turned the shower on and disrobed quickly and jumped into the shower. The steaming hot water beat down on his head as his palms lay flat against the tiles as he tried to make sense out of what happened. He was trying to figure out the time the money was taken and how long Muffin was gone. She was his first suspect because she was the only person, other than him, that knew the combination to the safe. The only thing that didn't set right with him about that was there would have been no need for her to kill Drama. He shook his head and lay it back and opened his mouth so the shower water could go inside then he spit it out. Bo, he was the only other person that had access into the house, shit, he's the one that gave him the house keys and he never came inside which was unusual in itself. That bad feeling he was having was coming from one or both of those muhfuckas and he had to find out which one. He lathered up and then jumped out the shower pat drying his body then wrapping the towel around himself and only taking his gun when he left the bathroom. He got dressed in his room, closed and locked the safe then beeped Muffin one final time putting 911 in the code back to back. He was going to fuck her up just for ignoring his calls. Like most muhfuckas, when something bad happens, they go back to something familiar. Before he

walked out the room he picked up the cordless phone and dialed some numbers and waited impatiently for someone to pick up.

"Hello?"

"Ay yo, what's up Mooka?" Junior said stiffly.

There was a long pause before she was able to say anything else. "Junior? You aiight?" Her voice trembled.

"Nah, not really. Can I holla for a minute? You busy?" He desperately needed to hear the voice of someone he knew he could trust, someone that never betrayed him; someone he truly loved.

"Of course, of course. What's wrong Junior?" Concern seeped out of her voice as she held the phone in her trembling hands.

"Shit fucked up out here Mooka. I'm just getting out the hospital and I come to my crib and find my safe broken into and all my fucking money gone! Every fucking dollar!"

"Oh my God! Do you know who took it? Does it have something to do with what happened between you and KB?" She was asking so many questions in succession.

"I don't know who did it but I got an idea and I swear if I'm right, I'm murking them out the gate; no questions asked. I'm not taking this loss, not chalking this up to the game 'cause this shit was an inside job! They took everything I own, I ain't got shit left but what I had on me when I got shot and that's short money." Junior was seething, the more he talked about it, the madder he got.

Shondra was on the other end of the phone beside herself with worry. She wished she could help him out financially but she was sure the little bit of money Chico was giving her for the baby wasn't enough for him to get back on his feet.

"If you need some money I got a little bit saved up that I can give you to help you out." Shondra offered.

"Nah Mooka, I'll scrape some ends together. This shit right here is temporary but what I'm gonna do to the muhfucka

who robbed me is gon' be permanent." Junior didn't want to take any of the money she had, it probably wouldn't be enough for him to get a brick much less a half a brick.

"Aiight but if you change your mind I'll give it all to you. It's about $8,000 I saved. I know that ain't a lot of money to you but it's all I have and you can have it if you need it."

Junior paused as his eyes got wide. Where the fuck did she get money like that to save eight G's? He shook his head and started rethinking what he was going to do. He had three G's he could put his hands on and with her eight he was sure he could pay for a half brick then get a whole one on consignment; his face was still good since he paid the connect on time with no shorts.

"You said you got 8 G's? If you let me hold that I'll get it back to you by two weeks." Junior paused as he looked out the window. "You sure you could let me hold that?"

"Of course. Why you ask?" Shondra asked puzzled. Junior used to keep quadruple that in the safe in her house, eight thousand used to be what he gave her to go shopping. This was money she saved.

"Nah it's jus I was wondering where you was getting money to save like that. I don't want to take your life savings and risk it just because mine gone, you know what I'm saying?"

"Don't worry about it Junior. It's just money and it can always be replaced." Shondra purposely avoided his question to where she got the money.

Since she had the baby Chico was giving her money every two weeks and it was more than he was giving her through her whole pregnancy. She didn't question him about it but knew it started happening after she saw that bitch Muffin talking to him. She figured the bitch was hustling for him or hitting him off with work but didn't care as long as he gave her money so she wouldn't have to get on welfare.

"Aiigt then. I just wanted to be sure. Hold onto that for me, I should be breaking out tonight or early in the morning depending on what I find out."

"Please don't do nothing crazy Junior, you just getting out the hospital." Shondra pleaded.

"I ain't gon' lie, if I catch the muhfucka tonight it's going down tonight."

"Well can you at least call me and let me know when you're on your way back here?" She asked.

"No question, I was going to do that anyway. While we on the phone I know how I left things and I think we need to talk, if you have time."

Junior was in his feelings about Muffin because she didn't come to the hospital when he was discharged, she wasn't there when he got home where he found out he had gotten robbed for all his money and to top it off whoever did it killed Drama too. It was almost instinctive for him to seek Shondra out in a time like this because he was confused, angry and hurt. Of course it wasn't fair what he put her through when it came to Muffin but he thought he was in love with her...at the time.

Shondra was standing in the hallway talking on the wall phone. She stretched the cord as far as she could so she could peek in on the baby to make sure he was still asleep. She could see his little back raising up and down in the bassinet then she walked back in the hallway and addressed Junior.

"I have time what you wanna talk about?" She already had an idea it was going to be about their relationship or what was left of it because he already told her the worst news; him getting robbed.

Junior sat down on the arm of the couch and rubbed his wound with his right hand. "I want to apologize for all the dirty shit I did to you Mooka. I'm so sorry for putting you through all that bullshit with that crazy bitch. I shouldn't of never made you feel like she was more important than you, I fucked up all the way and I'm sorry baby." Junior was getting emotional. His

feelings for Shondra never went away, he always loved her. "I'm not trying to make any excuses for none of that foul shit that happened but under the circumstances I wasn't thinking right and that shit affected my choices. So much was happening over in Baptiste and with that murder beef over my head I had to bail out and in the process I didn't really think it all the way through." His head lowered.

Shondra inhaled and exhaled deeply into the phone; her heart was fluttering uncontrollably. His apology seemed so sincere and because she loved him so much, her heart was all too willing to let him back in; unadulterated. "Junior I know you were going through a lot last year and I understand some of it but what I can't understand is how that bitch was able to pull you away from me. Me and you had so much history, we built a stable life and a sturdy relationship that shouldn't have been infiltrated so easily. I can accept your apology because I missed you so much, I was lost without you and I prayed for the day me and you would get back together. There are some things that we need to clear up before we do this." Shondra paused and breathed out a long burst of air. "Are you still fucking with that squeaky voice bitch?"

"Nah, not like that." Junior replied too quickly and regretted what came out of his mouth. No doubt that would take some explaining.

"What you mean not like that?" Shondra questioned, her heart shifting it's beat.

"It's like this with Muffin. She handle all my shit so I don't have to..." Shondra cut him off briskly.

"You gonna sing that same fucking song before 'bout that she mule your shit and the one that gonna take the fall for you? Please don't play me like that again Junior. If you seriously want this shit between us to work again then the first thing you gotta get rid of is that bitch. I already seen her creeping around her a couple weeks ago..." It was Junior's turn to cut her off.

"You said you seen her 'round your way a couple weeks ago?" Junior's voice raised unintentionally.

"Yea, right around the time you called and told me you got shot. To be honest I was wondering if you was still fucking with her 'cause why would she be here while you on your deathbed?" Shondra purposely added dramatics to get her point across. "If I was with you, you know I woulda never left your side for no reason!" That was the stake through Muffin's chest.

Junior half listened to what Shondra was saying because he was trying to figure out why Muffin would go to Baptiste. Shondra wasn't a threat because Muffin was the one with him down south. He couldn't figure out what other reason she would be around there for except Shondra, that was her only connection. He needed to find out more information from Shondra so he could try and piece the scattered puzzle together that had disloyalty and deceit written all over it. "Where you see her exactly?"

"She was across the street talking to somebody from my building then she jumped in a cab and started yelling some bullshit out the cab window when they drove by."

"Who was she talking to?" The wheels were turning in his head but he wasn't getting anywhere.

Shondra didn't know what to say, she was at a crossroad. Mentioning Chico's name would definitely shift the conversation but she couldn't lie to him. She wanted him back and she didn't want to start with lies because everything going forward would be built on that lie. "She was talking to Chico." It came out almost a decibel over a whisper.

"That's the muhfucka you was fuckin'!" Junior's voice raised. He rubbed his head with his hand furiously. "Fuck she out there talkin' to that lame ass nigga for anyway!" Junior paused then breathed out. "You still fucking him Shondra?"

Shondra paused then quickly said, "No! I been stop fucking with him Junior." She heard her baby waking up making soft gurgling noises. She walked over to her room and

peeked inside the bassinet and could see the baby still laying on his stomach, ass poked up in the air and flipping left to right as he made small noises. "Junior can I call you back in about a fifteen minutes." She needed to feed her son.

"Nah, let me call you back when I come back from the block." He said walking over to the window and looking out. "Don't think I'm flipping Mooka I just wanted to know if you still fucking with dude that's all. I ain't forget what that faggot ass muhfucka did, he still owe me some bread!" Junior remembered. "I'ma let you go and call you back when I get back, aiight?"

"Ok, please call me back. I really want us to finish talking." Shondra said sincerely then paused as she rubbed her son's back as he continued stirring in his bassinet. "I still love you." She almost whispered then disconnected the call just as her son's cries became audible.

Junior held the phone in his hand and looked at it wondering who baby he heard crying in the background before Shondra hung up.

Chapter 16

Bo slammed the door to his car and walked up to the store on the block. The scene out there had changed since Junior had come down supplying the town with weight. Instead of renting cars, the boys were buying luxury models vehicles, buying clothes from the most expensive stores in the mall and paying for extended stays in five star hotels. Although jobs were scarce in the small town, the revenue from drugs kept the businesses open and thriving, in turn keeping people employed. In one aspect drugs was a necessary evil in the wake of the bad economy because it kept the businesses in town profitable but the flip side was that it destroyed the small African American community families that became addicted to the highly addictive crack cocaine. It was not a recreational drug like powder cocaine and when it hit the scene users soon realized one hit could have you hooked and chasing it most of your life. Although it was a very profitable business, it left broken homes in its wake.

Bo walked into the store and slapped some of the boys five as he made his way to the back. Two boys shooting pool stopped when they saw him approaching and they all walked towards the bathroom in the back of the store.

"I need another ounce. You got one on you?" The first guy asked Bo as he pulled out a stack of money from his pocket and started counting. While he counted his partner pulled out a stack of his own and began counting bills. He wanted more work too. Bo took the money from both boys and counted it all out himself and when he was done dug into pocket and pulled out a small digital scale and placed it on the bathroom sink. He

pulled out a small Ziploc bag tied tightly with a rough round crystallized rock inside. He placed it on the scale and it read 28.5 and he passed it to the first guy then did the same thing again for the other guy. They both slapped him five after their drug transaction and went back to shooting pool.

"When you gon' let me get sumthin'?" A young guy sitting on the bench asked Bo as he passed him.

Bo looked down at the boy who was asking him the question. "Why you ain't in school boy?" He asked ignoring his question.

"Ain't no money in school." He replied defiantly.

Bo laughed. "You right 'bout that, all the money in here." Bo flashed his knot of money.

"So when you gon' let me make some?" The young boy pushed.

Bo scratched his head and looked around the store. Everyone in there was selling drugs and all the drugs came from one source, Muffin. All the work was being distributed by him so there was no reason the young boy couldn't get some. "Ok, I'm gon' give you something small when I get back."

The young boy's eyes lit up as a smile grew on his hairless face. "Thanks Bo man. I swear I'm gon' make more money than anybody."

"Just make sure you pay me what you owe." Bo said turning around and walking toward the front door of the store.

When he pushed the door open and stepped out of the store he sat down on the wooden picnic table and watched the boys running to cars making sales while crack heads stood around looking to run errands for hits. Suddenly everyone stopped what they were doing because they heard two gunshots. Everyone looked around not knowing exactly where it came from then some seconds later they heard three more shots and a loud scream that came from the direction of the barbershop. Everyone started milling out the store to see what was happening then they saw a crack head named Lizard running

out from the barbershop holding his ass. Then they saw the dude that owned the barbershop running behind him with a gun. Bo grabbed his gun from his waist as the boys started shouting threats to KB. They didn't know what happened but believed in sticking together. Bo walked out to the middle of the street and when KB locked eyes with him he raised his gun. KB stopped and Bo raised his gun as Lizard ran pass screaming he was shot in the ass.

***

KB pulled into the parking lot of his barber shop and parked his car in his designated spot. It was almost a month since he been there to open up and when Patricia quit, Gloria hired another beautician to replace her then put Jerome in charge of opening and closing the shop. She would have Jerome meet her at restaurants like Golden Corral to bring her the day's receipts and go over them while talking about improvements that needed to be made in the barbershop. Gloria was still wary of Junior and Muffin so she intentionally steered clear of the block and the barbershop when doing business.

KB unconsciously tapped his waist where his firearm was secured in his belt holster. He had purchased an arsenal of new guns after his weapon was stolen the day he had the shoot out with Junior. Gloria had wanted him to report the gun stolen but he decided against it because he still had a street element to him and considered it snitching. His gun was already off safety as he pulled it out its holster and exited his vehicle, gripping the firearm tightly as if it was a baton in a relay race. He surveyed his surroundings as he approached the back door cautiously, looking left to right out of rattled nervousness.

He put the key in the cylinder and turned it, unlocking the door. Pushing it inward, one of the hinges squeaked loudly and then he heard something scattering about inside. He froze for a second but instinct raised the arm holding the pistol and

had it pointing in front of him. His heart fluttered quickly as he ventured inside slowly his feet moving like he was wearing lead shoes. He stopped and listened once he was inside and looked down the hallway to where the barber chairs were. He scanned the area from where he was standing and sharpened the audio in his ears waiting to hear movement up front. The office door was to his right so he tried turning the knob to see if the door was locked; it was. He walked pass his office and the closer he got to the barber area, the more his legs shook. He kept his back against the wall as he neared the opening then was startled by a raccoon that came charging down the hallway at him. He pulled the trigger as he backed up and two of the slugs slammed into the back of the oversized pest downing him instantly. KB fell back onto his ass after the animal stopped moving, his smoking gun still trained on the animal. Before getting back on his feet he allowed time for his heart to stop beating so fast by taking some deep breaths. He stood up and looked down at the dead carcass and marveled at his marksmanship in the wake of fear.

He turned to go into his office to call someone to remove the road kill from his shop and before he reached the door, it flew open and a skinny man bolted from the office and high tailed it to the back door of the shop at break neck speed. KB was once again caught off guard but his instincts kicked in and he pointed his gun and let three shots go in succession. The third bullet discharged produced a blood curdling scream from the fleeing man as he stumbled out the door. KB sprinted to the back door and watched as the man ran up the block holding his ass as he ran.

"Fuckin' crackhead!'" He spewed as he half chased him to the corner of the block.

He stopped short when he saw a group of young guys gathering by the store. He knew some of the block boys that came to get their hair cut but he didn't know them well enough to cross the line.

"I catch you stealing something else out my fucking shop, I'll body you next time!" He screamed so the crack head could not lie about the reason he got popped in his ass.

He kept his gun exposed as he watched some of the block boys assist the shot crack head. They were making gestures toward KB letting him know they didn't approve of one of their own being handled in that manner, no matter what he did. His eyes locked on Bo, remembering the face of Junior's cousin, the one who passed him the gun. KB looked down at Bo's hand and watched as he raised it slowly towards him. Flashbacks of getting shot raced through his mind and instinct took over and he raised his firearm chest high aiming at Bo.

"What the fuck up muhfucka!" KB screamed as he inched next to a pickup truck to use as a shield. "That muhfucka stole out my fucking shop! You want to bang out over that muhfucka then let's go!" He screamed.

The boys who didn't have guns backed up. They remembered the dude from the barbershop, he was from Brooklyn and was in a shootout with Junior. There was no doubt he was no slow leak and was real familiar with pulling triggers. The unarmed boys backed away to the safety of the store while others stood with Bo and started drawing their own weapons.

"You don't want to do that partner!" Bo shouted. "You'll die right by that truck!"

"I'm ready to die muhfucka! You still talkin'! You think I'ma back down 'cause a crack head violated my shit! You buggin'! I'm ready to make it thunderstorm out this muhfucka over mine!" KB's anger was escalating as he kept talking.

"Yo Bo! Fuck that muhfucka, we can get him another time!" One of the boys said grabbing him and pulling him towards the store.

Bo turned around reluctantly but kept his eyes on KB. He was beginning to understand why Muffin wanted his ass dead, he was really a threat in their small town. They needed to

156

run his ass out of town which wasn't really difficult, they'd done that before. He backed away, face fighting KB who came from behind the pickup truck with his gun still pointed at Bo.

KB backed away towards the barbershop, never holstering his firearm in case one of Bo boys wanted to try and get a name for themselves by challenging the barbershop owner from New York. KB wasn't the least bit afraid of any of the boys on the block and would gladly empty his sixteen shot clip into anyone who wanted to make the headlines in the local paper. He wasn't afraid to bust his gun because he'd been shot twice already and he wasn't about to let another muhfucka shoot him again, fuck that! He was sure they knew that after the shoot out he had with the guy that was supplying them with all the drugs they were selling; Junior. When he got close to the shop he turned around and ran inside and locked the doors. He hated the big plate glass windows but they did provide a clear view to the block. He went into his office to check if the crack head got away with anything of value. As he surveyed his inventory he heard the door being jiggled and he cocked the hammer on his gun and ran out of his office pointing at the door. Jerome was standing outside of the door trying to open the door. When he saw KB pointing his gun at him he stopped what he was doing and raised his hands in the air. KB quickly walked to the door, gun in his hand and opened it briskly.

"What's going on bossman?" Jerome asked venturing into the shop slowly.

"Fucking crack head broke in." He answered closing the door and looking down towards the block.

"That's fucked up. Anything missing?" Jerome asked checking his station.

"I don't think so but I gotta take my time, know what I'm saying?" KB said walking back to his office. "Yo Rome?"

"Yea bossman." Jerome answered walking towards the office to see what KB wanted.

"You know who that nigga that be with Junior is?" He asked taking a seat behind his desk when Rome appeared in the doorway.

"Bo?" He answered absentmindedly.

"That's the niggas name huh?" KB nodded to himself going back into the shop. "What's that muhfuckas story? Before Junior got here selling all this drug shit, how was duke? I mean, what was his character? Was this muhfucka a gunslinger or a gangster?"

Jerome stood next to his chair and rubbed his goatee. "Wasn't really nobody down these parts gangster or gunslingers. When you cats from NY come down here some of these guys start trying to act like 'em. I never known Bo to shoot guns, he used to steal out of Piggly Wiggly just like we all used to but that's the most he did far as I can recall."

KB shook his head slowly. "Junior don' put a battery in these fool's back and gonna get them caught up in some shit they really not built for!" He waved his gun in the air. "These shits spit hot balls out the barrel that will end a muhfuckas existence, I know, this my second time getting hit and I'm not gon' let another muhfucka use me for target practice! This shit ain't no movie, these shits will stop your heart from beating! I was lucky, I used up two of my lives! A cat only get nine!"

"These drugs don' changed this whole town man. The old coons are the ones strung out on it and the youngins are the one selling them this shit. The money is the motivation, we a small town and we always last to get everything..." Jerome paused. "...'cept these drugs. That shit just came out of nowhere. Fucked up most e'erbody family in one way or another."

"I ain't never sold no drugs in Brooklyn. I used to rob them muhfuckas and my man Stump, God bless the dead, hated all drug dealers. He used to say it didn't take no skills to sell drugs, it was the easiest way to make money but it destroyed our people. I know what this shit does to people, it make bitches desert their kids, make sons rob their moms and turn daughters

into prostitutes. I don't respect those muhfuckas 'cause they let the love of money take over their common sense, I knew muhfuckas who would sell to their own mother and say if they didn't she would get it from somewhere else so they only keeping the money in the family." KB glanced out the plate glass window towards the block. "I don't know how serious that shit is down here but I don't give a fuck about none of them niggas out there selling that shit, young or old, I'll body them!" KB said shaking his gun in his hand.

Jerome took a seat in his barber chair and turned it around to face KB. "I tried selling that shit before, just because I seen the boys flashing a lot of money and since money tight and jobs is scarce I dibbled and dabbed in it. The money was good, I can't lie but shit changed when I started finding out that a lot of my kinfolk was on that shit bad. It's like it just transformed them into different fucking people. I saw what it was doing to my family and I had to stop 'cause it just ain't right. I'm not a fan of nobody that sells that shit either, not no more." Jerome said sincerely.

KB looked at Jerome for a second and wondered if being a business owner was a smart move right now. It was right smack dab in the middle of a area that was flooded with drugs and his beef was with Junior who was supplying the drugs to the boys on the block which meant his beef with him could easily turn into beef with the block boys. He didn't have anyone on his side; no one that would bang out with him against Junior. Jerome shared one of his sentiments, his dislike for drug dealers, and if he was willing to join forces with KB then he would have some help in shutting Junior down. His barbershop was too close to where Junior made his money and it was inevitable that they would bump heads again, there was no way around it. He could keep the barbershop open so he'll still have his money coming in then he'd hunt Junior down and body him, ridding him of a beef that followed him from Brooklyn.

"Yo Rome. I got a proposition for you bruh, if you're interested." KB said to him as he turned and looked at him in his eyes.

"What is it?" Jerome asked, his antennas up.

"You already seen what went down when I bumped head with that nigga I got beef with from NY right?" It wasn't really a question it was more of a statement. "This beef we got started in Brooklyn 'cause my man tried to rob him. I wasn't a part of that shit, I was there but never bust my gun at the muhfucka. He heard I was there so he was on some get back shit so I ain't have no choice but to be on watch for the nigga. The bitch he down here with him clapped me in a club 'cause she was with him and he probably told her to do it. That was my first time getting clipped until I saw the muhfucka come up in here. I gotta get rid of this dude fam and I need some help, just one dude that can hold me down; just be my eyes. I don't know this town like that, I don't know who's who but if I had somebody that could point out the muhfuckas I need to worry about then I'll have a better chance on making this nigga a distant memory and in the process once his ass is gone the supply of drugs down here will dry up. I know it won't stop but I'm sure it'll dry up, you feel me?" KB eyed him seriously.

Jerome stared at KB and nodded his head slowly and was about to open his mouth to let him know if he was on board or not but before he could say anything the dinging bell alerted them someone was entering the barbershop. He and KB both looked at the door as Patricia walked inside with two other girls. She looked like a shining star, dressed in a tight Tommy Hilfiger warm up suit that clung to her body like her second skin. KB's mouth dropped as he salivated while Jerome held nothing back and screamed out, "DAMN!"

***

Bo was surrounded by a lot of the guys from the block when Junior walked into the store.

"What's up New Yawk?" was heard from various guys as Junior made his way to Bo. He was sure all the guys from the block knew he had a shoot out with KB and got shot. Looks of respect mixed with surprise was on their faces. Bo was sitting on the bench next to the pool table when Junior approached.

"Yo cuz, I need to holla at you for a minute." Junior spoke in monotone.

Bo rose to his feet and followed behind Junior who was already headed back out the door. Junior kept walking away from the store going in the direction of the gas station. Bo tried to catch up to him with hurried steps then yelled out, "Where you going cuz?"

Junior stopped then turned around, a single vein going down the middle of his forehead. "I need to ask you a question Bo." His head leaned slightly to the left. "Where the fuck is Muffin?"

Bo's eyebrows raised high and his eyes got big. "I don't know." His voice sounded unsure.

"You lying!" Junior barked. "What the fuck is goin' Bo!" Junior inched up to him both fists balled up tightly.

Bo put his head down and shook it slowly. "Look here cuz I don't know what the fuck was going on after you got shot. Ole' girl started trippin' man." Bo frowned.

"Fuck you talkin' 'bout!" Junior's heart rate increased. He wasn't sure what he was about to hear but had a sinking feeling it was going to be something he wasn't going to like. "Go 'head, tell me!" He yelled impatiently.

"Awright man, I'ma tell you straight. I think your ole lady trying to take over your shit down here." Bo blurted out.

"WHAT!" Junior boomed. His voice caught the attention of some of the guys hanging by the store. "When all this shit started?"

161

FOUR SHADOUGH PUBLISHING

"From the time you was laying up in the hospital. I asked her did she know where the rest of the work was since I was running low. She didn't want to tell me and got all crazy making me go on a scavenger hunt to go pick it up. Then when she went up top she called down here and told me she had some more work and that if I got rid of it she would give me twice as much and pay me twice as much to move it. Soon as she got back she kept her word but told me not to say anything about it to you..." Junior interrupted him.

"So you didn't! You went against the grain on this one Bo. How you gon' move all fucked up like that? You supposed to be my family! You violated that by trading places for greed." Junior's face scowled. "What? You thought I wasn't gonna make it muhfucka!" He looked behind him for a second then back at Bo. "Where the bitch at, in New York right?"

"Yea. She left yesterday and said she was just gonna be gon' for a day and be back by tomorrow." Bo felt like shit. "Cuz, I ain't have no way of getting no more work, you was laid up in the hospital. I didn't know when you was going to get back right so I was looking at it like I was keeping shit in the family since she was your ole lady." Bo shrugged his shoulders.

Junior's breathing was heavy as he listened with lowered eyebrows. He was staring directly in Bo's eyes trying to see if he could detect any deceit. "What you know about the safe and my money?"

"You talking 'bout how much money she took wit' her when she went to cop? That I don't know."

"The work you got now, that's the work she gave you?"

"Yea." Bo said his head hanging and his speech lowered.

Junior reeled back then slapped Bo so hard in his face he lost his footing on the gravel beneath his feet and hit the ground hard. Junior stepped to him and quickly disarmed him before he realized what was happening. Crack heads and some of the boys on the block started to mill around to see what the commotion was. Junior stood over his cousin with the gun in his hand.

"You disloyal fuck!" Junior screamed at Bo who was looking up at him with wide pleading eyes. "How the fuck you gonna flip on me like that? That's some foul shit!" Junior kneeled down on one knee and gripped the gun tightly in his mitt. Bo's admission proved he couldn't be trusted and was capable of doing anything. Junior needed to find out if he was the one that robbed him and killed Drama; if he did his family was going to be dressed in black. The hammer in his hand was the tool he was going to use as his truth serum. "I'm only gonna ask you this once Bo and I swear on auntie if you lie she gon' lose a son to the streets! Did you take my money out my fucking safe?" Junior's eyes were piercing through Bo's like a laser.

Bo's eyes grew wider as he shook his head in protest violently. "Hell naw! Man I wouldn't do no shit like that to you cuz. I know you hot wit' me 'bout that move I made but you can't think I'll steal from you man, come on now!" Spit flew from his mouth as he pleaded his case.

Junior stared at him for a long time then stood up slowly. He reached his hand down and Bo extended his and Junior pulled him up to his feet.

"Somebody robbed my fucking crib and took all my fucking bread and killed Drama!" Junior told Bo with fire dancing in his pupils. Junior looked behind him at the boys that hustled for him and Bo then he turned back and said to Bo, "Any of these niggas out here copped a new whip, some diamond jewelry or tricking money lately?"

Bo looked over his back at his boy and tried to seriously think if he saw anyone spending paper like it was going out of style. "Nah cuz, I can't say I seen none of the boys spending a lot of money, no more than they usually spend."

Junior nodded his head slowly. "I need you to drop me back home to my crib." He passed Bo his gun and turned around and headed to his car. The boys backed up and wondered what the scuffle was about. Junior stood by the

163

passenger side of Bo's car while he went back inside the store. While he waited the rage he felt for his first cousin was eating at him. He wanted to put a hurting on him for his betrayal, he treated him good when he got down there, he let him become the "man" down there although everyone knew Junior was the one who bought the weight in town. One thing he did know, if Bo was the culprit, karma would settle his fate. Junior was in the game long enough to understand how fickle it could be; he experienced it first hand in Baptiste so he felt fucked up for slipping even though he thought he could trust family. He could understand Muffin flipping because their relationship was more dick to pussy than sincere love since them being down south. He came down there so he wouldn't get caught up for that body in Brooklyn and Muffin was with whatever he was doing. As soon as he blew up she started showing her colors but Junior ignored it and brushed if off as her wanting to be a 'boss bitch' always asking him questions about how much he sold his O's (oz.) for, how quick was the workers moving the weight and how much he was spending when he copped.

"*Shit!*" Junior yelled out unconsciously. "*Fucking bitch was probably plotting from the gate!*" He shook his head.

There was no excuse for him, he was supposed to peep what she was doing but she was so smooth; she fucked him then had pillow talk and he gave it up without even thinking.

"*Slick bitch!*" He thought to himself.

Muffin was taking him out of the game and he sat by and let her, never paying attention to her movements; until now when it might be too late. The shoot out in the barbershop worked out in her favor because it gave her time to move around without him being none the wiser. His slow ass cousin was just happy to get work so her shit couldn't have been any sweeter.

Bo walked to the driver side and got inside then looked at Junior. "KB shot Lizard earlier today."

Junior turned his head to the side and looked at Bo. "What you just said?"

"Your boy KB shot Lizard early this morning." He repeated.

Junior turned his head in the direction of the barbershop and reached his hand over to Bo. "Give me your gun and go drive by there before you take me home." Junior grabbed the ratchet and slid the slide back inserting a live round in the chamber as Bo made a U-turn and headed to the barbershop.

FOUR SHADOUGH PUBLISHING

Chapter 17

Muffin heard a commotion while she sat at the table bagging up the slabs of cooked up cocaine in front of her; it was coming from outside. She slid the automatic off the table and checked the clip, it was full. She cocked the hammer and stepped slowly to the window and pulled the corner of the curtain discreetly and peeked out. She could barely see but she could hear voices; she couldn't make out what they were saying. She began to panic as she looked behind her at the drugs on the table then her eyes scanned the small room; there was no escape. She looked back out the window and walked to the door slowly to look out the peephole and confirm whoever was out there was plotting to break into her room. She tiptoed to the door, the cheap burgundy commercial carpet silencing any noise. She closed her left eye then slowly put her right eye to the peep hole; she gasped under her breath. The peephole gave her a panoramic view of what was going on outside her hotel door. There were half a dozen men with windbreaker jackets standing in front of the door. One was carrying a battering ram and was running full speed at the door. She saw him swing it backwards and she backed away from the door just as it came crashing open.

"Freeze! Get down on the ground!" An officer screamed entering the room waving an assault rifle.

"Fuck that!" Muffin screamed backing up pass the drug filled table towards the bathroom. She raised her hammer and squeezed the trigger but nothing happened. She kept mashing the trigger repeatedly as more police rushed into the room with guns.

"Drop the weapon!" They screamed with their guns trained on her. She saw infrared dots dancing all around the walls; she checked the gun again and the clip was full. She pulled on the trigger again but no bullets flew out the barrel. The police kept screaming for her to drop her gun but she kept backing away pulling the trigger.

"Shoot her!" She heard them scream then she heard gunfire and saw bright flashes of light as her heart beat like drums in her chest.

Muffin sat straight up in the chair she was sitting in a cold sweat. The television was on and cast a hazy light in the room; Ziploc bags, razor blades and drug residue littered the table. The automatic was sitting on the edge right next to the pie sized crack cocaine. The dream she had spooked the shit out of her and she felt all over her body to make sure she was awake and not still dreaming. She pushed herself away from the table and stumbled into the bathroom and turned the faucet on. She looked in the mirror and the reflection was a red eyed girl who looked fatigued and worn out. She hadn't rested properly since coming to New York and it was catching up with her. She splashed cold water on her face with both hands trying to shock herself awake. Her face dripping with water, she grabbed one of the white towels that was folded up on the side of the tub and wiped her face; the texture was abrasive.

She checked herself in the mirror; the dream had felt so real and her heart was just getting back to its normal beating. She went back to the table and looked at the digital clock on the night stand; she had been there four hours already. She needed to hurry up and bag up the rest of the work for Chico then jump on the highway to North Carolina so she could hit Bo and Patricia off with the rest of the work. She sat down at the table and was about to start bagging up again then she jumped when she heard loud banging on the door.

"*Fuck!*" She thought out in a loud whisper. Was her dream a prelude to what was really going to happen? Her mind

was spinning as she grabbed her weapon off the table and pointed it at the door with shaking hands. Time slowed down to a crawl and she wondered if it was all worth dying or going to jail, her heart tried to burst through her chest as all the moisture left her mouth and dried it out. She swallowed hard as beads of sweat appeared on her forehead.

"Checkout time!" The voice behind the door screamed out as the door knocking continued.

Muffin breathed out; her nerves were rattled but she was relieved. "I'll be out in a minute!" She screamed as she jumped out the seat she was in. She took all the drugs that wasn't bagged up and put it inside the Ziploc freezer bag then put all the paraphernalia inside her oversized Louis Vutton bag. She ran into the bathroom, grabbed a washcloth, wet it under the faucet then went back and wiped down the table. She was about to put the hammer in her pocketbook too but fear made her decide to keep it in her waist; she tucked it securely and pulled her shirt over her pants. She threw her pocketbook on her shoulder and grabbed the room key and looked around the room to make sure she wasn't leaving anything. She peeked out the peephole before grabbing the door knob on door. Satisfied, she got the fuck out of the room; she was glad this part was over.

**

Patricia was by her old station looking through drawers for items she had left behind when she quit. She was sucking her teeth as she bent down unplugging hair dryers, curling irons and clippers that were laying on the panel of her old station.

"You letting other bitches use the shit I left here like my hair products and dryers?" She asked with an attitude when she stood up, staring daggers at KB.

"I ain't been in here Pat, this my first time back since..." He paused. "...since you left." He stared at her with a faraway look in his eyes.

Pat broke his stare. "Well your bitch should know better. She probably told whoever working in here now they could keep my mess but she sho' was mistaken 'cause all this shit leaving with me to...day." She snapped while the girls that came in with her cosigned by nodding their heads in agreement.

KB was thrown off by how she was talking even if she was still mad at him, her vernacular was never so abrasive and riddled with curse words. Patricia had changed and it was evident in how she was acting.

"Well if anything is broke or missing I'll pay to replace it." KB offered while Jerome kept his mouth shut but his eyes glued to her round ass.

"I don't need your fucking help nor do I need your fucking money!" She challenged then pulled out a large stack of money that was rubber banded.

KB's head went back slowly and wondered what the fuck she was doing with all that money. From where he was standing it looked like it was at least five gees easily.

"Wow! Where you get money like that from girl? Let me hold somethin'." Jerome said playfully but was serious.

The girls standing by the door pulled out some money too but their stacks weren't as big as Patricia's. There was no doubt that they were into something illegal but it wasn't really any of KB's concern although he was still feeling something romantically for Patricia. He had to let her know how he felt, he just needed her to give him a chance.

"Ay Pat. I just wanna say sorry for what happened." He started.

"Boy please! I don't hardly wanna hear your sorry. I just came here to get my mess. I'm 'bout to open my own shop." She rolled her eyes and looked over at the station she cleaned out. "Whoever working that station might come where I'm at 'cause I can promise you she ain't gon' have not one client once my shop open." Her smile had wicked intentions.

KB didn't care about nothing she was saying because he just wanted her to accept his apology. He knew he fucked up and just wanted to be sincere and have her accept his apology.

"Congratulations Pat. That's a good look 'cause you definitely was an asset here at New York Kutz." KB replied using professional business etiquette to break down her defenses. "That's why it was hard to see you leave us."

"Fuck you KB!" She screamed, her emotions were still bruised from him lying to her. She was more upset with herself because she almost broke her virginity under false pretenses. She hated that he lied to her then called her out of her name, there was no need for him to do that because she didn't carry herself like a bitch nor did she conduct herself like that. She honestly liked him and it was because he was so nice to her in the beginning but she realized he was no different than any other guy.

Now that she had money to open up her own shop and getting introduced to the drug trade, her attitude changed along with her financial situation. She was taking charge because Muffin told her men exploited weakness so to always stay in control and money was control. It seemed to be working with KB.

"I was being serious Pat. I know I fucked up and I'm trying to make it right by apologizing. I'm sorry." KB said sincerely.

Jerome tilted his head at KB and then looked at Patricia and wondered if they fucked the way they both were carrying on.

Patricia grabbed all her belongings and gave it to the girls and told them to take it in the car. They took it and left the shop, the bell dinging as they opened the door. Patricia went to embrace Jerome hoping her display of affection would fuck with KB's feelings. KB looked on wishing it was him her soft body pressed against. He watched as Jerome became animated and started moaning and making sex noises as she pushed him

off her playfully. She turned to KB and stared at him momentarily but then he blinked three times quickly as Junior's face came into view.

"Get the fuck down!" He screamed to Pat and Jerome.

Jerome and Patricia ran over to the chairs and hit the deck, KB pulled out his hammer and got low as the gunfire erupted. "*Not again!*" He thought to himself as he poised himself for another gun battle.

***

"That muhfucka must think I'm pussy huh?" Junior was heated. "He backed out on you and he ain't let the hammer go? I'ma show him that I ain't playing no more fucking games!"

The car approached the barbershop slowly and Junior could see clearly through the plate glass window as Bo slowed down to a creep right in front. There was a girl, a guy and KB was standing in clear view.

"Let me out right here!" Junior waved his hand for Bo to stop the car.

"What you gon' do cuz?" Bo looked at him one eyebrow raised.

"I'm gon' make it rain and that bitch as nigga 'bout to get wet the fuck up!" He sneered as he pushed open the car door and jumped out the car. He looked back at Bo. "Leave that door open just like that 'cause I'ma be back in a short!"

Junior walked up on the porch slowly and pointed his gun at KB and fired off four shots shattering the glass door on impact. Everyone in the barbershop ducked and screamed; KB pulled out his iron and peeked over the chairs and raised the arm with the gun and squeezed off six shots at the door recklessly. The sound of dinging metal from the bullets hitting the door frame could be heard as Junior stood on the side and waited for the shooting to cease. He peeked his head around and heard four more gunshots and ducked back for cover. "*That was*

like ten shots he fired already." Junior thought to himself. *"I can body that faggot muhfucka if I get him to empty his clip."* He peeked around the corner again and shot inside the barbershop again, using only three shots. "I'm gon' body your bitch ass this time muhfucka!" Junior shouted through the door.

"Ay man! Me and Pat ain't got shit to do with y'alls beef! Please let us get out of here man!" Jerome shouted as he and Patricia cowered by the chairs used by customers who waited for a cut.

"Tell that muhfucka to stop hiding then! The only way he getting out of there is if they zipping his ass up in a body bag!" Junior shouted back.

"Fuck you Junior! You die!" KB stood up and pointed at the door and started firing off his automatic until the slide on it extended and the trigger stopped clicking. *"Oh shit!"* KB thought to himself and panicked as Junior slowly appeared in the doorway with a sick twisted smile on his face. Patricia's eyes immediately watered as she realized KB was out of bullets and watched with a horrified expression as Junior appeared in the doorway with his gun pointing directly at KB.

"You die muhfucka!" Junior screamed as he pulled the trigger.

"NO!" Gloria came running from the back of the shop with a large automatic and started squeezing in the direction of Junior.

He backed away, caught off guard and ran to the car because he wasn't sure how many shots he had left. "Fuck!" He screamed as he made his way back to the car. "Let's get the fuck outta here!" He said to Bo and slid down low in the seat in case Gloria came out the front busting.

***

Chico was standing in the front of the building waiting on Muffin to come through. She called him and said she was

five minutes away and needed him to be waiting outside for him. Since she gave him that package things in Baptiste started to look up for him and it was his first real feeling of power. All the guys were respecting him because he was able to help them keep a fair amount of money in their pockets. He didn't have to do anything but count money and distribute work; the life of a young boss.

Muffin pulled up on the side of the building and exited the truck then opened the back door and grabbed the bag that was filled with drugs. She was still feeling a little edgy after having that fucked up dream but she couldn't focus on it because she had unfinished business to handle with Chico.

She walked around the side of the building and saw him standing in the front of his building. He started walking towards her and held his hand out for the bag and she gave it to him; if the noccos were around he would be the one to get caught with everything. Guess her nerves were still a little rattled.

"What's up Muffin?" He greeted her with a smile and she noticed his newly acquired gold teeth. He looked like a bumbling idiot to her but she kept her comments to herself. Guys that hustled and wasn't used to money always became slaves to money, buying the biggest and most shiniest thing trying to stand out when they should be trying to do the opposite and stay low key so they wouldn't be seen; it's called longevity. She shook her head as they rode the elevator up to his floor. She followed him into his crib and she immediately smelled food coming from the kitchen. He greeted an old gray haired woman he called 'abuelita' and kissed her on her wrinkled cheek. He introduced her to Muffin and she nodded her head and greeted her politely then kept it moving to his room.

"Give me the bag." She directed as soon as she closed his room door.

He handed it to her and she sat down on a chair by his bed and dug her hand inside the bag. She pulled out all the

173

bombs she bagged up minus the couple of ounces she was unable to finish. Chico readily counted out his package then looked up at her.

"This it?" He had a puzzled look on his face.

"Yea Ron Rico, that's it. I'm in a rush so I didn't have time to finish bagging the rest up so I'll probably double up next trip." Muffin explained.

Chico bit his bottom lip. "Why I gotta get short? I wasn't short or late when I hit you with the bread. What's really good?" He questioned.

"Look here Roberto." She turned to him. "Don't question shit 'cause if there's a problem we can just cancel all this shit and let you find somebody else. Don't let that li'l bit of money go to your fucking head, you not the real boss out here...ok?" She skinned up her nose. "This can all end with one phone call, understand? Stop worrying 'bout how much shit you got and make sure your count right. You'll get hit with more before you're done." She turned and left not wanting to hear his reply. Chico followed behind her as she said good bye to his grandmother and walked to the front door. The smell had Muffin's stomach grumbling, she was famished. Chico grabbed the doorknob and pulled the door open.

"Could you call me by my name, I mean you bein' mad disrespectful calling me out my name..." Chico was interrupted as Muffin's head jerked around as she pushed the button for the elevator.

"Them gold fronts got you feeling like you really a boss huh?" Muffin smiled. "Ok, what's your name?"

"It's Chico." He replied seriously.

The elevator came and she grabbed the handle and pulled it open but before getting on she turned and said, "I don't like Chico."

As the elevator descended to the lobby Muffin thought of how cocky Chico was getting. "Money really do change a muhfucka." She thought out loud. She walked out the building

174

and headed to the truck around the corner. She checked the time and she was a little off schedule but would try to make up the time on the highway but first she needed to stash the work. Junior would go to one his homeboys that owned a 24-hour used tire shop and have them put the drugs in the spare tire. She walked to the truck and opened the back door and placed the bag onto the backseat. She slammed the door then went to the back to check the tire then turned her head, she felt like she was being watched.

FOUR  SHADOUGH
PUBLISHING

Chapter 18

"I can't believe that bitch was bustin' back at me!" Junior remarked heatedly as he washed the dirt off his hand.

After the second botched hit on KB, Bo dropped him home and he helped him dig a hole in his backyard to bury Drama then left. While he was there they talked in length about what was going on in the streets and with Muffin those months he was laid up in the hospital. Bo apologized profusely about his betrayal but stood fast that he believed what he did was because it was still with the family. Junior showed him the empty safe - and with the death of Drama that was proof he wasn't lying about being robbed. As much as he didn't want to believe Muffin was behind it he couldn't shake the thought. Bo tried his best to make it seem like he was still on Junior's team but Junior's radar knew the switch had already been made. The only thing he could do to change the way the pendulum was swinging was to offer him a better deal and doing that would hurt the game.

Junior was aware of how Muffin got Bo onboard so easily, she used old fashioned greed as her catalyst. Where she was going to fail was not understanding that greed did not breed loyalty. Her tactic was to move in hard and fast and give the illusion that things were moving the way she wanted but from experience Junior knew she would bottom out because of the amount of pressure she would inevitably face; he knew it all too well. It seems good in the beginning until the shit storm hits you where you live and you're forced to eat it, accept it or flush it out. She was thorough but he was sure she wasn't prepared or

aware of what was getting ready to happen because he was going to be the one bringing it.

"Snake ass bitch!" He screamed into the mirror then walked into his room. He couldn't wait for Muffin to come because once she arrived he had a strong feeling he wouldn't be able to compose himself if she lied to him; he would hurt or possibly kill her on the spot. He grabbed the phone.

"Yo. Let me speak to Bo." He barked into the phone.

"Ay Bo! Telephone man!" The guy who picked up yelled out as he let the payphone receiver drop and dangle, banging against the wall. Bo snatched it up when he got to it.

"Yea." He answered.

"Be here in 15 minutes to take me to the bus station." Junior commanded then disconnected the call, not waiting for a response.

He started gathering some things he needed for his long ass bus ride to Brooklyn then dialed another number when he was done packing.

"Hello?"

"Yea, it's Junior." He replied pulling a long sleeve shirt out from his closet. "How the weather up there?"

"It's cool out, you just need like a jean jacket or something. Snorkel weather is over." Shondra replied. Inside she was excited to know he was coming home; not to her house but back to Brooklyn. "When you leaving?"

"Tonight." He stopped what he was doing as the thought of seeing her wafted through his mind. "I can't wait to see you." He replied thinking out loud absentmindedly.

Shondra's heart fluttered because she missed him terribly and was still very much in love. "I can't either. How long you think you staying?"

He scratched his head. "That, I don't know. It all depends on what kinda deal I can make with my cousin. I gotta see how all this shit plays out."

"I know it's going to work out for you because you always come back out on top." She bigged him up.

"Yea, but that's not really good. My stay on top always seems short, I need some longevity. You know what I'm saying?"

"Yea, I understand." She knew he was referring to his drug business but she was thinking about Muffin's role in his life, she wanted that to be short; over.

"We been through a lot when we were together right?" Junior was reminiscing about the love they both shared once upon a time, hoping it could be rekindled once he and her had a chance to talk things out. "I don't want to bring up old shit over the phone but it's been real different without you in my life. I know you might think everything down here with me was gravy and that's why you hadn't heard from me but that ain't the gospel 'cause there's not one day that passed that you weren't on my mind. I did try to forget you because of all the shit that happened that caused me to leave in a hurry but I couldn't get you outta my mind. I just need you to know that I never stopped loving you Mooka." Sincerity could be heard in his voice.

"I never forgot about you either Junior, I swear to God I thought of you every day. I missed what we had and I'm hoping that when you come here that you give us a fair shot. A lot of things have changed, it's been over a year since we've seen each other." She desperately wanted to tell him about her baby boy but she couldn't do it over the phone, she was afraid that would kill her chances of them even talking. She dropped her head wondering how in the world she was going to be able to tell him that she had Chico's baby, a man that he still had beef with and wanted to kill. She shook her head slowly. "Junior, I always loved you and will always love you...no matter what happens when you get here." Her emotions were leaking out haphazardly implicating a warning and Junior picked up on it from the previous conversation they had earlier.

"Why you keep saying that? Things are different, did something happen? Something you need to tell me?" Junior pushed.

"*Fuck! Fuck! Fuck!*" She thought in her mind as she hit her palm upside her head for getting too emotional and tipping him off that there was indeed something she needed to discuss with him. "I'm just saying that it's been a while since we've seen each other and not everything will be the same. I've been through so much since you left me and I can tell you have been too; you was shot." She expertly shifted suspicion.

"Yea." Junior rubbed his groin self consciously. "Crazy shit is how me and that muhfucka wind up in the same fucking town, almost like it was meant for us to bump heads again for some reason." He looked up at the ceiling. "Twisted fate or karma, either one, it's still crazy."

"I'm just glad you're ok Junior." Shondra squeezed out. There was knocking on her front door and her brother pulled it open and Chico was standing on the other side. Her jaw dropped when she saw him standing there with a box of Similac and pack of Pampers.

"Mooka, you heard me?" Junior asked.

"Huh? Um what you said?" She mumbled holding her hand up telling her brother to tell him to wait in the hallway. "I'm sorry, I didn't hear what you said." She tried to recover.

"I said I'm getting ready to get outta here, it's time for me to catch my bus."

"Oh ok. Be careful and I hope I can see you when you get here." She said eyeing the door.

"Aiight, I'm out." Junior said. He hung up the phone and grabbed his bag and walked out the door to Bo's car. He walked down the steps and held his hands up blocking his face from the headlights shining brightly. He opened the passenger side door and got in, throwing his bag in the back seat. He peered over at Bo who just threw his arm over Junior's seat, turned his head to

the back and reversed out of the driveway then pulled off just as a pickup truck pulled up and parked across the street.

"K." Shondra put the phone back on the wall and walked to the door and opened it.

"What's up Shondra?" Chico said with a half smile.

"Nothing." She replied dryly as he handed her the bag of diapers.

"Can I see my son?" Chico asked picking up the box of formula and holding it in both hands waiting for her response.

"He's sleeping Chico, why don't you come back another time?" Shondra replied reaching out to grab the box but he pulled back.

"So what he's sleeping, I'm his father. That's what all babies do anyways, eat, shit, sleep and cry." Chico said frustrated.

"That's right but he on a schedule and I don't want to be up all night with him 'cause you wanna see him." Shondra sucked her teeth.

"If you stopped your shit I'd be able to come and see him when he is up but you still on your bullshit. When you gonna get pass all that shit huh? I take care of him, bring him all the shit you ask for and need plus I hit you with bread and you still act like you can't forget that shit that happened." He sighed. "You the one that was so worried when he was born that I was gonna be a dead beat and not wanting to be around to spend time with him and you the one trying to keep me away from my fucking son!"

"Oh please!" Shondra waved her hand but was still focused on trying to take the box out of his hand but he refused.

"What is it? That muhfucka you was on the phone with, that's the reason why I can't come in to see my fucking son?" He accused. "I saw how you was all nervous and shit when you saw me standing at the door. What? You fucking with another muhfucka now?"

Shondra squinted her eyes and them humphed. "Yea muhfucka that's exactly what it is!" She snatched the box out of his hand then tried to slam the door but he stopped it from closing, outstretching his arm.

"Can't no nigga come 'round here and be up in your crib if I can't see my son!" He threatened pulling out his automatic from his waist. "I'll kill him first! Remember that!"

"Whatever Chico!" She hissed.

"Try me if you think I'm bluffing!" He sneered and pulled the door closed so hard it rattled the door frame.

"Fucking asshole!" Shondra screamed under her breath as screaming erupted from the back, the slamming door had woken her sleeping boy.

Chapter 19

Muffin pulled up in the driveway and hopped out of the jeep and walked to the door sluggishly, she was tired from the eight hour drive. She stuck her key in the lock and pushed the door open and sought the couch for comfort as she flopped down and let her pocketbook drop to the floor next to her.

"Wooo! That was some fucking trip!" She said out loud to herself.

Before she left New York she took the truck to Junior's man and had him place the drugs in the spare tire then she hopped on the road. She only stopped two times to fill up and kept trucking until she made it back this morning. She knew she should have called to check on Junior but she would do that as soon as she spoke with Bo and hit him with his package.

On the ride to North Carolina she had a lot of time to think and came up with a good solution to what she was going to do. She knew once Junior was well enough he was going to reclaim his spot but the taste of money and power had her desiring it more and more; she was obsessed. She wasn't about to give it up after all she been through with him especially since he was going behind her back calling that bitch Shondra then calling her name out like he miss her. He couldn't fault her, shit, his loyalty was in question just as much as hers. She was banking on her arrangement with Patricia to continue without interruption and suspected Bo would defect back to Junior once he was back home and at the helm; he was his family and she expected nothing less. She still felt she had at least a couple more trips in her with Bo until Junior fully recovered but she

was going to pull back on how much work she was giving him and make Patricia her concentration.

She stretched and yawned from fatigue but knew her day needed to start because both Patricia and Bo would be ready for her. She picked up the phone and dialed some numbers and waited for someone to pick up.

"Hey girl, what's up, you back?" Patricia asked readily recognizing the distinctive high pitched squeaky voice on the other line.

"Yea, you ready for me?" She was all about business.

"Umm, you need to come 'round here. I know how you said don't talk on the phone so you need to come here so I can tell you what happened." There was urgency in her voice.

Muffin's mind was processing all the possible things that could have gone bad in the last 48 hours that she was gone - someone got busted and was locked up, she fucked up some money, someone got killed or someone was snitching. None of it was good for her business and was definitely happening at the wrong time.

"I'm coming now." Muffin said quickly. "You home right?"

"Yes."

Muffin placed the cordless phone on the base and decided to get her bags out the truck, freshen up, then go meet up with Patricia. She got up and went to the door and when she opened it there was a red and white pickup truck sitting across the street idling. She didn't pay it any mind as she walked to the back of the truck. Her hand was on handle as she pulled the door open towards her and she looked to her right again and the window of the F150 rolled down slowly and a hand came into view holding a black automatic handgun. Fire erupted from the barrel as hot bullets were released with a thunderous sound. Muffin instinctively ran for the front door and could hear the dinging from the bullets hitting the truck. She fell before she reached the door and screamed out in sheer terror as the booms

from the gun seemed to never stop; then instant quiet fell upon her ears until she heard squalling tires. Her whole body was shaking and she was crying hysterically. She managed to get to her feet and when she looked at the front door it looked like Connect The Dots and she wailed as she rushed inside and locked it then fell to the floor wondering who wanted to kill her.

***

KB was tired of the bullshit beef he and Junior was going through. Because of it he had been shot twice, once by his crazy bitch Muffin and then by him in his own barbershop. He and Gloria moved down south to get away from all the madness in Brooklyn and to land in a stewing pot of ongoing beef was just ridiculous.

It had only been a couple of months since he and Junior had the shoot out; his tender shoulder was a daily reminder. When Junior walked into his shop again busting his gun like they were in the OK Corral his life flashed by his eyes again and he was getting tired of it happening again like a movie on repeat.

He always had a strong feeling Junior would come back to exact his revenge but for some reason he thought it would happen somewhere else, not in his barbershop where he had to make a living. The first time they bumped heads in the shop he said the town was not big enough for both of them to be there; his message was clear, he wanted him dead or out of that town.

If it hadn't been for Gloria coming in when she did, KB knew Junior would have gotten his wish because he had him pinned down but the shells she dumped from the gun she was carrying changed the tide and the outcome of the gun battle. After the smoke cleared she was still gripping the gun tightly but her eyes had shifted to Patricia who was cowering by the chairs. KB quickly disarmed her and held her close to him in a loving embrace out of gratitude for saving his life and to

prevent her from squeezing off additional shots in Patricia's direction, literally.

"Ahh man Glo, if you didn't come when you did..." KB had tears glistening in his eyes as he held her and she could feel his body trembling slightly.

"I heard about a shooting down here on the police scanner and after all the shit that happened I couldn't take the chance of it being you again. I was on my way to the mall so I grabbed my gun and came rushing down here instead. I pulled up and I saw that muhufucka Junior standing on the side of the door with a gun in his hand and I knew he was coming for you so I pulled into the back and prayed I could get to you first and warn you but when I heard the shots I panicked." She paused and took a deep breath. "When I heard a lull in the shooting I figured that was the best time to come in to try to help you but when I saw him shooting at you all I could think about was him hurting you again and I just saw red baby and tried my best to end his worthless life!"

While she was telling him her story, Patricia and Jerome were just getting themselves together. The door dinged and everyone's heart skipped but calmed down when the girls who were with Patricia came rushing in.

"You awlright Pat?" One asked acting all concerned now that everything was over.

"I'm fine, I'm fine." She replied but her nerves were rattled.

"Oh good 'cause we was worried he was coming in here after you..." The other girl started saying before getting a stern look from Patricia.

"What the fuck she doing here?" Gloria asked KB pointing at Patricia, her focus no longer on what happened just minutes ago.

"She came to pick up some of her stuff she left..." KB tried to tell her but was cut off.

"She just now coming to pick up her shit? Why the fuck she didn't get it when her ass left?" Gloria was talking to KB but her eyes were locked on Patricia. "Did she get everything, 'cause if she didn't she still gots to get the fuck up outta this shop!" Gloria's tone was threatening.

"Who the fuck is that bitch talkin' to like that!" One of Patricia's friend belted out.

Gloria snatched the gun out of KB's hand and pointed it at the three girls. Jerome dived for the waiting chairs again while Patricia's friends beat it out of the barbershop leaving her looking at a deranged woman pointing a pistol at her.

In her mind, Gloria wanted to pull the trigger and watch her head explode for payback of the ass whipping she received from her months back and all the disrespect up until the time she resigned. KB grabbed the hand holding the gun and lowered it and when Patricia saw it was safe, she got the fuck out of the shop.

KB shook his head because all the shit that was happening was starting to affect Gloria in a bad way and he had to put a stop to it. He looked into her eyes and led her to the office and sat her down then told her he would be back then went out to Jerome who was once again just getting himself together.

"Now you see what I'm talking 'bout." KB had said to him.

His voice shaky, Jerome replied. "In living color."

"Look, I need you to do me a favor Rome."

"Shoot boss man." He replied.

"I'm gonna need you to handle the police report 'cause I know them muhfuckas on their way. I'm gonna take my girl home and go handle this clown ass nigga later. This shit right here gotta stop. When the heat come just lie and tell them you came after everything went down." He rubbed his chin. "This dude is reckless in how he doin' shit and he fuckin' with my

186

money with this bullshit! Customers gon' be scared to come get their hair cut."

"Don't worry bossman. I got you." Jerome assured him.

KB placed his hand on his shoulder and patted it gently. "Thanks Rome. I appreciate this."

KB went back to the office where Gloria was sitting with her head in her hands. He walked over to her then kneeled down and grabbed both her hands, they were moist from her tears, then kissed them both gently and pulled her to him. Her cries weren't audible but he could feel the heat from her breath on his shoulder as she wept silently.

"I made a promise to you when we left Brooklyn," he spoke in a low tone but loud enough for her to hear, "and told you I would move you away from the bullshit, give you a better life and keep you safe. I tried to keep my word Glo' but Junior trying to turn me into a liar!" He gritted his teeth. "I can't let this happen again, this is the last time and my last promise to you!" KB pulled her up and draped his arm around her shoulders like a shawl and walked her out the back door to her car. He opened the passenger side door and was about to seat her when she stopped and looked into eyes, hers were still watery.

"NO! I'll drive myself home, you go handle that shit! I'm tired of this shit too! Do what you have to do but make sure you come back to me...PROMISE ME!"

"I PROMISE!" His lips tightened.

He turned with renewed gusto and went back into the shop. "I'm gonna need two more favors from you Rome."

***

KB had fallen asleep but was awaken by the sound of a door closing. He sat upright in the seat and saw a woman walking up the stairs going into the house. He couldn't tell who she was because he was seeing her from the back; the tinted windows was also a factor in hindering identification. The sun

had come up and was shining brightly and he rubbed his eyes to adjust his vision. He shook his head and was now alert waiting for Junior to emerge from out of his house. Thanks to Rome he was able to find out where Junior stayed; Bo wasn't that smart in giving up his cousin's home address especially after what happened at the barbershop. It was all going to end today, Junior would no longer be a threat to him.

His patience paid off when the door opened and the same woman came out the house. She was heading to the jeep and KB squinted trying to see who she was because she looked familiar. She stopped momentarily and stared at the truck and that's when he recognized her, it was Junior's bitch, the one who shot him. Although he was there to kill Junior the bitch would be just as satisfying. He kept his eyes trained on her while he rolled the window down with his left hand and felt around on the passenger seat with his right until his fingers touched the handle of his gun. He grabbed it and cocked the hammer and when the window was down all the way he anchored his shoulder on the door and leaned out the window, arm outstretched. He steadied his aim as quickly as he could then he pulled the trigger repeatedly hoping his accuracy was on point; he wanted to cut her down. He heard screams over the explosion that came from the gun. She scurried out of the way like a scared mouse as he kept pulling the trigger. While pulling the trigger he saw her drop to the ground and he pointed the barrel down in hopes his slugs would tear into her. He didn't know how fast he was pulling the trigger and emptied his clip quickly. He pulled his arm back inside and rolled the window up quickly then stomped on the gas pedal and peeled out just as neighbors started peeking through their curtains while others decided to come out and see what happened for themselves. The only thing they saw was the smoke and dust left from the F150 KB borrowed from Jerome.

Chapter 20

Junior got off the elevator and put his key in the door then pushed it open. Midnite barked loudly as he closed the door quietly and hushed the dog. It had been so long since he saw Junior he was excited. He pat the huge pit bull on his head and sighed heavily, thinking about Drama then walked into the living room and put his bag down on the couch. He walked to the back of the apartment and knocked on Craig's bedroom door. A couple second later the door flew open with Craig standing in white ankle socks, Polo boxers, bare chested with a massive Desert Eagle pointed in Junior's face.

"Oh shit! What's up boy!" Craig hugged Junior around his neck, gun still in his hand.

"Hol' up cuz. Put that shit down before it goes off by mistake." Junior squeaked watching the gun that was dangerously close to his face.

"Oh my bad. I know your ass spooked being around these things since you been hit." Craig acknowledged as he removed his arm from around Junior's shoulder and held the gun down to his waist.

"Damn right!" Junior replied seriously then frowned his face with a perplexed look.

"So what's good? I didn't even know you was out the hospital and shit."

Junior's expression didn't change, he was wondering how Craig knew he had been shot...Muffin.

"Yo put something on so we can politic in the living room." Junior said abruptly turning and heading to the living room.

Craig looked at him for some seconds then went back into his room and grabbed his sweats and followed behind his young cousin.

"What's the deal?" Craig asked when he got to the living room.

Junior was staring out the project window down into the parking lot then turned around and rested his back against the window sill. "How you knew I was shot? Who told you?"

Craig's head turned sideways and looked at his cousin, he wasn't a slow leak and figured he found out that Muffin was going into business for herself. He was a guilty party but wasn't rooted in deep as her, he was just supplying her with the product and was reaping the rewards because if it wasn't him it would have been somebody else.

"Your girl told me, why?"

Junior stared square in his eyes and didn't say anything, he pouted his lips.

"You seen her when she came to Brooklyn?" There was no need to beat around the bush. He knew she was copping big weight but he didn't know from where and wanted to make sure Craig wasn't in on her deal.

Craig lowered his head and licked the front of his teeth with his tongue then folded his hands in front of him. "She came here wanting to cop some weight. She called me out of the blue one day telling me you got shot then said she had to keep your business going and needed some weight to make it happen." Craig admitted. "I wasn't going to fuck with her because I knew you was incapacitated but she promised me she would tell you once you was better." Craig nodded his head. "I guess she lied."

Junior balled his fist tightly. "Fucking bitch! I knew it!" His eyebrows lowered and he gritted his teeth. "She got to Bo too! Why would y'all..." Craig cut him off.

"Don't come at me with that why I fuck with her bullshit because money has no loyalty! I told that bitch as soon as you

190

get better this deal would be dead between us. This my business muhfucka and I always told you this game has no loyalty! Don't get in your feelings now because she wanna play the game." Craig smirked. "What you came here for cuz, to find out if she moving weight?"

"Bitch robbed me blind! Took all my fucking stash and killed my pit! I'ma body that bitch!" Hot beads of sweat littered Junior's forehead.

Craig's head jerked back. "She robbed you? Fuck would she do that for?"

"Take over everything. Leave me crippled. Turn the tables on me. I don't fucking know!" Junior was pulling at straws.

"That's a dirty bitch son. What the fuck you do to make her flip like that?" Craig asked.

"Shit was good 'til I got blasted. Something musta happened then, I don't know cuz but right now I don't give a fuck! I'ma hurt that greazy bitch when I catch her. When the last time she came here to cop."

"She just left last night." Craig told him.

"Fuck! She was here. Damn! How much she spend?"

"Five bricks, all cash." Craig revealed.

Junior shook his head slowly. "I gotta call down there to Bo stupid ass. I'm gonna need you to do me a solid Craig."

"I already know just make sure you thinking straight before you start making moves again. Being sloppy will get you knocked or murked."

"I know but this shit got me buggin'." Junior grabbed his head with his palms. "Can't figure out why the bitch would flip like this."

"No need to catch a headache over that shit. Get focused and get back to work. I got you, whatever you need." Craig assured him.

"Thanks cuz. I'm glad I can depend on you."

"How much bread she took you for?" Craig interrogated.

"Almost half a mil." Junior bit his bottom lip.

Craig let out a long whistle and scratched the top of his head. "That's a man loss cuz. You know that right?"

A man loss was a way of saying that the violation was to be met with death. Craig didn't mix words when it came to business and how to handle it accordingly. No one was off limits when it came down to it and he spared no sympathy because dealing with emotions caused hesitation and that lead to indecision. Craig didn't play when it came to his money and straightened anyone who tried to play or disrespect him so what Muffin did was inexcusable in his eyes and she would go missing if it were up to him.

"Yea, I know." Junior whispered. "Trust me, I'm gonna handle that."

Craig's head cocked to the side. "You better. You tell anybody else what she did?"

"Nobody but Bo." Junior informed him.

"Bo?" Craig gazed up at the ceiling in deep thought. "You said he changed sides on you for the bitch right?"

Junior harumphed. "You did too."

"The fuck I did! I sell weight muhfucka! Don't get this shit twisted li'l cuz. I don't work for that bitch, I supplied her with some weight. She came at me under false pretenses using your name and shit. You wasn't around to cosign it and she had the bread so I made the transaction. There's no disloyalty in that so stop your shit! Bo is a worker and knew the takeover was happening, she baited him with the work and I'm sure she paid him more to seal the deal." Junior nodded his head slowly in agreement. "Smart bitch! Gotta give her that."

"Before you get me right, I need to make a run over to Baptiste to holla at my old shorty." Junior proposed. "I need to borrow one of your whips and a hammer."

"So you running back to something familiar now, huh? I ain't mad atcha cuzzo. But you better be careful, you still got those homicide D's looking for you right?"

"Yea. I missed my court date so I'm sure I got a warrant. I don't think they still riding through there looking for me like that though. It's been a year already, my scent over there should be gone by now." Junior supposed.

"It should be but don't you still got beef with a young muhfucka over that way that owe you money or something? If he see you he definitely gonna put them bloodhounds on your trail and that scent gon' be strong again. Be careful." Craig warned.

Junior almost forgot about Chico. Craig mentioning his name brought back feelings he didn't want to think about before going to see Shondra. Chico did owe him money but he was also fucking her and for some reason it seemed to be bothering Junior more now than when he found out a year ago. Could it be because Muffin betrayed him? He tried to shake off the feeling but his anger was rising.

"I'ma be careful but if I see that muhfucka out there he gon' flatline!" Junior threatened.

A fine Puerto Rican girl sashayed into the kitchen with a petite white silk robe tied loosely about her body, the top of her breasts spilling out the top. She stopped abruptly seeing Junior and gathered the robe around her tighter.

"I sorry, I don't know you have company." She said in her fucked up English.

Craig turned and walked over to her putting his arms around her shoulder. "It's ok baby." He kissed her passionately on her lips as Junior's bottom jaw dropped because he never seen Craig kiss any of the hoe's he fucked. "This is my cousin Junior." He looked at Junior. "This is my fiancé, Scarlet."

Junior burst out laughing. "Fuck outta here! You almost got me muhfucka!"

Craig's look was unmistakable. "I'm not playing. Scarlet is my fiancé cuz." His eyes were fixed on Junior, steady and piercing.

"You serious?" Junior's voice lowered.

"As two slugs in the heart." An evil smile formed.

Junior walked over and shook her hand. "Nice to meet you Scarlet."

"Thank you. Nice to meeting you." She replied consistent with her fucked up English. "You want me to cooking you breakfast papito?"

"*Papito*?" Junior thought to himself. "*This nigga crazier than a muhfucka from the G Building. That bitch a hoe! She don' sucked the whole crew including me!*"

"Nah mamita. Me and my cousin talking before he go out and take care of some business. Me and you will go out and get something." Craig kissed her again and patted her on the ass gingerly. "Go 'head in the back, I'll be there in a li'l while."

When she disappeared in the back Junior's facial expression prompted Craig to explain Scarlet.

"She's the one. I been with a lot of broads in my life so I know what I'm feeling for her is real. I can look at you trying to figure out if I lost it or if I'm pussywhipped but that could never be because I never splashed," he paused and stared at Junior intently, "and nobody else has either. Everybody know she got fire head but that's all they know. I know her intimately."

"I hear all that shit but I'm not sure if I understand why you would wife her." Junior looked at Craig sideways. "I'm not judging her, I'm questioning your judgment. You always said you wouldn't fuck with a broad seriously because of your business but here you telling me you and Scarlet 'bout to get married. I don't understand that shit."

Craig placed his hand on Junior's shoulder. "I'm in love with her, that's all you need to understand. I can't fight this shit or figure it out, believe me I tried and it spooks me because for the first time in my life I'm dealing with something I don't know how to control." Craig stated honestly.

"Congratulations and welcome to my world." Junior replied shaking his head slowly and hugging his cousin.

***

The hot water beat down on her body and massaged her neck and back; she was tense and anxious. She was hoping Junior was going to stop by because she wanted to see him face to face so they could talk; they needed to talk. Too much time had passed. She lathered up then let the water rinse her clean as she bent over to turn off the faucets. She grabbed her beach towel off the top of the toilet and wrapped her body completely then stepped out the tub and stood in front of the mirror. It was fogged up from the steamy hot shower, she wiped it with her hand and looked at the image of a confused woman staring back at her. "*What!*" She screamed to herself in her mind. "*I know I need to tell him! I'm not stupid and I'm not expecting any miracles!*" She had a mental conversation with herself, battling with her wits. She sucked her teeth loudly then turned and grabbed the bathroom door handle and pulled it open walking to her room. She pushed her door open and gasped.

"What the fuck you doin' in my room Chico!" She screamed holding her towel up by her breasts.

"Your brother let me in. I came to see my son." He responded nonchalantly holding the baby in his arms not looking up at her.

"Well you gonna have to leave until I get dressed..." He cut her off.

"Hol' on, when I come by at night I can't see him, in the afternoon the same shit and now in the morning it's still a problem? What the fuck Shondra, you don't want me to see him?" Chico was ice grilling her.

She shook her head and walked out the room and banged on her brother's door then pushed it open. She was met with a thick, strong scent of marijuana and stinking pussy.

"Randy, why the fuck would you let that muhfucka in!" She screamed at him.

He sat up in the bed throwing the cover over his morning conquest. "He your baby father, he was coming to see his son. What's the problem with that!"

"I was in the fucking shower and I didn't know he was in my fucking room!" Shondra barked.

"What difference do it make, he your baby father, he already saw your ass naked!" Randy giggled.

"Get that bitch outta here too! This ain't no fucking hotel!"

Shondra slammed his door and headed back to her room. "Can you take the baby and go sit in the living room while I get dressed please?" She wasn't really asking Chico. She stood by the door waiting for him to get out before she went all the way in. He looked at her momentarily and lay the baby in the bassinet then wheeled it into the living room and Shondra closed the door behind her; her back resting on it as she breathed out. She locked it then grabbed the pink baby lotion and sat on the edge of her bed and unraveled the towel then squeezed some in the palm of her hand. She rubbed her hands together and smoothed her calf and foot as she thought of a way to get rid of Chico. She wasn't sure of the time Junior would make an appearance if he came at all but if he did she didn't want him to see the baby yet, she wanted a fair chance of telling him herself. She quickly finished putting lotion on her body then got up and went into her top drawer and pulled out her black lace panties and matching bra and slid both on comfortably. She looked at herself in the full length mirror that was tilted up against the wall and stood sideways, her profile showed the pouch in the front she didn't get rid of since the birth of her son. She frowned thinking she would look unattractive to Junior once he saw her. She went to her closet and pulled out a pair of Used Jeans with the rips in it and a matching shirt. She fought to button the too tight jeans and sucked her breath in as much as she could as she struggled to button it up before she passed out from asphyxiation. When she

breathed out she looked in the mirror and her stomach fat hung over her jeans; muffintop. She looked around her room then grabbed one of her Gucci signature scarves and wrapped it around her waist trying to conceal her stomach bulge, it didn't work and she sucked her teeth then flopped on the bed. The house phone rang and she reached for her cordless handset.

"Hello?"

"I'm here." Junior spoke without a greeting because he recognized her voice.

"W-where, outside?" Her stuttering was not only a result of her anxiousness in hearing his voice but of her fear of him being right outside and Chico being in the house.

"Nah, I'm at the phone booth down the block. I need you to just check outside real quick before I pull up over there, I don't want no surprises." He informed her.

Her heart thumped through her chest so hard her shirt moved up and down. "Ok. You gon' wait by the phone booth 'til I call you back or..."

He cut her off. "Nah, I'ma hold on. Just go check for me real quick."

"Um ok. Hold on." Her palms were sweaty as her mind raced trying to figure out how she was going to get Chico to leave. She placed the phone down on the bed and walked out the room and closed the door behind her.

"I gotta go meet my mother downtown at the check cashing place so you gonna have to leave now." Shondra told Chico as she reached for their son.

"I swear it's always something with you! I'm getting tired of this shit wit' you about my fucking son!" Chico stood up holding his son to his chest.

"I don't have time for this Chico! Give me him and leave!" Shondra barked with urgency.

"Fuck outta here! If you leaving I'll take him with me until you get back! Go get his baby bag, I got pampers and shit at the crib, all I need is formula." Chico ordered her.

"Ok, fuck it but you better bring him back as soon as I call your house." She threatened. She didn't have time to argue with Chico, Junior was on hold waiting for her to come back to the phone. She went in the kitchen and pulled open the refrigerator and grabbed three eight ounce bottles that were already made and rushed back to her room to make the baby bag and let Junior know it was ok to come over.

"I don't really know what I was supposed to be looking for but I didn't see nothing out of the ordinary like police or detective cars anywhere." She said catching her breath and putting the bottles inside the baby bag along with powdered formula and pampers.

"Ok kool. Sounds like you just ran around the whole building." Junior laughed. "I'll be there in five minutes."

"All right. I'll be waiting." She sang into the phone.

"Leave the front door open for me." Junior said quickly before disconnecting his call. "Don't do like you did last time." He stated seriously.

"I will, I promise." She answered.

"Good. I'll see you in a minute." He hung up the phone.

"*Shit!*" She thought to herself. "*I gotta get him outta here before Junior gets here, fuck!*" She slung the baby bag over her shoulder and hurried into the living room to where Chico was standing holding their son. "Here's his bag." She passed him the bag; he took it and flung it over his shoulder then looked at her.

"You not gon' give me his stroller?" Chico questioned.

She moved swiftly to the closet that housed the baby stroller and pulled it out and flipped a lever on the bottom that opened it up automatically. She pushed it over to him and he leaned into the bassinet and pulled out a powder blue baby blanket and laid it inside the stroller. He seemed to be having a hard time holding the baby and putting the blanket in properly so she assisted him then took the baby and strapped him into the

stroller. She bent down and kissed him gingerly on the lips as he cooed and smacked his lips.

She looked up at Chico. "When I call please bring him right back. If you give me any problems then you ain't never gotta worry 'bout seeing him again."

"Whatever!" Chico screamed grabbing the stroller and backing it up to the door. "I know you better get your fuckin' mind right when it comes to me seeing my son. I'm not gon' keep playin' these fucking games with you!" He pulled the front door open and wheeled the stroller out into the hallway as Shondra watched him disappear out of the building. She closed the door and rested her back against it breathing out and feeling a wave of guilt blanket her because she felt relief that her son wouldn't be there when Junior arrived. She just wanted to be able to tell him instead of it being dumped in his lap; she tried to make herself believe that but in her heart she knew the truth, she was putting a man before her child and she vowed never to do that. She looked down at the bassinet and pushed it back to her room, she couldn't risk Junior see it.

***

The grey Audi 5000 pulled up to the curb and parallel parked. Junior fixed the gun in his waistline then emerged from the driver's seat cautiously looking left to right and up on the roof of Shondra's building and the adjacent buildings. He strolled to the corner of the building and turned right and headed to the front. Paranoia took over as his steps quickened to the entrance. There were a few people outside, some staring while others gave a head nod in recognition to who he was. He lowered his head but walked with confidence and was near the building entrance when he heard, "Yo Chico." He stopped and immediately turned around and scanned the area quickly trying to see if he saw him. He zeroed in on Chico and his face balled up from anger. Chico was standing across the street standing in

front of a baby carriage and it looked like he was talking to a crackhead. Junior wondered what he was doing standing on the block with a baby until he observed Chico reaching into the stroller then placing something in the crackhead's grubby hands; undoubtedly drugs. *"That's what the stroller's for; smart."* Junior thought as he stood in front the building and watched the transaction. His eyes kept darting back and forth looking at passing cars and some of the people walking by. *"That nigga still selling over here. I should go over there and body his faggot ass!"* Junior didn't forget he owed him money especially now that he was broke. He couldn't remember how much he owed him but now that he knew he was still hustling in Baptiste he was definitely going to make him pay him back.

He turned and walked into the building but seeing Chico upset him because his feelings wandered to him fucking Shondra and it made him want to hurt him just that much more. He grabbed the doorknob of Shondra's door, knocked lightly and turned it then pushed the door inward. He peeked his head in first before stepping into the apartment. The door closed softly behind him and he locked it and was about to call out Shondra's name but she was coming down the hallway. She stopped abruptly and grabbed her chest with both hands and it looked like she was taking a deep breath. Their eyes locked, Junior's heartbeat sped up in his chest and he began to feel nervous all of a sudden. Love. Their feelings were on full display, there was no hiding what was in the air, their love didn't end, it never did, it was too strong. Standing there for what seemed like hours, Shondra took off running and jumped into his arms. She squeezed him so tight around his neck, he could feel her body trembling and her hot breathing on his shoulder and neck. He squeezed her hard too, his embrace gentle but firm. The two lovers held onto one another, afraid to let go, afraid letting go would bring the reality of their situation back to the forefront. Junior let her down on her feet after the long embrace and stood back and looked at her.

FOUR SHADOUGH
PUBLISHING

"You're still beautiful to me Mooka." He half whispered.

"I miss you so much Junior." It sounded like she sang the words.

She walked up to him slowly, her eyes steady and when she was close enough she grabbed his hands in hers and closed her eyes then leaned up for a kiss. Junior's head automatically lowered and he met her lips and they both kissed passionately, the fire of their absence from one another evident in the sloppiness and erratic movement in how they kissed. Junior grabbed a handful of her soft derriere and she pressed against his rising hardness, periodically grinding her front while moaning each time he hit the bone atop her vaginal area. Nipples hardened and panties soaking from her juices, Shondra had to gasp for air.

"Oh my God!" She squealed. "I want you to fuck me! I want to feel you inside me, please!"

"Not here Mooka. Let's go to your room." Junior said between breaths as he fondled her tits in his palms.

"*Fuck am I thinking?*" She thought to herself. "*He'll see all my son stuff in there.*" She instinctively dropped to her knees and in one motion unzipped his pants, fished for his manhood in his Calvin Klein boxers, pulled the hardened tool out from the cotton fabric then stuffed it inside her mouth. She heard him whimper and she tried to swallow his entire mass.

Junior's head fell backwards immediately as his palms gripped the sides of Shondra's head and he pushed her off. It was the first time his dick was aroused since the shooting and he was feeling a little discomfort although her mouth felt so inviting.

"I'm still a li'l sore down there Mooka." He whispered. "That's where I got shot." He explained so she wouldn't think he didn't want her sexually.

"You can't have sex?" She asked standing up and wiping her mouth with the back of her hand.

Just as she stood up her brother Randy walked out the room with the smut he was sleeping with the night before.

"Oh, it's ok you giving a muhfucka head in the fucking living room but it's a problem if I fuck in my bedroom." He cackled to his sister holding the waist of the young girl who looked like she was high on something other than weed. "What's up Junior?" He reached his hand out to give him five.

"What's good Ran?" Junior used his right hand to slap him five while the other was used to pull up his pants awkwardly.

"Fuck you Randy!" Shondra screamed out. She looked at the zombie faced girl and sucked her teeth. "Get that crack smoking bitch outta here!"

Randy grabbed the girl by her hand and led her to the front door, opened it then looked at Junior. "She still the same ole' Shondra kid. You ain't miss shit!" He walked out the door, slamming it behind him.

"Fuck you!" She screamed as she twisted the locks to make sure he didn't double back. She slowly turned back to Junior and shook her head slowly. "I think he smoking woolas."

"Word?" Junior exclaimed as he zipped his pants up. "That's fucked up."

"Yea I know. He be coming in late nights with all different kind of dirty bitches and they all be looking like they zonked out. That shit fucking up my family, first my oldest sister now this young dumb ass." She sucked her teeth loudly.

Junior remembered it was her sister being strung out on crack that made him start selling in Baptiste. She would run all night to get drugs and he figured if he could get her to cop from him as many times as she went he would make good money. Now the very thing he started selling was destroying her family.

"You sure he smoking woos? Maybe he like fucking with them heads because they don't require much persuasion to get the pussy. A promise of a hit or two usually does the trick."

"Nah, he smoking them woos or he hitting that pipe. I'm just waiting 'til something of mine get missing in this bitch and then his ass is out, fuck that!" Shondra took a seat on the red velvet couch.

Junior walked over to where she was sitting and stood in front of her. "I'm sorry you going through this." He took a seat next to her and put his arm around her and she welcomed it by leaning her head near his shoulder and chest.

"I love you so much Junior and I hope we work this out." She spoke sincerely.

He breathed out and slightly leaned his head forward so he could look into her eyes. "I love you too Mooka, never stopped. I'm not sure if we can pick up from where we left off but we can try and start over. I know I made mad mistakes with your heart but this time it's gonna be different, I'm gonna be different and I'm gonna treat you better. I won't put nobody before you, I won't lie about shit I'm doing and I won't step out on you again." He grabbed her hand. "I promise baby. I know what real love is and I want it with you."

Shondra sucked her bottom lip inside her mouth and began tearing up. Her emotions were so high strung that she was unable to control the tears that flowed freely like a waterfall. She sniffled as Junior draped his other arm around her; this was all she wanted but now feared it would all be over once she told him she had a baby...by Chico. Shondra loved her son more than breathing but she also loved Junior and didn't want that to be the deal breaker for them.

"What about your money?" She asked. "Are you going to be going back down south once you take care of what you need to up here?"

"Yea. I'm going to bounce soon as I get me some work but I needed to talk to you first so we can figure out what this is going to be." He pointed back and forth between them. "I want you to trust me and know that I'm going to do the right thing from now on."

FOUR  SHADOUGH
PUBLISHING

"I..." She paused and closed her eyes then opened them slowly. "I'm scared Junior. I don't want to lose you again now that I have you in my life." She squeezed his hand tightly.

"You not Mooka. I'm here to stay this time...for good." He assured her.

"No matter what?" She asked in a lowered voice.

Junior sat up then grabbed her by both shoulders and turned her around facing him. "What you gotta tell me Shondra?" His eyes were steady but they looked fearful. "What is it?"

She lowered her head and closed her eyes again slowly. She couldn't lie to him, she couldn't keep something like that a secret from him. She didn't have an explanation, she lied and denied she was fucking Chico. She was going to have to tell him the truth and pray he would stay with her. She lifted her head up and opened her eyes slowly and her lips trembled but as she was about to tell him his beeper went off.

"Hold on let me see who the fuck this is." Junior said pulling the device from his belt and looking at the numbers. It was Muffin calling from his crib in North Carolina. "I need to call this number back but go 'head and tell me what you gotta tell me first." He said clipping the pager back on his belt.

"If it's important you can use the phone in the hallway." She suggested hoping to buy her some time.

"Nah, it can wait. Just go 'head and tell me." Junior urged.

Chapter 21

After the initial shock of what happened wore off, Muffin walked into the bedroom and stopped at the door. Her heart started to beat feverishly in her chest again as she eased into the room slowly. It looked like someone had broken into the house and ransacked the room, the closet door was wide open, clothes were everywhere and when she peeked inside the closet the safe was wide open and empty. She instantly thought whoever was just trying to kill her had most likely broken in hoping she was there. Terror consumed her as she looked under the mattress for the gun she hid there once Junior got shot. She fished it out from its hiding spot then slammed a live round into the chamber by pulling the slide back. She walked out the room and slowly walked to the front window and pulled the curtain back slightly and peeked outside. There were a few neighbors outside standing around talking and pointing at the truck and the house. She picked up the cordless phone and quickly dialed some numbers as she made her way to the kitchen cautiously hoping there were no surprises lurking there. She looked around nervously as the phone rang in her ear.

"Hello?" Someone answered.

"Yea, let me speak to Bo." She responded making her way to the back door.

"Hol' on." The voice said and she could hear them calling out to Bo.

She pulled the curtain back by the back door and gazed out the backyard. She scanned the area and noticed Drama wasn't out there. She looked up unconsciously wondering what the fuck was going on.

"Hello?" Bo answered.

"Hey what's up?" Muffin answered not sure if she wanted to tell him what was going on.

"What's up witcha? You back?" He asked.

"Yea but some crazy shit just happened."

"What's goin' on?" Bo asked.

Muffin opened the back door and walked into the back yard towards Drama's dog house.

"Drama's gone." She half whispered into the phone.

"Yea, I heard."

Muffin almost dropped the phone. "How you hear that?"

"Oh, you musta not spoke with Junior yet then."

"He's out the hospital?"

"Yea, he got out yesterday."

"*Shit!*" Muffin thought to herself. "Where the fuck is he? Oh my God!" She figured the bullets were really meant for Junior and whoever broke into the house was looking for him.

"Calm down Muffin. I took him to the bus station last night."

"Huh?" Muffin said confused. "Yo, what the fuck is going on Bo?"

"It's a lot goin' on but you know I can't really say over the phone."

"I know." Muffin lowered her head and walked back into the house and closed the back door. "I need to meet you somewhere so you can tell me all of what's been going on since I left two days ago."

"Meet me at the game room in the mall and bring that food with you if you got any." Bo told her.

"I'll be there in fifteen minutes."

"Awlright. I'll be there." He confirmed then hung up the phone.

"Fuck he going to New York for and he just got out the fucking hospital?" Muffin said out loud to herself. "I know he went to see that bitch with his stupid ass! He gon' get his heart

blasted the fuck open and that'll be good for his dirty ass. And to think I was keeping it real with him all this time and he was probably just waiting for the chance to leave me." She dialed his beeper number and put in her code then went to the front door. She pulled it open and saw a police cruiser parked on the street and the cop talking to one of the neighbors.

"*Oh fuck!*" She thought to herself as she dropped the firearm behind one of the pillows on the couch before stepping outside. She walked to the truck and pulled open the back door and grabbed her bag cutting her eye at the officer talking to a neighbor who was pointing in her direction. "Shit!" She mumbled under her breath as the police came towards her.

"'Scuse me ma'am. If you don't mind I'd like to ask you some questions about what happened out here." He said trotting up the driveway.

Muffin turned to face him and sucked her teeth. "I don't really don't know anything. All I know is that somebody was shooting, I don't know if they were shooting at me or not." She said quickly then turned around to go in the house.

"You didn't see the person that was firing the weapon at you?" He asked.

"I didn't see nobody and don't know if they was shooting at me. Please sir, I have a lot to do. I have to take my truck to the shop to be repaired. Thanks for your concern but that's all I know." Muffin said grabbing the door handle.

"Ok. If you happen to remember anything just give me a call." He said handing her his card with his number on it.

Muffin took the card from him and smiled weakly then walked into the house and closed the door behind her. She knew the cop didn't really give a fuck about what happened because it took him all of twenty minutes to respond. From what she knew from being in the town for a year, the police didn't really care about the blacks and any violence done to them or their property, they were only concerned with their own and she knew her brushing him off was exactly what he wanted because

he wasn't going to do any investigation even if she did tell him she knew something. She picked her gun back up and the cordless then dialed Junior's number again, put in her code and went into the bedroom to get the number of the guy Junior used to take the drugs out of the spare tire.

***

The game room was packed when Muffin entered, the sound of the Ms. Pacman song rang in her ears as she walked through looking for Bo. It was dark inside and packed with young kids. Muffin spotted Bo talking to someone and it looked like he was making a transaction. She stopped and watched for a second then realized the guy was hitting Bo with work. She backed away and walked over toward the entrance of the game room and stuffed her hand inside her pocket and pulled out a quarter and inserted it in the machine. She hit the one player button and grabbed the joystick and maneuvered Ms. Pacman around the maze. She cut her eye when she saw the guy Bo was talking to walk towards the entrance of the game room. When he walked pass she noticed he wasn't dressed like how most of the country folk dressed, he was dressed like he was from New York. He had on a Polo badge shirt and Guess jeans and was wearing suede Bally's. He was about to exit the game room but stopped short when someone asked him something.

"Nah kid," she heard him say, "I'ma get ghost in a minute."

His lingo confirmed he was not from North Carolina. The game alerted her that Ms. Pacman was eaten by a ghost and she tried to focus her attention back on the game. The guy from New York pushed open the door and left the game room and after playing the game for another minute or so she felt a hand resting on her shoulder.

"I didn't know you played video games." Bo said.

"I love Ms. Pacman. Soon as I saw it I had to play one game." She replied maneuvering the joy stick while she stuck her ass out. "This my last man, I'll be with you in a second."

"You ain't gon' take down that high score." He said watching her pattern to get away from the ghosts.

"Not today but if I had time I would." Muffin said turning to Bo and letting Ms. Pacman get eaten by the ghost Blinky. "Come on let's go outside to my truck."

When Muffin pushed the door open and walked towards the mall exit, which was a few feet away, she noticed the guy Bo was talking to standing next to a potted tree talking to one of the local country girls. He was a handsome specimen of a man and she noticed he had a fair complexion and smooth wavy hair; he was a NY dime. She made her way to the exit and he caught her looking but she didn't care as she pushed the second door with her eyes glued to him until Bo interrupted her thoughts.

"Did that happen when you was in New Yawk?" He asked pointing to the bullet holes in the door of the truck.

"No, that shit happened when I got back this morning. Why did Junior go to New York Bo?" Muffin questioned as she opened the driver's side door.

"What you mean that happened when you got back this morning? What happened?" He ignored her question for his own.

Too much had happened in a short period of time and things needed to get straightened out or Muffin was going to self destruct. She was beginning to feel overwhelmed, there was too much unknown shit happening to her and she needed to, at the very least, find out. She would have to answer Bo's question then hope he would give her information so she could piece the jigsaw together.

"When I pulled up to the house this morning I got out the truck and went in the house for like fifteen minutes to stretch and shit. Then I went back out to the truck to get my bags from the back. There was this pickup truck sitting across

the street from the house but I didn't pay it any mind and then the window rolled down and all I saw was a gun and heard shots. I tried to run to the house but I fell then the shooting stopped and the pickup broke the fuck out with no explanation." Muffin breathed out. "Your turn. What happened when Junior got out of the hospital."

"When he first got out he came on the block tripping. He thought I stole money out the safe and killed y'all dog." Bo's second sentence had Muffin's eyes wide as saucers. "He asked me to help him bury the dog, I said I would then I told him KB had shot one of the crack heads and came on the block like he wanted problems. Junior got mad at that and went to the barbershop and had another shoot out with KB."

"What!" Muffin couldn't believe what she heard. "He shot out with that muhfucka and he just came out the hospital? Did he hit him?"

"I don't think so 'cause he came back to the car mad saying his ole' lady started shooting too." Bo informed her.

Muffin nodded her head. "That's probably who was shooting at me at the house, it was KB! I wonder how that muhfucka know where we lived." She looked at Bo with accusing eyes then shifted them to the sky as she thought. "And you said somebody robbed the crib too? Took all the money out the safe, right?" Bo nodded his head and she showcased a half smile. "Who knew about the safe and that nobody would be home?"

Bo was beginning to see that everything was getting out of control. First he was being accused by Junior and now he was being accused again by Muffin for stealing money from out the safe. He was getting frustrated with all the accusations and finger pointing.

"You think just like he do. I ain't gon' steal from my kinfolk and he already know I didn't take his money." Bo had half a mind to tell her Junior suspected her of taking the money

but decided against it because he wanted it to come as a surprise to her.

"Well who stole his money?" Muffin breathed out and curled her lips up on the side then looked at Bo. She was about to say something then hesitated. She needed to focus on taking care of business. She still hadn't spoken to Junior and needed to find out what the status was between them. His trip to New York had Shondra written all over it so for her to guess that they were done was a logical thought. "You still gonna move this stuff for me?" She asked Bo.

"Yea. Where you put it this time?" He asked ready to go to the location and pick it up.

"I got it right here." She reached inside her bag and pulled out a plastic Belk's shopping bag then handed it to him.

"It's in here?" He asked grabbing the bag and looking at the contents inside. "Don't look like the same thing you been hitting me with. What's up?" Bo knew he was right in his thinking that things were changing, now she was willing to do hand to hand with him but she was shorting him on the work. He knew it would be just a matter of time before it all came to a crashing halt.

"It's not." She sucked her teeth showing aggravation. "I didn't have time to bag shit up with a muhfucka shooting slugs over my head, you selfish fuck!"

"Easy, I was just wondering why, that's all." Bo said in defense.

"Nothing to wonder about. When you done come see me and I'll hit you with the rest." She told him closing the passenger side door. She had no intentions on fucking with him again, she was going to put all her energy and time into building herself up with Patricia and her crew.

"No problem, I'll be done in a couple of days." Bo stated before walking off.

Muffin jumped into the front seat and stuck the key in the ignition but watched as he went inside the mall and started

FOUR  SHADOUGH
PUBLISHING

talking with the guy from New York again. She shook her head with a nervous sinking feeling overcoming her. She could almost see the change coming but she didn't have any other choice but to try to shift it back to her direction. All her focus had to be on Patricia, she didn't have any ties to Junior and no affiliation to Bo.

***

The truck pulled into a parking space of the Holiday Inn hotel. Muffin jumped out and grabbed her bag and the duffle bag filled with work. She walked up to Room 114 and rapped on the door three times quickly. She saw the curtain move to the side then the door swung open. She stepped inside then the door closed behind her; Patricia locked the door behind her and stared at Muffin strangely.

Muffin sat the duffle bag and pocketbook on top of the table then pulled the chair out and took a seat.

"So what happened?" She finally said to Patricia who had taken a seat by one of the twin beds in the room.

"Girl, what didn't happen?" Patricia sat up. "You know since we been doing all this dealing I been making some good money and I been saving all of it, not spending anything because my goal was to get my shop right?" She paused to catch her breath. "Well, me Dasia and Rose went to the barbershop to get the rest of my beauty products and stuff I left when I quit and while I was in there, Junior came in there and started shooting at KB again. He didn't care who was in there either!" Patricia was waving her arms as she spoke.

"I heard. That's what you had to tell me?" Muffin was waiting for something she didn't know.

Patricia had a puzzled look on her face. "Um yea. You actin' like what I just told you wasn't bad."

"No, no, no." Muffin held her palms and waved furiously. "Don't take it like that because some crazy shit

happened soon as I got back to town. Somebody was shooting at me when I pulled up to my house and after hearing what Junior did I can pretty much guess it was KB." Muffin said emphatically.

Patricia's jaw was stuck in the open position as she stared at Muffin with a blank expression. Muffin ignored her and went into the duffle bag and pulled out bagged up ounces of crack and laid it on the table. After she was done counting she turned to Patricia who was still staring at her with her jaw opened like it was locked in that position. Muffin waved her hand in front of her and snapped her fingers a couple times like she was bringing her out of a trance.

"You gonna have a little bit more than usual but that shouldn't be a problem since you ran out so fast last time." Muffin said nonchalantly then started putting the ounces back in the duffle bag. When she was finished she turned to Patricia whose head was shaking slowly left to right. "What's wrong Pat?" Muffin now had a puzzled expression.

"I don't wanna do this anymore, too much bad stuff happening. Your boyfriend shooting at KB in the barbershop and you getting shot at soon as you get home, all this mess ain't worth the money or my life. I just don't wanna do this no mo'." Patricia affirmed sincerely.

"Hmmph! That shit that happened is all part of the fucking game Pat but none of that shit you talking 'bout happened to you. KB and Junior the one that got beef, you ain't got no worries, you just happened to be at the wrong place at the wrong time, that's all. You act like Junior was shooting at you, he ain't got no beef with you!" Muffin tried to be convincing but the look on Patricia's face was telling her she wasn't buying what she was selling. "Look Pat you can't just stop doing this shit right now, I need you to help me move the rest of this shit."

"Uh uh. I don't wanna mess with that stuff no more. I really 'preciate you for letting make some money so I can open

my own shop but I just can't do this for you no more, I'm sorry Muffin." Patricia continued shaking her head slowly.

Muffin couldn't believe what she was hearing. This couldn't be happening, what was she going to do? She didn't have anyone else she half way trusted to move all those bricks for her. Her stomach felt like it was tying up in knots, fear was becoming her companion. She looked at Patricia and shook her head, the bitch used her to make a little bit of money and when shit started to get a little thick she was all too ready to bail out with the money she made. No, she couldn't make getting out that easy for her, she should have never got involved in the first place. She moved over to her pocketbook and pulled out her automatic and held it down by her waist.

"I ever tell you what I did to KB?" Muffin said gritting her teeth. Her demeanor had changed almost instantly. "I wish I could but if I did, I would have to kill you Pat and I really like you." She slowly rubbed the nose of the barrel up and down her thigh. "It's real fucked up you want to bail on me 'cause of some shit that don't have nothing to do with you or what we're doing. You can't anyway!" Muffin voiced raised scaring Patricia. "It don't work like that, you can't just say I quit like you was working in that fucking barbershop, this the streets! There's rules to this shit! This ain't a job, this is a fucking lifestyle and you can't just jump up and leave 'cause you scared or you feel like you made enough money; that's selfish! What about me? What about my money? Bottom line you can't quit 'cause this ain't no fucking job!" Muffin was staring at her with icy eyes.

"You didn't explain all these rules to me before I decided to do this. Why are you actin' like this now towards me? Why are you trying to force to me to do this when I told you I don't want to anymore?" Patricia was whispering and realized she was in over her head with Muffin.

"Boo hoo! You want out for real?" Muffin nodded her head slowly.

"Yes, please." Patricia pleaded.

"No problem. Give me three hun'ed cash right now and you can walk away and forget all this shit!" Muffin proposed.

"Three hundred dollars?" Patricia asked slowly with hope in her voice.

"No you stupid cunt! Thousand!" Muffin retorted.

"Three hundred thousand dollars?" Patricia murmured.

"Yea. Give me that and you out and you ain't never gotta worry 'bout somebody trying to kill you." Muffin threatened subliminally.

"How did you come up with that number?" Patricia questioned.

"Because that was my goal amount I wanted to make. Now since you trying to bail out on the deal after all that money I spent to make sure you could make some money you gonna pay me my shit back, period or there's gonna be a lot of slow singing while your feet are pointing up towards the church ceiling." Muffin threatened.

Patricia suddenly became terrified and wished she never fucked with the crazy Brooklyn girl standing in front of her with a gun forcing her to sell her drugs. She was afraid if she didn't Muffin would hurt her. She had plans to open her own beauty shop, she wasn't planning on selling drugs for the rest of her life. All she wanted was enough money to buy her own building and start her business. She shook her head slowly.

"Is that a no?" Muffin asked, her eyebrows raising along with the arm holding the gun.

"No, no. I just can't believe you're really doing this to me." Patricia breathed out. "I don't have a choice so I'll do it." Patricia relented.

"Good! Now let me explain something to you in case you think you slick. If you think about moving this shit slow then I'm gonna make your fat head explode like a pumpkin and I ain't bullshitting! I know how long it takes boo boo. If you tell anybody what's gonna on, instead of your grandma walking through the church doors, she gonna be carried by six niggas

215

wearing black suits! Don't fuck with me!" Muffin roared. She grabbed the duffle bag off the desk and dropped it on the floor next to Patricia's feet. "I want mine first so that means full payment by the end of the week! Now fuck around and don't have it for me." Muffin slid her pocketbook off the table and swung it across her shoulder and unlocked the door then grabbed the handle. She turned it and was about to pull open the door then stopped and looked at Patricia.

"Oh I forgot. If you even think about calling the police trying to get me locked up just remember that it's not just me. I have a team of shooters down here already waiting for shit like this to happen so you better think real carefully before you do any dumb shit. Ain't no police down here gon' be able to protect you from the gorillas I fuck with!" She pulled the door open then slammed it shut. She looked around then stuffed the gun in her pocketbook and hurried to the truck.

"Shit! Shit! Shit!" She mumbled to herself as she pulled off. She hoped Patricia bought her bluff game enough to finish off the package she gave her so she could get the fuck out of that town and go back home to Brooklyn with all the money she made. She loved Junior but there was no telling what the fuck he was doing in NY.

"Fuck that!" She thought out loud. "That muhfucka broke now anyways!" She pulled into traffic and was headed to the house to pack her clothes because in a week she was to be back home in Brooklyn and more than likely she was going to be without Junior.

Chapter 22

The door was pushed open and the living room was empty and quiet except for the low chatter coming from the television set. KB walked towards the bedroom and placed his palm flat against the bedroom door and pushed it open slowly. Gloria was bent over folding clothes, her ass shaking as she moved vigorously.

"What you doin' Glo'?" He asked.

His voice startled her and she dropped the shirt she was folding and grabbed the gun on the bed and pointed as she turned to him.

"Whoa! It's me baby!" KB screamed elevating his voice and hands so she would recognize it was him.

"I'm sorry." She breathed out lowering the firearm then dropping it back on the bed.

He walked over to her slowly and she moved to him and lay her head against his chest as he hugged her and lowered his nose into her shoulder and closed his eyes rocking her gently back and forth. He opened his eyes and his eyes fell onto the bed and noticed two suitcases, one partially filled with clothes and folded clothes next to the other one. He pushed her off him holding her gently by her arms.

"Where you goin' baby?" KB asked with a baffled expression.

Tears had already fallen and she was restraining from letting the downpour happen.

"I'm going home." She said bluntly.

"You leavin' me Glo'?" KB took a step back blinking his eyes quickly.

Gloria grabbed his hand and held it tenderly in hers. "I need a break from all of this K. I thought I was escaping all that bullshit in Brooklyn when we got here but it's like shit got worse since we been here. That crazy muhfucka Junior is down here in the same town and shoots you then this sick fuck comes back again and tries to finish the job. My nerves is shot! I can't deal with this shit anymore, I'm on pins and needles out here, scared to go to OUR shop and scared to ride around in town because I don't want to bump into that crazy muhfucka or his crazy bitch. I knew I was losing it when I came in the shop shooting like I'm in the streets, it's too much for me. We can't raise a family here." Gloria's tears cascaded down her face given it a glazed over look as she sniffled and wiped her nose. "I want to get away from this place just as much, if not more, than when we was in Brooklyn. I can't believe all that's happened since we moved down here, it's just fuckin' crazy!"

KB lowered his head and fought the emotion that was welling up inside. He knew in his heart if Gloria went back to Brooklyn she wouldn't be coming back. He couldn't blame her because everything she said was true. He lifted his head back up and looked her in her eyes, his was glassy.

"I don't want you to leave me Glo'. I don't want to be down here without you. This move was supposed to be for the both of us. I understand exactly what you're saying and you're right, I can't argue that point." His chest heaved up and down.

"I'm sorry K baby but I just don't want to get sucked in with all this bullshit. We're alone down here and outnumbered and honestly, I'm scared." She rocked back and forth and bit her bottom lip. "I'm scared that I'm going to kill somebody or they're gonna kill me! That's the truth."

"I was supposed to take care of you." He whispered more to himself. "This is my fault, I shoulda handled this shit from the jump." He rubbed his hand over his head. "Ok, I'll leave with you, just let me shut down the barbershop...."

"No!" Gloria interrupted him. "I don't want you to do that K. It's your business, you made it what it is today. Don't shut it down." She shook her head slowly.

"I don't have a choice, I'm not going to let you leave me, we came here together and that's how we're leaving." KB said with finality.

Gloria looked up at him and had mixed emotions, she didn't want him to give up his business but she also didn't want him to give up his life or freedom fucking with Junior.

They embraced and she buried her head in his chest and squeezed him around his waist tightly.

"We goin' back home baby?" She looked up at him.

"Yea ma, we gon' blow this wack ass town!" He forced a smile. "I figure we keep the house and use it for a vacation spot or we can rent it out. What you think?"

"I say rent it out. I don't think I'm gon' want to come down here to vacation, too many bad memories." She pushed away from him gently. "We don't have to worry about finding a place right away once we get there, we can stay at my mom's crib." Gloria suggested.

"I ain't gon' be comfortable stayin' with your mom Glo', you know that." He protested slightly.

"It won't be for long baby." She walked over to the bed and sat down then picked up the cordless phone. "I'm going to call her right now and let her know. It'll save us a lot of money and headache, ok baby."

"Aiight." KB relented then turned and walked out the room. "*I don't want to go to no fucking Baptiste.*" He thought to himself as he opened the closet and grabbed his automatic.

***

The tension in the room was so thick it was stifling. Shondra stared in Junior's eyes and tried to gauge his feeling but his look was too intense. Her throat was dry and palms clammy

but she was at a impasse and had to reveal her truth hoping the honesty, however brutal and hurtful, would balance out the high strung emotions that was sure to follow.

Junior felt perspiration under his arms and was getting more and more anxious wondering what the hell Shondra was so afraid to tell him. He was leaning strongly towards her coming clean about fucking with Chico, it was a sore spot for him but as a man he had to eat it because he knew what he had been doing with Muffin. He sighed heavily to give her an indication that he was getting tired of her stalling.

"I had a baby; a son." She blurted it out. It wasn't done tactfully it came out crass and sudden. Silence. Junior's body went completely cold; his limbs felt heavy. He stared at her with a faraway look; he was looking pass her as if she weren't standing there. His left leg moved backwards slowly then the right followed, his left hand reached out to the armrest of the red velvet couch. He couldn't feel it and stumbled backwards awkwardly and landed on the edge of the couch; his legs crossed at the ankles. His back arched and his head felt like he was wearing a solid steel helmet and it lowered slowly, his eyes burned and his nostrils were enflamed. The palms of his hands caught his descending head and then a loud and low growl erupted from somewhere deep inside his body. The pain he felt was too great, he could no longer contain it and he cried like he lost a parent, his body shook as he wailed without shame, his emotions were naked and on full display; he was crushed.

Shondra ran over to him and planted her ass right next to him. She slid her arm around his back and could feel his whole body shuddering, she rocked him side to side slowly as his cries grew louder and more uncontrolled. He was wounded by a cut that was invisible to the naked eye but went deep and hurt worse than any laceration a man could be given. It was her first time witnessing him in so much pain and knowing she caused it incited her tears of sadness to appear. They both sat on the couch in a crippled heap sobbing and purging themselves of all

the years of hurt that had been bottled up inside, it was a baptismal of pain being excavated from their body; it was needed and long overdue.

Five minutes passed and Junior with a tear stained face courageously looked at Shondra sniffling.

"Who's the father?" His pained expression could not be denied.

She grabbed his hand slowly and placed it in her own and squeezed it. "It's Chico's."

"Aww no! No! NO! NO!" The volcano of tears erupted as he snatched his hand away from her. His body fell backwards and he bawled out again for another five minutes. It was heartbreaking to see his devastation and it hurt her to the core. She felt guilty for causing his pain and wished to God he would still give them a chance. His pain was a show of how deep in love he was with her, that's what she was hoping. She tried to touch his hand but he brushed her away and she understood, maybe he needed time. She scooted over to the other side of the couch and she cried along with him, her pain was similar so she was justified in sharing her tears as well.

Junior finally gathered himself together and sat upright on the couch. He brushed his pants off and attempted to wipe his face and eyes dry with the palms of his hands but he wasn't doing anything but smearing his face with salty tears. He turned his head slowly to Shondra then shook it and sniffled.

"I'm so fucking hurt right now." His eyes were crimson and his voice was weak with pain.

"Junior, I'm so sorry. I don't love him, I don't want him." She cried out in desperation.

"You don't love or want him?" Junior's face screwed up. "What kind of mom would say..."

"No, no." She waved her hand to interrupt him. "I'm talking 'bout Chico." She clarified.

"You had to feel something, you fucked him and had his seed." He sounded dejected when he spoke.

"Please Junior. Don't let this change anything between us, please." Shondra implored.

"Of course it changes everything." He rubbed his head with both hands. "You have a baby and it's by the muhfucka I want to kill! How that's gon' work? You going to be with the man that kills his father or wants his father dead?"

"I don't care Junior. I love you! I want us to be a family!" She professed.

"How Shondra? You want me to play daddy to another man's seed? I can't do that shit! You was supposed to have my baby, he was supposed to be my son." Junior's tears and howling started again, he was an emotional wreck.

"Oh God, I'm so sorry Junior." Shondra sobbed. "I didn't plan this, you gotta believe me but I didn't know what to do. I was so lost and alone."

Junior looked up at her, eyes fire red and his heart shattered in a million parts. He nodded his head suddenly like something got through to him. "You know something, you're right." It was time for him to man up. "I did leave you alone, I left for a year knowing you were fucking with that lame. I knew but at the time I guess I didn't give a fuck because I was doing me. I just never thought..." He paused to gather himself. "I always thought I would be the father of your first child. I thought I would be the one to share that with you. I always thought you and me was gonna get married and raise a family of li'l Juniors and Juniorettes." He forced a half smile as he looked at her with weakened eyes. "I really can't blame you, I shoulda been here."

Shondra looked down at her ring finger and the light spot where the engagement ring Junior had given her used to be before Muffin robbed her then sighed heavily. "I can't let you take all the blame baby because it takes two hands to clap. If I didn't let my anger get the best of me and give your name to those cops you wouldn't had been forced to leave and maybe things between us would have been different." She grabbed his

hand in hers and held onto it. "I'm so very sorry for hurting you Junior but I couldn't lie to you. I'm still in love with you." She confessed.

"And I'm still in love with you Mooka." Hearing her pet name brought a smile to her face and she believed that they may be ok after all.

***

The traffic outside began thinning out as Chico watched from his living room window. It faced the back of the building where his workers hustled and since he was watching his son, he was monitoring their movements by checking the scene every so often. He was holding his son in his arms unconsciously rocking back and forth. Standing there holding him and hearing the gurgling noises he made, he realized that he produced life and it was his job, no, it was his duty to be a father to his first born seed.

He didn't like the way Shondra was treating him but he still wanted to be with her because he did love her. He only tolerated how she treated him because he was broke but now that he was making money and running his own spot he wasn't going to let her keep disrespecting him like he was bummy; he was caked up now. He looked down at his son and smiled then gazed out the window again. He felt like he was looking out the window of a penthouse high rise because things were good for him at the moment although it didn't start out that way; life was funny like that. A couple years ago he was working for Rock who was Junior's lieutenant and he was a worker running down crack addicts for five dollar hits turning in percentages that didn't make sense to him. After Rock was murdered he was forced to work for Lakim and got mixed up with he and Junior's ongoing beef but while he worked for La he made less money and was under more pressure and was ready to get out of the game because he couldn't handle it. He turned into a snitch

because that was the only way he could get out of the game without La killing him. After La was murdered he tried to be his own boss but he soon realized he wasn't built to be a boss because he didn't know anything about how the business ran from the inside. Everything seemed to be crumbling right before his eyes and he had a baby on the way then Muffin appeared out of nowhere and brought him back to life. He wasn't going to allow this opportunity to die out on him, he was planning to stay on top because he already knew how being broke felt and he wasn't going back there. His son looked up at him and smiled before he threw up some milk. Chico laughed and wiped his mouth with his bib then walked over to the couch and sat down. He was thinking about keeping him for the night but he knew Shondra would wild out on him and he hated that. He hated he had to jump through flaming hoops just to see his son and now with the status he held in Baptiste, she was going to stop playing him like he was a sucker. It was time to put an end to her bullshit once and for all.

Chico grabbed the house phone and beeped his lieutenant then got his son ready because he was going to Shondra's crib to talk to her about keeping him for the night and he wasn't going to take no for an answer.

Chapter 23

Since Junior hadn't returned any of her calls when she paged him, Muffin figured he was with laying up with his slut Shondra. It infuriated her that he wasn't man enough to let her know he wanted to go backwards, she deserved that much. She still loved him but wasn't going to let that cloud her judgment because she was obviously not a priority in his life anymore, him not calling was a clear indication of that fact. She wondered how much he knew about what she was doing because there was not telling what his cheese eating cousin Bo told him. She had to at least find out when he was coming back so she could at least hide out until she was done collecting all the money on the street.

She picked up the phone and dialed his beeper number again leaving her special code. She got up and looked in her bag and pulled out the money Patricia had dropped off to her already. Everything had been going so good when she first started and then it seemed to change overnight. As she counted the money what seemed like the tenth time she was beginning to realize how much it changed her and her thinking. What supposed to have started out as her holding her man down turned into her trying to take over and solidify her own spot in the drug game. She felt the power of brokering her own deal with Craig, the power and influence the money had in getting Bo, Patricia and Chico to work for her and she felt the respect of being a female boss in a game where most men ruled. Now she seemed to be losing that edge she once had because she didn't factor in any sudden changes so it was all coming at her sideways and she wasn't equipped to handle it, things were

definitely threatening to spiral out of control and she had no
clue on how to stop it. She was in limbo with Junior, she had no
idea if they were still in a relationship or not.

The phone rang and startled her out of her thoughts. She
went over to the nightstand and picked it up.

"Hello?" She answered in her high pitched squeaky
voice.

"What you doin' in a hotel Muff?" Junior asked
immediately.

"Junior? What the fuck is going on?" She ignored his
question because she needed her questions answered first.

"What you mean what's going on?" Junior's tone was
distinct and Muffin picked up on it immediately.

"You with that bitch!" Her claws came out and she was
ready for battle. "You get out the fucking hospital and the first
thing you do is hop a fucking Greyhound to cuddle with that
hoe!" She wasn't sure but if that's what he did, her rhetoric
would surely get him to confess.

"Where the fuck were you when I came out the fucking
hospital? Tell me that!" Junior shot back.

"Taking care of your fucking business that you was
unable to do! I was in NY making sure when you did come
home from the hospital your shit would still be the same, that's
where the fuck I was at!" She screamed into the phone her high
pitched voice squawking noisily.

"Then where's my fucking money! You took care of that
too!" Junior barked.

"Your money? You think I stole from you muhfucka! I
been down here with you over a year and never once took a
fucking dime from you and you wanna accuse me of stealing
now? You ain't shit! I was here for you the whole fucking time,
I nursed you back to health you ungrateful fuck! I was the one
in the hospital when you had all those tubes running out ya ass!
And I'm the one that made sure your thieving, slow ass cousin
ain't take you for your fucking money! You got me real fucked

up Junior to sit here and accuse me of stealing from you." Muffin's anger had hot tears running from her eyes as she screamed.

"You're a liar!" Junior growled gritting his teeth.

"I'm a liar too? Oh that bitch musta sucked your fucking brains outta ya head for you to be calling me a liar! Now I'm a liar and a thief?" His words were slicing through what was left of her heart.

"Yea you a fucking liar! When I was in the hospital you stole some money then and lied and said it was for your mom's and..." Muffin cut him off quickly.

"I took that money and bought more work for you you fucking asshole. Keep letting that bitch fill your head with bullshit. You so fucking stupid!" She couldn't camouflage her hurt any longer. "How can you accuse me of all this shit when all I thought about was making sure you was ok when you came out the hospital. I was with you through some of your hardest times nigga! I held you down and was willing to lose everything to protect you! I can't believe you would flip on me like this for nothing!" She was bawling. "Do you even care that somebody tried to kill me when I got back here? That's why I'm in this fucking hotel if you really want to know." She was hoping that bit of information would soften him up, if he still cared one iota for her.

"Word? What happened?" Junior's interest suddenly shifted.

"I pulled up in the driveway and got out then went into the house. I came back out to get my bags and somebody in a pickup truck started shooting at me. I almost died. The front door is full of holes. After they left I went in the house and that's when I saw the safe was empty. I didn't know if you took the money or not so I went to see Bo and he told me some bullshit about you thinking I stole your money and shit."

"Did you who it was?" Junior asked.

"No 'cause I was too busy ducking." She responded sarcastically.

"Who took my money Muff?" Junior asked getting back to his purpose for calling. "You know it was a half a million in there so I'm willing to die or go to jail to get it back. I'm not playing."

"You threatening to do something to me nigga? I can't believe this shit is happening! You over there sucking that bitch pussy, the bitch that's fucking the little boy that beat you out of your money. I was the one that went with you over there to hold you down when you had no fucking body! I was the bitch that stuck around when your family and that bitch kicked you to the fucking curb! Now you back sniffing that bitch ass? Well you stay your stupid ass with her, she gon' be the one to break your fucking heart like you just broke mine bitch!" Containing her anger was no longer an option, full throttle and full speed ahead.

"All I want is my money Muff! Where is it!" Junior bellowed into the phone. "I want my fucking money or..."

"You know what Junior. I can't do this shit no more with you. I ain't steal your fucking money and you know that shit but you better stop threatening my life or yours'll be over!" Muffin slammed the phone down on the receiver shaking the desk.

"Oh my God! This bitch must got that nigga brainwashed 'cause he really thinks I stole his fucking money!" She whimpered to herself as she put the money she counted back in her bag neatly wondering if ten thousand was enough money for her to leave.

Desperation set in almost immediately and she wondered what her next move was going to be. She wasn't sure how long Junior was going to be in New York but she knew he couldn't leave on the Trailways bus or Amtrak, it was after 9pm and she knew the schedules by heart. She had at least one more day to try and collect all the money from Patricia and Bo. She had no idea what Junior's threat meant, she didn't want to believe he would physically kill her but she didn't want to take

any chances; he sounded angry and was short with his words. The adrenaline rush she got from her short run as a female boss wasn't worth the fear and confusion she was currently feeling. Despite what the streets said about the money, power and respect obtained through being a drug dealer, none of that could replace the one thing you could lose...your life.

There had to be a way she could even the playing field for Junior. She was deep in thought, too many things were running through her mind and she needed to stop and concentrate on one thing at a time. What was her priority? Money. She grabbed the phone and dialed some numbers.

"Hello?" Someone answered.

"Let me speak with Bo." She replied quickly.

"Hold on. Hey Bo, telephone mane." The guy who answered screamed out.

There was some chattering going back and forth in the background then the guy came back and said, "Yo, he ain't here."

"He not there huh? Ok." Muffin hung up the phone. The bullshit started already. She wasn't about to take no losses on the work she gave Bo, she was going to get all she could out of his lying ass then bounce back to Brooklyn. Junior's threat rang loudly in her head and she knew once she got back to Brooklyn she could buy her some time to keep him away from her. She grabbed her jacket then stuffed her automatic inside her pocketbook then peeked out the curtain then opened the door and stepped outside. She was paranoid as she walked to the truck but not that afraid that she wasn't going to get her money from Bo.

***

Junior slammed the phone down as he looked around the room he lived in so many years ago. The steel gray he painted was starting to fade and the carpet looked worn. The television's

images weren't as sharp as before and were blurry, the color no longer crisp and the volume button broken off. He shook his head slowly as he closed his eyes trying to figure out how Muffin knew about Shondra having a baby by Chico. He gritted his teeth as he thought of how he didn't have anyone down there he could trust to really hold him down while he was in the hospital.

Shondra came in the room and he stood up from the bed.

"Everything ok? I heard you screaming." She asked sincerely.

"Nah, everything not all right but it will be once I get back down there." Junior's eyebrows lowered. "I gotta make that bitch pay for crossing me."

"I don't know the whole story but maybe you should just let that bitch fizzle out on her own." Shondra suggested.

"Too much bread involved, she gotta pay one way or the other." Junior said seriously.

As much as Shondra couldn't stand Muffin she didn't want Junior to kill her; the bitch would still win in death because Junior would have to go on the run or would be spending the rest of his life behind bars and she still wouldn't be with him.

"I just don't want you to do anything that will keep you away from me another minute Junior. I want us to build a life together...all of us." She included her son on purpose.

It would take some getting used to but he felt he was ready to take on being with her and her son.

"We will." He grabbed her hand. "I just have to handle this one thing and I promise you we'll be together as a family." He was serious as he stared into her eyes.

"I hope so Junior 'cause this time I'm not letting you go." She wrapped her arms around his neck and pulled him close to her. As he hugged her he gazed down at the bassinet and sighed heavily.

"Where's the baby?" He whispered in her ear.

She released her hold from him and said, "He's with his father."

The word stung in his ears as a frown instantly appeared on his face. This was going to be hard getting used to but his love for her would eventually soften the hurt. The one thing that needed to happen was him handling the situation with Chico, there was no need to prolong the inevitable. Chico had to go by any means necessary.

"You know I'm gonna kill that muhfucka right?" Junior said straight faced.

Shondra nodded her head slowly and Junior looked at her wondering if she cared anything for her baby's father.

***

Patricia was sitting inside her new Mazda 626 listening to Babyface serenade her through the speakers. In the passenger seat sat one of the many girls that she distributed Muffin's drug to. The girl, Ebony, was smoking a blunt while Patricia counted out the money she had to pay Muffin. She didn't need to do it anymore and would have stopped but after the threat Muffin made on her grandmother's life, she was going to keep doing it just until she figured out how to get from under her grasp. She wasn't afraid of her, she just worried about her grandmother getting pulled into any of her mess. She sucked her teeth loudly as she recounted and saw that Ebony was short $1,500.00. She turned to her and turned the volume down.

"How you fifteen hundred short Eb?" She asked annoyed.

"I take shorts. You said don't turn down no money." She said with glassed over eyes.

"Yea, I said don't turn down money but that don't mean give the shit away either!" Patricia shook her head. She would have to give up her money to make the count right for Muffin.

231

She didn't want to risk her making no more idle threats against her grandmother.

"You gon' have to pay me that money back from this last package I'm giving you." She told Ebony.

"I'm not gon' get paid off that one then?" Ebony asked with a befuddled look on her face.

"You think you still 'posed to get paid even after you short so much money? Are you that stupid girl?" Patricia's head cocked sideways.

Ebony sucked her teeth and took the package Patricia handed to her and grabbed the handle on the vehicle to exit. "You need to stop smoking that dope girl, it's fucking yo' mind slam the fuck up!" Patricia chastised.

"Hmmph!" Ebony expressed as she walked away towards the recreational center.

"What's up Pat?"

Patricia turned to the voice and smiled wide. "Hey Ronnie. What you doin' up this way."

"Came to see what you doin'." He smiled harder.

"I ain't doin' nothing but listening to some music, as you can see."

"When you get this?" He said rubbing his hand on the hood of the midsized car. "I thought you said you wasn't gonna buy nothing expensive, said you was gonna concentrate on opening your own shop."

"It's ok. Ain't nobody watching me. I'm good Ronnie." She told him.

"Ok, I just wanna make sure 'cause..." He stopped talking as he made eye contact with the woman riding in the jeep. It backed up and pulled alongside Patricia's car.

"Ay Pat, what's up?" Muffin said getting out the jeep, leaving it running in the middle of the street. She walked over to the driver's side but her eyes were glued to the guy she was talking to.

"Hey Muffin." Patricia spoke as she hurriedly got out of her vehicle.

Muffin walked over to both of them and smirked when she looked at the car. "When you get this?" She asked Patricia pointing to the Mazda that displayed thirty day tags in the back window.

"Oh it's not mine." Patricia answered quickly.

Muffin looked at Ronnie. "It must be yours then."

"No, it's not mine." He replied quickly.

"I need to talk to you." She looked at Ronnie but was speaking to Patricia. "In private."

Ronnie took the hint and picked up the bike he was riding and rode off down the street.

"I need the rest of the money by tomorrow. You have anything else on you now?" Muffin asked.

"Yea, give me a minute." Patricia bent down and reached inside the car and pulled out her pocketbook and handed Muffin a stack of money.

"How much is this?" Muffin asked looking at the neatly stacked of bills.

"It should be twenty five thousand." Patricia said nonchalantly.

"Let me ask you something? Since you been working for me how much money you saved up?" Muffin asked.

"Huh?" Patricia's face screwed up at the question.

"You've been dressing really nice all of a sudden and now you with this new car that you lying and saying isn't yours but I bet if I look in your glove compartment I'll see your bill of sale. I'm far from stupid Pat. If you don't want to tell me it means you hiding something and I swear I woulda never put this shit together if I didn't see that muhfucka that was talking to you." Muffin said with her mouth twisted.

"What you talkin' 'bout Muffin?" Patricia's heart started beating quickly.

"That's the muhfucka that came to my house to change my fucking locks. You and that muhfucka broke into the safe and stole all my fucking money. That's why you want out now, that's why you started dressing better, that's how you bought this fucking car and that's how you going to open up your own beauty shop!" Muffin's eyes were bright from anger. She pulled out her automatic and grabbed Patricia to her forcefully. "You gonna take me to get my fucking money bitch! All of it!"

Patricia was dragged over to the passenger side of the jeep and got inside then Muffin tucked the gun back into her pocketbook and was about to open the door when she saw headlights in front of her approaching. The door of the vehicle opened and Bo appeared and called out to Muffin. She stopped and looked at him with hate filled eyes.

"What you want?" She asked sarcastically as he approached her.

"Where you going?" He asked moving to her slowly.

"I was on my way to see you to pick up my money." She said matter of factly.

"Oh ok. What you doin' wit' Pat? You was taking her with you to see me?" Bo was standing five feet away now.

"Why the fuck you worried 'bout who ride with me all of a sudden to pick up my money? You got my money?" Muffin asked, her mouth balled up.

Bo cocked his arm back and slammed his fist into the center of Muffin's face. Her nose looked like it broke on impact and blood squirted from it like a punctured hose. The noise that came out of her mouth was unidentifiable but the pain she felt was reminiscent of when she had fought Shondra in the back of her building in Baptiste. She stumbled backwards and reached out to grab the closest thing to her, the spoiler on the trunk of Patricia's car. She stood upright on shaky legs as Bo advanced on her quickly. Her eyes watered but she could see Patricia jumping out the jeep and running over to the front of her car.

"I always wanted to do that so I could see how tough your city ass really is!" Bo hissed.

"She got a gun in her purse Bo." Patricia informed him.

Bo picked up her purse and took out the automatic weapon and tucked it in his waist. He fumbled inside and grabbed the money Patricia had given her and threw it to her. Muffin was still seeing stars when another blow was delivered by Patricia. It was a vicious right hook that literally spun her in full circle then her shoulders were grabbed and Patricia leaned forward and head butted her then let her spill to the ground like road kill. Muffin moaned as she heard them talking amongst themselves. She turned over and blood drained from her nose like an open faucet. She cupped her hands under her leak and crawled to the curb. Although dizzy she could make out the guy Ronnie standing and talking with Bo and Patricia. "Fuck!" She gurgled before passing out.

Chapter 24

"When you supposed to get your son back?" Junior asked as he prepared to leave.

"When I call him he's supposed to bring him." Shondra said cautiously. "Why? You got plans for us?"

"I wanted you to go back to Tompkins with me but I'm not sure if you'll spend the night without your son. You ever do that before?"

"Honestly? No, but I never had a reason to." Shondra said quietly. "I'm sure he'll be fine with him."

"Nah, I wouldn't want you to do that. It wouldn't be right, your first time doing it would be for the wrong reasons. We got time." Junior said changing his mind.

"I'm out, I'll call you when I get back to..." The knocking of the door both interrupted and startled them. Junior gripped his firearm instinctively while Shondra's heart started rattling in her chest. She looked at her watch then looked at Junior, her eyes were already pleading with him.

"If that's him can you please not do anything to him right now, he has my son." Shondra asked with sincerity.

Junior's teeth gritted and his mouth balled up. "This is his first and only pass. Don't take too long 'cause I'm not gonna sit back here waiting like no lame." Junior stated with emphasis.

"Ok, thank you baby. I won't be long, I promise." She hurried to the door.

She looked through the peephole and was shocked to see Chico standing in the hallway with their son. She unlocked the door and pulled it open and looked down at the stroller and smiled instantly. She reached out for it and Chico pulled it back.

Shondra looked up at him surprised and grabbed the front of the stroller and pushed the canopy back to make sure her son was in there. Seeing him bundled up in his blanket she breathed a sigh of relief and gazed up at Chico.

"What the fuck you doing?" Her voice was strong and bold.

"I came here to tell you he staying with me tonight. I'm tired of this dumb shit with how you control when I see him and shit. This our son and I got as much right to have him with me as you do." Chico stated forcefully.

"Ok, he can spend the night with you tonight but I want him back in the morning. Do you have enough formula and diapers for him?" She asked.

Chico was expecting a long drawn out fight, he was thrown off by her change in character.

"You all right?" He asked looking at her carefully. "You high or something."

"No muhfucka! But if you keep asking me stupid fucking questions I'ma change my mind and he won't be going nowhere with you!" She sassed.

"Ok kool, aiight. I'll have him back in the morning. I'll call before I bring him."

"Nah, I'll call you in the morning." She bent down and unstrapped her son then picked him up and squeezed him in her arms and kissed his tiny face. "Mommy loves you. You be a good boy ok?" She rocked him in her arms for some seconds then strapped him back in. "Don't have him 'round your li'l bitches trying play house neither!" She said then shut her door denying him a chance to respond.

"Fucking bitch!" He muttered under his breath as he turned and headed out the building with his son.

Shondra placed her back against the door and breathed out heavily. As much as she didn't want Chico to take the baby for the night she knew she had to agree in order to avoid an argument that more than likely would have brought Junior

running from the back and she didn't want to chance her son getting caught in any cross fire. She leaned up off the door and started towards the room just as Junior was coming out.

"Where's your son?" He asked seeing her empty handed.

"He's keeping him for the night." She answered softly.

"Why?"

"I been giving him a hard time about seeing him. He hasn't really spent that much time with him since he was born so to avoid an argument I let him keep him for the night." Shondra grabbed Junior's hand. "Now we can spend the night together."

Junior looked into her eyes and then a smile appeared on his face. "Yea, we can spend the night together. Get your jacket and we'll get outta here. I'm parked on the side of the building in a Audi 5000."

Shondra walked pass him as he made his way to the front door. He opened it and went out in the hallway and out the back door to the car. He was still on alert, his eyes darting back and forth, low and high as he opened the door taking a seat and inserting the key in the ignition. He left the door open and looked down the block then turned his head and looked up the block and spotted Chico with the stroller once again making a sale. He got out of the car and didn't know why he was so infuriated at what Chico was doing but he knew it endangered that little boy's life. Junior walked in a fast pace towards the corner with fire in his eyes, Chico still didn't see him as he crossed the street. Junior walked up behind him and the worker eyes lit up. Chico turned around holding the package he was about to give the worker in his hands. Junior snatched it and gritted his teeth.

"I would kill you right now if you didn't have your son with you! I want the rest of the money you owe me muhfucka or next time your lights gonna be put out! I don't care who you with next time neither!" Junior sneered as he stuffed the drugs in his pocket and showed the handle of his firearm.

"Y-y-yo I thought we was straight with that." Chico countered nervously.

"How you feel?" Junior asked.

"This your shit I'm selling. I thought you knew." Chico informed him.

"What! What the fuck you talkin' bout?"

"Muffin said you was cool with putting work back out here and me handling it and that's how I could pay off what I owed. You didn't say that?" Chico had a confused look on his face.

Junior thought for a second, Muffin was making power moves all behind his back. As much as he wanted to peel Chico's wig back, he had to see how much work she gave him.

"I didn't say none of that shit! I put work out here but I didn't know it was going to you. How much you got for me now?" Junior's eyes were piercing.

"I got a little over twenty thou. I'll have the rest of it by the weekend and the count will be right, not like before you put me back on. She was supposed to be dropping off more work since she shorted me the last pack. That's what I thought first when I saw you." Chico told him.

"Let me get that twenty." Junior said hurriedly.

"Right now?" Chico asked curiously.

"Yea muhfucka! Right now!" Junior growled.

"Aiight, let me run my son upstairs and I'll be down with it in a minute." Chico turned and pushed the stroller then stopped. "You not gonna hit me with nothing else?"

"Just get my money nigga!" Junior barked as Chico turned and pushed his son towards his building.

When he got to his building he turned back and wondered why Junior came over there. He thought he was over there to see how things was going himself and to hit him off with more work but he didn't seem to know what was going on so before he gave up that money he was going to beep Muffin and see what was really happening with the work.

Junior couldn't believe Muffin was working all angles of his drug business, she was trying to lock down his out of town movements as well as his old Brooklyn spot. He shook his head and as much as he disliked what she was doing, he had to applaud her efforts, she moved like a real boss. She was smart enough to use his name to ensure payment.

Shondra came out the building and Junior crossed the street and met her at the corner.

"What you was doing across the street?" She asked looking at him strangely.

"I was saying what's up to some of the dudes out there." He lied. "I need to go back and holla at him for a minute. The car door is open and on so just sit in it 'til I get back."

"What you up to Junior?" She didn't believe him.

"Nothing. I'm just gonna get something from one of them real quick. It'll be fast."

"You said you not going to do nothing to that boy, remember?" She reminded him.

"Why you worrying about what happens to that fucking lame anyway?" He shifted the tone of the conversation in hopes of shutting her up.

"I'll be in the car. Please hurry up and be careful." She said walking towards the Audi.

"Don't worry."

***

Chico was waiting on the call back from Muffin. He peeked out window in his room and saw Junior standing on the corner. Something wasn't right with him being over in Baptiste all of a sudden. He picked up his phone and dialed Shondra's house and it rang out. He dialed the number again and the phone just rang and rang.

"*Fucking bitch!*" He yelled. "*That muhfucka came over here to see her! That's why she didn't beef with me about taking*

the baby for the night. Hmmph! That muhfucka not 'bout to get nothing else from me. Fuck him!" Chico was hot with jealousy. He had been trying so hard to be good to her and all she was doing was shafting him and now he knew why; she was waiting on Junior the whole time.

He lifted up his mattress, grabbed his gun from under it and stuffed it in the small of his back. He tightened his belt then walked out his room and knocked on his grandmother's door, and in Spanish, told her to watch his son until he got back upstairs. Then he left the house in a huff, his plans was to eliminate Junior.

Chapter 25

Muffin's eyes opened and everything was blurry. She couldn't get her eyes to focus but pain was shooting from her entire face. She lifted her hand and touched her nose gently and knew it was broken or at least felt broken. She tried to turn around and get up but she felt stiff.

"Here, let me get you up." She heard a male voice and turned her head to it. Her eyes still hadn't focused yet so she couldn't make out the man standing over her.

He gently grabbed her by her arms and lifted her slowly to her feet.

"Look like you need to go to the hospital and check that out." He advised.

"Who are you?" She asked ignoring what he said.

"Bones." He answered stepping back. "That's your truck over there in the middle of the street?"

"Hmm hmm." She answered blinking her eyes into focus. "*Oh shit!*" She thought to herself. "*That's the same muhfucka Bo was talking to in the mall.*" She backed up fearfully.

"What's wrong ma? You aiight?" He asked reaching his hand out to her.

"I'm good." Her voice sounded extra high and nasally since she couldn't breathe through her nose. She started making her way to the truck.

"You sure you aiight ma? You look a little dazed. What happened, who did you dirty like that?" He asked.

"Your peoples!" She accused figuring he was trying to be funny.

"My peoples?" He asked bewildered. "I ain't got no peoples down here. What make you even say some wild shit like that?"

"I seen you with him." She continued accusing him grabbing the door handle of the truck.

"Seen me with who? You buggin' ma, I ain't got no homeboys down here with me. I'm rolling dolo." He confessed.

She stopped and looked at him through squinted eyes. "You don't know Bo?"

He stopped and thought for a second. "Oh you talking 'bout the big country cat. Yea, he cop weight from me but I don't know him like that. He did that shit to you? Wow!" He said surprised.

"Yea, him and a bitch. They jumped me!"

"What you do for them to bust you down like that?"

"Why you wanna know, you gonna help me?"

"You never know, I might." He smiled. He was digging her even though her face looked like she was smacked with an iron skillet one too many times. "How you know I fucks with Bo?"

"I saw him get something from you in the game room at the mall." She said while searching for a napkin or cloth.

"Damn! Shit was that obvious. I'm slipping." He said more to himself than to her.

Muffin found a napkin and pulled down the visor on the driver's side and looked into the mirror. Tears erupted when she saw the damage to her once pretty face.

"I'm gonna kill them!" She screamed. "Look what they did to my face."

Bones walked over to her and tried to comfort her. "You want me to take you to the hospital so they can bandage you up?" He offered sincerely. Her crying made him feel bad for her.

"No, thanks." She cried.

"Let me at least take you home." He pushed.

"I don't have a home down here. I'm staying in a hotel."

"Let me drop you to your room. Park your car here and you can ride with me." He grabbed her hand and lead her out of the truck then jumped in with the driver's door still open and parked it right where she was laid out. "Come on and get in my car and I'll take you to your room." He said grabbing her pocketbook then handing it to her along with her keys.

***

"So you're from Brownsville?" Muffin asked.

"Yea, Blake Avenue and you from the Stuy?" He responded.

"Yep. Do or die." She stated proudly as she wiped the blood from her face.

"Never ran, never will. We get busy in the 'ville." He boasted. "I guess that dude Bo don't respect where you from." He chuckled.

"Nah but it's aiight 'cause I ain't letting this shit slide. He gon' get his melon peeled back!" She threatened squeezing the cloth out in the sink.

"You still ain't say why they duffed you out like that. If I was to guess I would say it had to do with either you was fucking with somebody man or you fucked with somebody bread. Am I right?" He questioned.

Muffin let out a slight chortle. "It damn sure wasn't over me fucking none of these muhfuckas."

"So it was over money, how much you took from them?" He quizzed.

The light bulb went off in Muffin's head. "I didn't take shit from them, they robbed me."

"They robbed you then whooped your ass?"

"No, they robbed me about a week ago while I was away in New York. They plotted the shit out to the wire because..."

She stopped and looked at Bones. "Would you be willing to help me get my money back from them?"

Bones laughed. "Not for short money. I don't wanna get caught up in no bullshit 'cause I got something good going down here already."

"This is definitely not short money. It's over three hun'ed thou they clipped from me." She boasted.

Bones face lit up when he heard the amount she claimed was stolen from her. "How you know they the ones that stole it from you?" He questioned.

"Before I tell you anything are you down to help me get it back?" Muffin was desperate. She didn't know Bones from a can of paint but her circumstances was calling for her to take a risk with him because she had no money and there was no way Bo or Patricia was going to pay her after what just happened.

"If it's really three hun'ed K then I'll consider it." Bones replied bluntly.

With no other recourse Muffin gave the details of what happened. "Me and my man was down here selling weight. We been making good money for over a year with no problems but then my man ran into this cat he had beef with from Brooklyn and they had a shoot out. My man got hit up and was laid up in the hospital so I was left out here to handle shit myself. I was making trips and muling shit back all by my lonely still hitting his snake ass cousin Bo with work. On one of my trips O.T. (out of town) my man was released from the hospital too soon and called an ambulance before he passed out but since nobody was home the police had to break the door down to get to him. When I got back in town that morning they were rushing him to the hospital so I called a locksmith to come change all the locks on the house but I also called his cousin Bo over to hit him off with the work. I put this bum ass country hoe Pat onto getting some money since her pockets were fucked up too. I knocked everything off and was on my way back up the way within a week. I do my thing and come back to some a muhfucka busting

at me when I pull up in my driveway, an open safe with all the bread gone and a dead pit that would tear the limbs off any muhfucka that came through the door." She paused and caught her breath then continued. "I asked Bo did he know what was going on and he played slow but I had a funny feeling he knew something then I hit the bitch Pat with some work and she started acting like she didn't need no more money when I knew the bitch wasn't caking like that from the jump. Shit started looking real crazy to me 'round 'bout this time so I went to collect all my bread before any more bullshit went down and on my way to pick up my money from Bo I sees this bitch Pat sitting in a brand new whip with 30-day tags. I hop out and she's talking to the fucking locksmith that changed the locks on my door. I put it together right then, the locksmith and Pat stole the money out the safe. He's a fucking locksmith so I was sure if he could open locks he damn sure could open a safe. She was a dead giveaway 'cause she wanted to stop working for me all of a sudden. I just couldn't figure out how the locksmith knew there was a safe in the room but after he rode off and Bo appeared a short time after, I figured out Bo the one that set the whole shit up 'cause he the only one that knew we had a safe in the crib, Pat didn't." She looked at Bones trying to see if her story was one he would be willing to help her with. "If you help me get my shit back I'll give you 40%." She spoke in percentages because Junior always told her when negotiating money, most niggas wouldn't know how much if you used it instead of a dollar amount.

"How you know they still got all that bread? You said she copped a whip so I'm sure they all split between them. You gonna have to get them all at the same time." He figured.

"Not necessarily. We can pick them off one by one." Muffin thought quick on her feet when it came to the subject of money. "We get Bo first then Pat who will bring the little timid locksmith in. I believe they both beat him anyway. I think he only did it because he was sweet on Pat." Muffin harumphed. "I

bet that's what that muhfucka was plotting when I saw him talking to the bitch in the car. Wow! They set me up sweet. That's why that bitch came at me with that sob story, that faggot ass Bo probably knew I would try to expand." She was speaking unconsciously in front of Bones but her discovery had her hype. "I'm gonna make them fuckers pay...NO MORE FUCKING GAMES!" She turned her attention to Bones. "You wit' it or what?"

"Fuck it, I'm down." He replied smacking his lips.

***

The night air blew softly while people passed by chatting and laughing. Junior's eyes were glued to the building Chico went into. He wasn't sure what was taking him so long to come downstairs with his money but he was growing impatient. He looked down to the car and then focused his attention back on the building's entrance. He saw the door open but a Spanish girl came out. Junior headed towards the building and paid attention to the workers as he passed, they were staring at him with a look of respect and fear. He walked around the back of the building and pulled his hammer out when he was by the courtyard. He slowly made his way to the back door and he stood there peeking through the wired glass. He squinted every time he heard a noise in the lobby then he saw what he was looking for, Chico emerged from the elevator empty handed. Junior didn't hesitate and snatched the door open pointing the gun to lead the way.

"What was you thinking about doing?" Junior placed the barrel at the back of Chico's head. "I asked you a question!" Junior gritted.

"Nothing." Chico managed to squeeze out from fear.

Junior smacked him upside his head hard with the butt of the gun, the noise sounded like he cracked his cranium. Chico cried out in agonizing pain and Junior checked him,

relieving him of his concealed firearm. Junior smacked him upside the head again.

"This is nothing!" Junior's hot breath rang in his ear. "I should kill your ass right now!" He wrapped his braids around his hand and yanked his head back towards him. "We're gonna go upstairs, we gonna get my all my fucking money and all my drugs. If you so much as twirl the wrong way, everybody in your crib gonna be rotten meat! Come on!" Junior pushed him to the exit holding his hair like reins on a horse.

They reached Chico's floor and when they got to his door Junior pulled his head back again.

"Who in there?" He whispered in his ear. "You lie and your head the first thing that catches this hot slug!"

"Just my abuela and my son. Don't hurt my family man, please." Chico begged.

"Shut the fuck up and open the door!" Junior pushed his head forward.

Chico nervously opened the door and Junior put his arm around his shoulder then jammed the gun in his ribs hard. His eyes scoured the small apartment then they walked awkwardly down the hallway towards his room.

"Chico es que usted?" His grandmother yelled from her room.

"Si abuelita. que me." He responded in Spanish telling her it was him.

Junior followed him into the room and Chico reached for the handle on the closet.

"Whoa muhfucka!" Junior stopped him. He looked around the room and picked up a sneaker. "Take the laces out, hurry up!" Chico unlaced the sneaker then Junior snatched it out of his hand. "Lay flat on the bed and put your hands behind your fucking back. If you give me any resistance I'm going to splatter your thoughts all over these fucked up walls." He tied his hands up tightly then turned him around on his back. "I'm

only gon' ask once and once only. Wrong answer equals a slow and agonizingly painful death. Where's the money!"

Chico blurted out, "It's in a Gucci shopping bag, the drugs. The money, it's in a black duffle bag on the floor in the closet."

Junior opened the closet slow and cautious looking back and forth at Chico to make sure he didn't try anything stupid. He grabbed the shopping bag first with his right hand while pointing the gun steadily at Chico. He placed it on the ground and peeked inside and there was bagged up work inside. He grabbed the duffle bag next and placed it on the floor and unzipped it and it was filled sloppily with different denominations of money. He shook his head and stared at Chico with hate in his eyes and Chico started to shake. Junior was poised to squeeze the trigger because he hated that Chico was the father to the woman he truly loved and he wanted him out of the picture, Shondra should have never fucked with him in the first place.

It was if Chico was reading his mind because he blurted, "Please don't kill me. Please."

Junior cocked the hammer back and curled his index finger over the trigger and skinned up his nose. He was gonna end his life so he could start a new one with Shondra without no bullshit from him. Chico's eyes closed tightly and he tensed up, stiff as a board. Tears rolled down his face as his lips trembled. Junior was about to pull the trigger when he heard a baby scream. He turned his head briefly to the cries then back to Chico who was huddled in a fetal position.

"Please don't do this here, not here, please. Not in front of my family." Chico begged.

Junior smashed the gun against Chico's face then dumped the drugs into the duffle bag along with the package that was in his waist. He could hear the child screaming and his grandmother yelling something in Spanish.

"Get the fuck up!" Junior swung the duffle bag over his shoulder then grabbed Chico by the shoulder.

Chico struggled to get up and stumbled out the room towards the door. His grandmother's door opened just as Junior pushed him out into the hallway of the building and he could hear her screaming, "Chico!" as he pushed him towards the exit.

"Go up the stairs!" Junior commanded as he pressed the gun in his back.

Chico could feel impending doom and his legs gave way as he fell onto the stairs in a miserable heap unable to control the movement of his limbs; he was immobilized. The pain from the butt of the gun jerked his senses and got his legs to start working again. He climbed the stairs unsteadily, each step closer to death. He shivered although it was warm and he could feel the trickle of blood down the front and sides of his face; it was a bloody mess. At the top of the landing was the orange metal roof door and Junior shoved him forward. Terror enveloped his whole body as Junior reached around him, turned the knob and pushed the roof door open exposing darkness from the night. He was pushed onto the roof forcefully and fell on the tiny rocks as Junior grabbed him by his shoulder and pulled him across the roof, sliding him through the sharp tiny rocks towards the metal railing. Junior bent down and loosened the shoestrings then tied it around the railing and secured it. He pulled on it to make sure it was tight then smashed Chico in the face repeatedly with the gun until he stopped making noises. He stood up and kicked him in the mouth then turned to leave. As his foot crunched the gravel beneath it Chico's eyes fluttered open.

"This ain't over muhfucka! I'm gonna get you back!" Then he shut his eyes slowly.

Chapter 26

The trailer park was deep in the country down a dirt path that lead deep into the woods. Single wide trailers were set up all around with dirt ditches so deep it could knock the transmission out of a car if it went faster than five miles an hour. It was a drug gold mine because the country boy dealers would be able to see the law way before they reached their trailers and had ample time to stash their drugs in the woods behind where they lived. Mostly poor people lived out in the trailer parks and their country accent for some reason was heavier than the city folk. The drug trade in the country was financially beneficial and only one person capitalized on it. Users in the trailer park had difficulty getting to town to cop any drugs, after finding someone who would go for them, the cost of the trip, gas and the possibility of getting caught on the way back by the law made it more advantageous to pay the additional cost for the comfort of getting it from someone in the trailer park.

It was late into the night when someone rattled on the trailer door.

"Ain't got nothin' 'til the morning!" The voice screamed from behind the door.

The rattling continued and once again the message, "Ain't nothin' happenin' 'til the morning!" rumbled through the trailer.

The lightweight metal door was kicked in and a towering figure entered the slender trailer with an assault rifle ready for action. Bo heard the crashing noise and thought for sure it was the law and bailed out the back door he had installed

on the trailer. He jumped down to the dirt and was met with a crashing blow that had him laying flat on his stomach.

"Ugggh!" He cried out before turning around on his back. "Awwww hell!" He screeched when he saw Muffin standing over him with a gun pointed to his forehead.

"Where the money you stole Bo?" She questioned with fierce eyes.

"I ain't stole..." His sentence couldn't be finished because pain was shooting from crack in the jaw he received from Muffin.

"Don't really have time for this. You gonna get one more chance to answer and if you choose to be greedy, I'm the last thing you'll ever see!"

"In the woods buried." He whimpered.

Bones jumped down from the back door and looked at Muffin with surprise. She handled the situation better than most niggas would. He smiled at her gangster and wondered if she had done anything like that before because she seemed so comfortable in her environment.

"Get the fuck up!" She ordered and stepped a few feet back from him in case he got jittery and tried to grab her firearm.

Bo got to his feet and looked at Bones then spit on the ground. Bones hit him with a vicious right cross that brought him to his knees and showered the dirt with droplets of blood. Bo reached out and grabbed at him, scratching Bones' hand.

"Spit again muhfucka!" Bones dared as Bo struggled to his feet.

Muffin waited for him to gather himself then screamed, "The money muhfucka!"

Bo trudged through the woods about 300 yards from his trailer and kicked some leaves around and said, "I buried it here."

Bones looked at Muffin and she nodded while keeping her gun trained on Bo. Bones started digging in the spot Bo

showed them with the butt of the assault rifle and a minute or two later pulled out a black hefty bag filled with money.

"How much in there?" Muffin asked Bo.

"'Bout a hundred 'n fifty gees." Bo said guessing.

"Good enough." Muffin squeezed the trigger twice and Bo's body fell like a tree in the woods.

"Let's go get the rest of it." Muffin said to Bones nonchalantly as she stepped over Bo's body like it was tree stump.

Bones looked at her with unbelieving eyes as he threw the bag over his shoulder. He was fucking with a lethal bitch.

***

The smoke coming from the pots on the stove caused the smoke alarm to go off. Bones used the butt of the assault rifle to crush it and the noise stopped. Muffin turned off the burners and turned around and handed Patricia her cordless phone.

"Call him and tell him you coming over." Muffin said picking up the other phone and placing it to her ear. "Say anything else other than that and I'm gonna splatter your brains all over this kitchen. Make sure you ask if he's alone."

Patricia made the phone call while Muffin listened in on the other line. Her and Bones had ambushed Patricia early in the morning at her grandmother's house. Once the grandmother pulled off Bones went to the front door and rang the bell while Muffin went around the back and broke in through the back door. There was breakfast cooking on the stove as she made her way through the kitchen into the dining room. She heard Patricia asking who was at the door as she crept up behind her silently. Patricia was holding a shot gun in her hand when Muffin saw her at the front door peeking through the curtains. She prayed Bones distracted her long enough to get closer so she could disarm her. When she felt she was in striking distance she charged and swung the hand holding the gun with precision

and caught Patricia square on the side of her face. Patricia fell to the floor out cold and Muffin let Bones in. He immediately picked Patricia up and carried her into the kitchen then sat her in the chair while Muffin tied her hands behind her back with wire she took from a speaker in the living room. Muffin filled up a cup of water then threw it in Patricia's face and when her eyes focused she was staring down the barrel of Muffin's gun. Sheer terror was plastered on her face and a puddle appeared under the chair she was sitting on. It was too easy for her to give up what Muffin wanted because she was deathly afraid of the consequences she would face if she didn't comply. She gave them the location of the money she hid in the attic and Bones retrieved it promptly. Although she spent ten thousand out of it, ninety thousand would do just fine. Patricia was even willing to give up Ronnie in exchange for her own life and told Muffin she was sure he had all the money he stole because he was already 'scary' about someone finding out.

Patricia was finished with her conversation and Muffin and Bones were ready to move on Ronnie and get the rest of the money. Patricia was shaking like a leaf and pleading with Muffin to let her go.

"Don't worry bitch, I'm gon' cut you loose soon as I get the rest of my fucking money!" Muffin assured her.

"Please Muffin. I didn't have anything to do with it, Bo was the one that plotted that whole shit out. He used me because he knew Ronnie liked me, that's the only thing I did." Patricia admitted.

"The only thing!" Muffin shouted. "Because of that shit you got my man flipping on me!" Muffin slapped her viciously. "You're the reason why this muhfucka mad with me now!" Muffin spoke too freely and glanced at Bones and his expression showed he caught what she said. "Let's get this bitch outta here so we can get the rest of the money." She said to him as she yanked Patricia up by her arms forcefully.

254

Bones went out the back and pulled the car closer to the back door so no one would notice Patricia with her hands tied behind her back. He opened the back door and Muffin pushed her out the door and towards the car then shoved her inside. Muffin slammed the door then went on the other side and got in the backseat next to her while Bones got in the front and drove.

Ronnie was inside his crib trying to clean up real quick before Patricia came over. He always liked her since middle school but because he was so nerdy she always looked over him and when they reached high school her popularity soared while his steadily declined. His father was a handyman and owned a small business doing home improvements. When Ronnie was young he would help him out in the summer, holidays and on the weekends and this is where he became an expert in repairing locks, breaking locks and a newly acquired skilled; safecracking. He started his own security and lock business hoping having his own business would impress Patricia; it didn't. When she came to him with a proposition to do a job with her and Bo, the motivation was not the money, the motivation was the possibility of hooking up with her. Everything seemed to work in his favor because she called and said she wanted to come over and asked if anybody was home; he knew that was a sign she wanted to give him some pussy, finally.

He continued cleaning up his small home in anticipation of Patricia's arrival. He made his bed and straightened up his living room quickly then went in the bathroom to wash up. The door knocked while he was in the bathroom and he got excited and grabbed a towel and wrapped it around his waist, he hoped it would be a considered a sexy move on his part when she saw him. He unlocked the door then pulled it open and Patricia was standing there looking disheveled and shaken. Her hands were behind her back and her eyes seemed to be pleading with him to help her. She was shoved inside, knocking him backwards to the floor. Muffin and Bones walked in and slammed the door.

"Oh shit Romeo! You got a thing for this bitch!" Muffin laughed paying attention to all the lit candles and sweet smelling aroma wafting through the air from the romantic ambiance that was trying to be created.

Ronnie's eyes almost popped out of his head when he saw Muffin and Bones standing in his house. He immediately knew Patricia set him up and his head shook slowly left to right. In a panicked state the towel dropped revealing his nakedness and Muffin ogled him for some seconds.

"Damn shorty, you packing a lotta beefcake with that small frame." She commented before getting down to the business at hand. "You know why we here so tell me so I can get my shit and be gone."

"I...I...didn't want to do it. Bo came and..." Ronnie stuttered.

"Save the plea, it don't matter. I want my bread, where is it!" Muffin boomed while Bones grabbed Patricia up and threw her onto the couch.

Ronnie gathered the towel around him and pointed to the back room. "It's in a safe in the hall closet. You want me to get it?"

Muffin wanted to send Bones to retrieve it but her level of trust in anyone has been removed when Junior shitted on her for Shondra so she wasn't going to chance getting played again.

"What's the combination? I'll get it myself." She said in a voice that couldn't be mistaken of who was in control.

Ronnie read out the combination and Muffin had him lead her to the safe.

"You put the combination in and I'll open it." She instructed not wanting any sudden surprises.

Ronnie put in the combination then backed away as Muffin pulled the handle down and saw all the money stacked neatly inside. She looked around the closet and grabbed a black garbage bag then handed it to Ronnie.

"Fill that shit up!" Her eyes were wide, this was the last of the money. She was doing exactly what Junior accused her of stealing but it was a forced decision on her part. There was no need to worry about the consequences because he already sent her a shout out that if she didn't give him the money he was going to do something to her.

"Let me ask you a question." Muffin said to Ronnie as he stuffed the bag with the money. He looked up at her with question marks in his pupil. "Why did y'all kill Drama though?"

He finished packing the money in the bag and stood up and looked at her. "The dog kept barking when we came in the house. Bo said the constant barking was going to wake the neighbors and they would call the police to stop the noise so he went out there and killed him." Ronnie explained.

Muffin nodded her head at his explanation then asked, "You like Pat huh?"

He looked at her with a weird expression.

"You didn't hear me?" She quizzed pointing the gun at his head.

"Yea, I like her." He replied.

"You ever fucked her?"

"No, she wasn't into me like that..."

"Not until she figured she could use you to crack that safe huh?" Muffin shook her head. "She played you. How long you been trying to fuck her? Let me guess, high school right?"

Ronnie nodded his head sheepishly.

"You probably thought she was coming over to give you some ass today huh?" Muffin shook her head. "Instead the bitch set you up to get killed. You do know that's what's gonna happen don't you?" Muffin's eyes were piercing showing truth.

"P-p-please..." He started stuttering.

"I feel sorry for you Ronnie, seriously. Seems like you caught the fucked up end of this shitty stick she handed you and you don't even look like the type of nigga that get involved with bullshit like this 'cause you woulda already been making money

off of safecracking." Muffin scratched her head and thought for a minute then smirked. "I got an offer for you that can work in your favor but not guaranteed. The only thing you're gonna be guaranteed is that you're going to be alive after it's all said and done. You ready to make a deal with the devil?"

With no choice Ronnie nodded his head in agreement and Muffin grabbed the bag and pushed him towards the living room. Patricia was sitting on the couch crying silently while Bones stood ogling her. Muffin walked over to him and dropped the bag by the door staring at Patricia and Ronnie. She looked up at Bones.

"What you wanna do with them?" She whispered in his ear covering her mouth so Patricia and Ronnie couldn't read her lips.

Bones shrugged his shoulders as he stared at the couple sitting on the couch with terrified looks plastered on their face.

Muffin was ready to jump on the road and head back to Brooklyn now that she had the money. She knew she crossed the line when she killed Bo but he was the reason behind all the shit she was going through. She laughed to herself because he wasn't as slow as she thought in the beginning; he fooled her. By the time Bo's body was found there would be an investigation but she would be long gone. She had to worry about Ronnie and Patricia. She looked at Bones and wondered what his plans were. She had just met him and appreciated him helping her but she no longer had any use for him.

"You staying in this town or you blowing?" She asked him.

"I was planning on staying here for a minute but after that body you caught I think I might just bounce too. I don't want to stick around and get caught up in that shit." He said thinking about his own future.

Muffin nodded her head. "Ok. So you wanna do, keep them breathing?"

"That's up to you. I'm just holdin' you down. We got the bread so whatever you gon' do you do. I don't want no parts of no bodies." Bones said bluntly.

"I thought you was from Brownsville nigga!" Muffin laughed. "Fuck it then! Tie both of 'em up and put them in the back room. I ain't leaving no witnesses." She said out loud, sealing the fate of Ronnie and Patricia.

Chapter 27

"Where'd you get that from?" Shondra asked Junior as he placed a shopping bag in the backseat.

"It's what that faggot owed me!" Junior remarked pulling out the parking space headed to Tompkins.

It was a silent ride to their destination, Shondra was worried about her son because he was still with Chico. She didn't think he would do anything to her son but he might play games when it came to bringing him back and she wasn't up to playing no games when it came to her son.

Junior pulled into an empty space in the parking lot and grabbed the Gucci shopping bag out the back of the car then went on the other side to open Shondra's door. She followed him into the building and when they got on the elevator she looked deep in his eyes. It was undeniable, she could still see the love he had for her. She smiled and lay her head on his shoulder and he welcomed it as he hugged her and pulled her close to him.

Inside the house Craig was in the living room having drinks with Scarlet. Junior introduced Shondra to her and they smiled warmly and shook hands then they both went into the back room where Junior immediately started in on her. He took her jacket off and kissed her passionately pushing her towards the bed. She didn't resist and put her arms out so she could catch herself and lay on the bed pulling his shirt over his head. Their passion was ignited and the flame was roaring out of control. His hands were all over her body unable to focus on any one part, he fondled her breasts, squeezed her ass and cuffed her pussy in rotation. She moaned as they both fought to get out

their clothes but without ungluing from each other. She was in her bra and panties and he was bare chested in his boxers as they paused to look at each other.

"I love the shit outta you Mooka! I'm not never gon' let you go again! That's on everything!" His words penetrated her like bullets ripping through a paper target.

Their bodies slammed into each other and intertwined like Twizzlers, his member went into her easily like a screw in a hole. She whimpered and squeezed him hard and pushed her pelvis forward. Their bodies became one, the ecstasy reached levels they both never imagined, their rhythm was in sync and their love was overflowing. Bliss. Nothing and no one could come between the connection they were making, this new bond was impenetrable and it was going to last forever.

"I want you to have my baby." Junior cried out as he grinded into her with precision and lust.

"Give it to me!" She whined. "Give it to me."

Junior thrust harder and soon his rhythm increased. Sweat dripped from their bodies as the moisture acted as a lubricant and he slid in and out of her with ease. Her moans were getting louder and the sounds caused him to pump harder and faster, his heart rate increasing. She dug her nails in his back and he let out a muffled scream from both pleasure and pain. Their bodies began to convulse as the buildup of orgasm approached. He latched onto her breast with his warm and wet tongue grinding his hips in a circular motion while his friction caused her lower region to move simultaneously with him until an eruption came from both of them and they exploded in orgasm. They both collapsed out of breath onto the bed, sprawled out like they reached the finish line after winning a marathon.

Junior propped up on elbows after regaining some energy and his breath.

"I meant what I said." He looked down at her laying across his belly.

"I know." She said looking up at him starry eyed.

"Let's go take a shower and go out there with cuz." He suggested moving her gently and grabbing a towel off the headboard.

***

"Y'all ain't leave nothing to the imagination." Craig laughed when Junior and Shondra came into the living room both wearing robes.

Shondra blushed slightly and took a seat across from Scarlet while Junior sat across from Craig. He reached for the Hennessy V.S.O.P. and poured himself a generous glass and twirled the brown liquid around in the cup before bringing it to his lips and taking a swig. His face screwed up slightly from the strong taste but after two or three swigs the flavor would be acquired.

"Looks like everything between y'all worked out." Craig acknowledged seeing they were both together.

"Looks that way." Junior said smiling.

"I know what that smile means cuz." Craig joked. "She got me smiling like that too." He said motioning to Scarlet.

Shondra sat quietly as she stared at Scarlet smiling.

"You want a drink?" Junior offered Shondra but she refused.

"So y'all made any plans? Any date when this gonna go down?" Junior directed his question to Craig referring to his engagement to Scarlet. "Oh my bad Mooka. Craig is engaged to Scarlet."

"Really? Congratulations to both of you." Shondra smiled warmly as she continued eyeing Scarlet.

"Thanks Shondra. We don't have a definite date as of yet but it might be as soon as next year." Craig informed them.

"Never thought I would see the day that this dude settle down and get married." Junior announced. "I'm glad though."

Craig nodded his head in agreement. "I gotta be honest, I never understood when people said you can't help who you love because I thought if you were strong mentally, you could control your emotions but with Scarlet," he looked over to her with loving eyes, "I ain't have no control. I love her."

"Awww." Shondra purred looking at Scarlet smiling. "Can I see your ring?" Shondra asked as Scarlet obliged and walked over with her left arm outstretched. "Wow, this shit is nice Craig."

"Five carats and that shit ain't no Bugs Bunny!" He laughed. "Nothing but the best for mine."

"It's such a good feeling to be with someone you love and trust because it completes you as a person, makes you a team. You can count on them to watch your back, hold you down and be there for you when nobody else will. It's a great feeling when you know they have your best interest at heart in all they do, right wrong or indifferent." Craig preached as Shondra looked at Junior nodding her head at Craig's last sentence. "You don't have to worry 'bout no disloyalty because y'all one and the same, what will hurt them hurts you and vice versa. You share everything, there are no secrets so there will never be any surprises. The union and bond is unbreakable, the love cannot be tested and the relationship is strengthened. Man, I love this woman for real." Craig professed sending airborne kisses to Scarlet. "This feeling she introduced to me has me widin' but in a good way. I'm just glad when the love bug did bite it was her teeth that sank in me."

"Go 'head with all that mushy shit!" Junior belted. "You-'I'm lost in love ass nigga'!" He hollered.

"Fuck you cuz." Craig laughed.

"Yo, you handle that other thing too?" Craig asked.

"Yea, I need to holla at you 'bout that real quick." Junior said grabbing his drink off the table and walking towards the back. Craig excused himself and followed him to the back room.

"What's up?" Craig asked.

"I got the bread and some work outta the muhfucka." Junior pulled out the Gucci bag and emptied everything onto the bed.

"How much is that?" Craig was pointing at the money.

"If I was to guess that's about $30,000."

"And the work?" Craig questioned.

"That was all of it bagged up." Junior did a quick count and guessed how much it was. "Probably a big eighth left."

"What you gonna do?" Craig asked seriously.

"I was thinking I'll get two bricks from you and one on consignment. Go back down there, body that bitch Muffin for violating and finish that muhfucka KB off then bubble out and get my money back right then go from there."

Craig scratched his head. "That's your plan? That shit sounds like some put together shit with no real agenda my dude. Stop and think for a minute. When you first got into this shit I told you this game has no loyalty and that you couldn't trust nobody. Your supposed man Kendu flipped on you and tried to get you murked, your first mistake but you survived. Then I told you that since you had muhfuckas looking to body you that if you still wanted to make money you had to have in you to hustle for life and eliminate all threats and keep your name relevant in the streets. Your man La flipped on you too and you escaped that shit 'cause of that shorty you was fucking with, Muffin. You got shit twisted with Shondra then went to your other bitch thinking she was your ride or die not knowing she had another agenda, your money. You was all in your feelings with her and I told you love is pain because your guards are down when you're emotionally caught up. You went down south and blew up again but karma is a mother fucker and you run into old deadly beef and you try to handle it but you get clapped up and gotta spend months in the hospital putting all your shit on standby. The bitch you think you love seizes the opportunity and says fuck you and goes out on her own and

uses the shit you taught her, to do it. She watched you and copied your style knowing she would be successful in her takeover. Now you're sitting here with revenge on your mind and you ready to take it to war with a body count.

Cuz you're not that same naive li'l dude from a few years ago. You don' grown up in the game, you don' survived most shit niggas fall for. You weathered most of the storm, this game is unpredictable, there is no rules, no refs, no winners - everyone loses one way or another." Craig put his hand on his shoulder. "I know you love Shondra kid, I see it in your eyes. You have to learn from your experiences. I'm not saying you ain't cut out for this shit no more, what I'm saying is this - Invest that twenty gees with me, take over three of the workers over here and bubble that way. Take the rest of the bread, go find a nice crib for you and your girl, away from the hood and all the bullshit and set up your family there. You gave out of town hustle a try but it's run its course; time to move on. That beef with homie, leave it down there and you'll bump into shorty again and when you do you, that's when you handle her. You supposed to be looking for longevity and stability fam, that much I can offer you here. Think about it."

"I hear you cuz and that shit sound good but the reason I went down there in the first place was because of those homicide D's looking for me for that body. That shit don't just go away 'cause I was MIA for a year." Junior said.

"Sounds like an excuse fam." Craig stated seriously. "I can get you lawyered up and find out what kind of evidence they have on you. If you know of anyone who can put that body on you then you know what you gotta do 'cause in order for them to charge you with it, they need witness testimony and dead men don't testify. And as far as anything you left down south, you can leave that shit there, whatever it is can be replaced, they never make one of anything."

"You make it sound simple cuz but there's some other shit I need to tell you." Junior's face frowned.

"Tell me." Craig responded with sincerity in his voice.

"When I went to Shondra crib she told me she had a baby." Junior started and he saw the surprised reaction on Craig's face. "Yea, but the fucked up part is the baby is by that muhfucka Chico!" Junior's teeth gritted unconsciously.

"Wow!" Craig lamented.

"I know. That shit crushed me so when I saw scrams outside he came over to me like everything was gravy and he hit me with some bullshit. Muffin been hitting him with work too cuz! She used my name to make it happen!"

Craig nodded his head. "I told you."

"He didn't know she was doing that shit behind my back so he thought all was forgiven with that bread he owed me. I told him no and to get the rest of my bread. He had the baby with him but when he left he was taking too long to come back so I figured he mighta made a phone call and told her what's up so I dipped into the building and caught him coming out the elevator, took him upstairs, got the rest of the bread and yayo then took him on the roof whipped him out decently then tied him up. I don't care nothing 'bout this nigga cuz, I hate this dude and I want to slump him out but that's her baby father. I don't know what kind of repercussions will come back to me if I leave her son without his pops, you feel me?"

"That's a hard call cuz. You don't have to body duke though because if the nigga really a marshmallow he will stay out your way." Craig reasoned.

"I think shit different when it comes to his seed, I think his heart grew since having him. You know what I'm saying? It's like he won't bust a grape in a fruit fight if me and him beefing but when it comes to his blood, he might go all out just on GP." Junior surmised.

"That's true, muhfuckas grow balls when they have someone to live and die for." Craig cosigned. "What you gonna do as far as he's concerned?"

"I just want scrams to be outta the picture. I'll try and be diplomatic first just for the sake of his seed but if he don't agree then I gotta make him a memory." Junior stated bluntly.

"That'll have your DNA all over it. No one will second guess you were a part of that then what? Ain't no happily ever after with her if you move like that." Craig challenged.

"Ain't no happily ever after if he still breathing either!" Junior said with attitude. "I don't know what I'm gonna do, it's a lot to think about but I know I wanna be with Shondra and if that means Chico got get put on a milk box then that's what the fuck it's gonna be."

"Ok cuz but take some time to think about everything. My offer stands and I think it's the best solution to your immediate problems right now." Craig said opening the room door preparing to leave.

Junior was shocked to see Scarlet standing by the door.

"What's wrong baby?" Craig asked lovingly.

"Nuthin'. I ask you if you no drinking again no more. If yes, we go to store for more." She said in her fucked up English.

"Nah baby, we have mad liquor in here. Look in the cabinet in the kitchen over the stove, it's a liquor store in there." Craig laughed as he and Junior followed her to back into the kitchen. Junior went and sat down next to Shondra and draped his arm around her.

"You aiight?" He asked gazing into her eyes.

"I'm groovy. Just waiting on you." She answered rubbing under his chin with her fingers. "His girl look mad familiar but I can't place her face."

"She used to be the neighborhood skeezer but this muhfucka gonna wife her." Junior shook his head. "I don't know what she did to him but he way gon' off that shit, talking 'bout love." Junior chuckled.

"Hmmm. I can't remember but I know I know her from somewhere." Shondra said thinking hard.

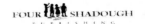

Junior grabbed the liquor and poured himself a nice serving. "That bitch blind and can't talk."

"What you talkin' 'bout?" Shondra asked giggling.

"She came in the back room talking about the liquor was almost gone and the shit right where we left it." Junior cackled.

"That's weird." Shondra answered looking over at the kitchen at Craig hugging Scarlet while she stared at her.

Chapter 28

Muffin looked out the window of the hotel. There weren't many people out since it was so early in the morning. She stared aimlessly at the few people who looked like they were on their way to work or school. She closed the curtain then turned around and sat on the bed. The bag fell off the bed and she reached down and picked it up and put it back on the bed. She zipped it open and took out all the money that was stuffed inside and dumped it out. She decided to count and stack it neatly since it was thrown haphazardly into her bag because she was in such a rush to leave. The only neat stacks were the ones she got from Ronnie. She started separating the bills as she counted the money out, she had no idea how much of it she and Bones had gotten back that was stolen from Junior's safe. She smiled to herself because she was able to come out on top with all the money although she took a major beating from Bo to get it.

When Bones tied Ronnie and Patricia up Muffin already knew what she was going to do. After they were all in the room she told Bones to undress Patricia since Ronnie only had a towel covering him. As he undressed her he became aroused by her beautifully stacked body. He fondled and groped her as he lay her on the bed then he turned to look at Muffin as if asking could he get his nut off. Muffin nodded and he jumped on her eagerly and started fucking her like a mad man. The rape lasted every bit of ninety seconds before Bones groaned like a wounded bear then shook as he lay inside of her after cumming. Patricia lay in shock, she was non-responsive almost as if she was in a coma. She stared blankly at the ceiling and that's when

Muffin remembered her telling her she never had dick inside her before.

Bones got up and pulled his pants up and backed away breathing heavily like he put in major work. Muffin went over to Ronnie and untied him then whispered in his ear.

"He don't have his gun. If you want to live when I untie you, you better go over there and fight him for raping your girl, do you understand?"

When he was untied, he charged Bones who was totally off guard. He hit him with rights and lefts that literally did no damage whatsoever. Bones grabbed him and struck him with three hard rights that immediately burst his lips and had blood shooting from them. Ronnie fell down to the ground and Bones pounded his face in, then Muffin screamed for him to stop. Bones was in a rage and continued pummeling him then finally stopped and stood up winded. Ronnie rolled around on the ground writhing in pain and Bones was about to stomp him but Muffin stood in front of him and pulled the trigger and a slug entered his chest. His eyes bulged and he gasped for air then she raised the gun and squeezed again this time the slug entered his forehead and he fell backwards. She released the clip and took out the rest of the bullets then slid the slide back and extracted the bullet in the head. She quickly wiped the gun off, went over to Bones and put the gun in his hand and pressed his fingers onto it then turned to Ronnie who was struggling to get to his feet.

"Here." Muffin stuffed the gun in his hand as he stood erect. "He came in looking to rob you and stole all you had in the safe then raped your girl. He had y'all at gunpoint and you fought with him and you got the gun and you shot him twice. Tell that story you won't go to jail, you'll be a fucking hero." She looked at Patricia laying on the bed. "What you do with that bitch is up to you. I got my money and I kept my promise, you still alive."

Muffin grabbed the guns and the bag full of money and jumped on the highway immediately, she wasn't taking any chances. When she made it to Brooklyn and went to a hotel instead of going home because she needed to figure out what she was going to do.

After counting and stacking the money neatly she had $289,505.00. She had absolutely no idea what she was going to do with all that money but knew it was more than she ever had.

She had experienced in two years what most dudes never experienced in a life time. She was going to miss Junior but she wasn't going to chance trying to see him, I mean she did take his money. She had no plans all she knew was that she didn't want to deal with drugs anymore, it was too unpredictable and changed her life forever, it had turned her out like a pimp does a young innocent promiscuous girl.

She packed the money neatly in the bag then looked in the mirror. She sighed and rubbed her growing belly. She had beaten the odds and got out of the shit, she was scott free. She smiled and would never forget what Junior had taught her, "This Game Has No Loyalty!"

Chapter 29

Junior and Shondra pulled up on the side of her building. He was dropping her off to pick up her son. They kissed passionately then she got out of the car. He watched as she walked around the corner to the front of her building.

Shondra went into her house and immediately called Chico's crib.

"Hello?" She said when she heard someone pick up the phone.

"Hola? Shondra?" His grandmother asked in her broken English.

"Yes, is Chico there?" She asked.

"Yes holy on, please." She said struggling with her English. Just then Shondra remembered where she knew Scarlet from, she was Chico's cousin. She remembered she saw him talking to her one day and thought she was one of the girls he was fucking and he briefly introduced her as his cousin. She didn't remember her being unable to speak English well, in fact, she remembered her speaking English just as good as anybody else. Chico had told her she was a high priced hoe and had come to see his grandmother because she wasn't feeling well at that time.

"Yea, what the fuck you want bitch?" Chico crowed into the phone.

"Who the fuck you talking to muhfucka!" Shondra shot back.

"You! You dirty bitch! I know you fucking with Junior! Tell that muhfucka this shit ain't over neither! Trust me, I'm

272

gonna get my fucking money back!" Chico screamed in the phone.

"What? Where my son Chico?" Shondra asked nervously.

"You told me not to have my son around no bitches playing house. So you and that nigga not gon' play house with my son bitch. Know that!"

"Fuck you, I'm coming to get my fucking son." Shondra barked and hung up the phone.

She headed out the door, her priority was getting her son from him just in case he wanted to start acting stupid. She made it across the street and was upstairs knocking on his doors in minutes. When he opened the door she was shocked to see his face. It looked like someone beat him in the face with a sledgehammer; it was a horrid mess.

"I came to get my son, is he ready?" She asked trying to ignore his gruesome mask.

"I shouldn't give him to you!" He screamed. "You really think you and that muhfucka 'bout to play house with my fucking son! Not gon' happen bitch! He gon' have to kill me!" Chico bellowed.

"First of all, you not my man so whoever I'm with is none of your business! You're only his father, that's it! And if you don't get my son I promise you you'll never see him again after I call the police and they take him outta your fucking house!" Shondra threatened.

"Yea, I know you'll tell the police, you told on the same nigga you trying to play house with now. You a stupid bitch! He bounced with another bitch and left you out here all fucked up! I was the one that took care of your bum ass after that. You forgot that shit too huh!" He walked away not giving her chance to say anything in rebuttal.

Shondra stood in the hallway heated at all the shit that was just thrown at her. She shifted her weight from one leg to the other as she waited for him to bring her son. Then the door

opened and Chico wheeled the stroller out into the hallway then handed her their son then abruptly slammed the door in her face. She kissed him a thousand times in his face before putting him in the stroller and rolling away down the hallway.

***

Junior watched as Shondra came out of Chico's building pushing the baby stroller. He didn't leave when he dropped her off because he believed she was going to have problems getting her son back because he was sure Chico was going to do the bitch shit and tell her everything that happened. When she got inside the building he got out the car and went through the back of the building and caught her just as she was wheeling the stroller through the door.

"Ay yo!" He yelled out before she closed the door.

She turned around startled and was shocked to see Junior standing in the lobby.

"What you doing back here, what happened?" She questioned.

"I thought you was going to have a problem with that bitch nigga so I stuck around just to make sure." Junior said as he climbed the three steps to her door.

"Now why would you think that?" She asked pursing her lips in a small smirk.

"I know he squealed like a bitch but he owed me money and gave a little resistance so I tipped him up a little bit." Junior said stepping inside and closing the door while she took her son out of the stroller.

"That was no tipping up, looked like he tapped out Junior." She unlocked the straps and was about to pull him out then turned to him. "Oh, you remember what I said about your cousin's fiancé, what's her name again? Oh Scarlet right?"

"Yea, what about her?" Junior asked focusing on her directly.

"I know where I know her from. That's Chico's cousin." She informed him.

"You sure?"

"I seen her over here with him and he introduced her to me as his cousin. She was over here visiting his grandmother when she was sick."

"Small world. You think she remembered you?" Junior asked.

"I kinda think so because she was staring at me too. I'm sure she knows who I am."

"Aah shit." Junior started thinking. "When I was talking to Craig in the room I mentioned that nigga's name and when I opened the door she was standing there. She mighta been ear hustling and overheard our conversation. I don't know how much she heard but that's why she was all mumbling and shit." Junior surmised.

"Oh and when I spoke to her, she spoke perfect English." Shondra added.

"Get the fuck outta here!" Junior shook his head. "Let me call this muhfucka right now and let him know what the deal is." He walked to the wall phone and picked it up.

While he was dialing Craig's number, Shondra finished taking her son out of the stroller and took him in the back to her room to undress and inspect him.

"Yo cuz." Junior said to Craig when he picked up the phone. "I gotta holla at you about some shit I heard. It's not confirmed but the source is legit and can be trusted."

"Ok talk." Craig said sitting up in his chair.

"Is your girl around?"

"Yea, she getting ready to make a move. What's up Junior?" Craig was getting anxious.

"Nah, can she hear your conversation?" Junior stressed.

"No man, she in the room getting ready." Craig said agitated. "Spill it man!"

"Ok, check it. When Shondra was over there she was telling me that Scarlet looked familiar to her but she couldn't remember from where. She just told me where she remembered her from. She said she's Chico's cousin and she was introduced to her and said she was sure she was talking regular not like how she talk around you like she came over her on a inner tube and shit."

"Fuck outta here!" Craig exclaimed.

"I know how you feel about her cuz but I had to tell you so you can check into it yourself. I didn't think nothing about her standing by the bedroom door when we was talking 'bout that lame but now that Shondra told me that, her reaction was kind of suspect. She was mumbling 'bout she wanted to see if you wanted to get more L-I-Q but when I went back in the living room the bottle we was drinking was still where we left it - damn near full. You feel me?" Junior made his point.

"Yea cuz. You right, I gotta check this shit out myself. I appreciate the heads us fam." Craig said sincerely. "I'll let you know if she's diseased or not."

"Say no more man. Handle yours." Junior said before ending the conversation.

***

Craig hung up the phone and held his head in the palm of his hands. He didn't want to believe Scarlet was playing him, not after he warned her what would happen to her. He was in the drug game but one thing he didn't do was play games. Life to him was way too short for that. She introduced him to love, something he swore against because of this very issue he had to face. He walked into the bedroom and Scarlet was just finishing putting on the rest of her make up.

"You 'bout ready baby?" Craig asked her.

"Jes baby. I ready going soon." She replied in her fucked up English.

"You sure you don't want me to drop you off?" Craig offered rubbing her ass softly.

"No papi. I fine by with myself." She babbled incoherently.

"Ok. You have everything you need? You need any more money?"

"No, no. I fine baby. I thank you."

"Ok, I'm gonna carry your bags to the door until you ready to leave." Craig said grabbing two suitcases and pulling them to the door.

He breathed out heavily then walked to Junior's room and went inside closing the door behind him. He opened the closet and looked inside the Gucci bag, it was empty. He looked down and shook his head left to right slowly. He couldn't believe what was happening. He was in love with Scarlet, he broke his cardinal rule for her. He closed the closet and walked out the room slowly. Scarlet came out his room and looked gorgeous standing there in front him smiling. He grabbed her close to him and kissed her passionately.

"I call cab he being here in ten minutes. I wait downstairs now." She told him.

"No problem. I'll help you to the elevator with your stuff." Craig grabbed her bags and opened the front door and pulled the suitcases in the hallway then pressed the elevator. She hugged and kissed him and his heart became heavy. The elevator opened and she boarded with a smile as Craig placed both bags inside. He waved at her and the doors started to close then she put her pocket book in between the doors. The doors opened and she stepped out and looked at Craig and said, "I love you so much Craig." It sounded sincere and the look in her eyes didn't deny that truth then the doors closed.

Craig turned and rushed back into the house and made a phone call. He sat in his chair by the window and looked down at the parking lot. His phone rang again and he picked it up and spoke briefly then walked to his room and went to his safe. He opened it and tears immediately escaped his eyes. He now knew how Junior felt when he came home from the hospital. He left it open and looked in the closet then pulled out the drawers, majority of Scarlet's clothes was still in there. He went back to the window in the kitchen and watched as a green and white cab pulled up into the parking lot. He saw Scarlet pulling the two heavy suitcases to the cab and watched as the driver got out and popped the trunk once he saw her coming towards the vehicle. Before she could put the luggage inside the trunk two guys walked up on her and grabbed her by her arms. She tussled with them then the cab driver came over to assist her until one of the guys pulled gun and waved him off. He jumped in his cab and backed out of the parking lot recklessly. The two guys forcefully dragged her back to the building while another guy grabbed the bags and followed behind the trio.

Craig went to his front door and unlocked it and sat back down in his kitchen and poured himself a much needed drink. He heard the door knock about a minute later.

"Come in!" He barked.

The door opened and Scarlet was shoved inside. She was screaming loudly in Spanish, no doubt cuss words. Craig never got up from where he was sitting. The suitcases were brought in.

"Where you want these at?" The guy asked.

"Pull them over here by me." Craig instructed.

He placed them right in front of Craig and then he disappeared out the door. The other guys were still holding on to Scarlet who continued going off in Spanish. Craig slowly got up from his chair and walked over to her then slapped her viciously. She shut up instantly and all of a sudden her eyes began to water like the slap explained to her what she already knew. Her lips quivered.

"Why Scarlet? I just want to know why?" He asked softly.

"Why what papi?" She asked.

Another thunderous slap knocked spit and blood from her mouth.

"I just want to know why Scarlet, why?"

Her head lowered then she looked back up at Craig.

"I didn't plan to do this, it just happened this way." She said in perfect English.

"So is Chico your cousin?" He asked.

"Yea, that's why I was getting out of here. When I saw that bitch I knew it would be a matter of time before she blew my kool so I left before it jumped off."

"But you was leaving me fo' dead. You took everything, you ain't leave me shit." Craig's eyes watered but no tears fell.

"I was supposed to take everything. You know that." She said softly.

"I know but I thought you loved me. By taking everything, that's how I know you didn't." Craig said nodding his head to the guys who were holding her by the arms. "Don't let her suffer. I want it clean but I don't want her body found." He walked over to her and stared in her eyes then leaned in slowly for a kiss but instead he hocked spit in her face. "I told you don't play me bitch! Now you dead!"

***

The red lights from the ambulance brought back memories of when he was shot. Junior helped Shondra and the paramedics load her son inside the truck. Junior had no idea he was severely anemic but was going to go with Shondra for support. She was a nervous wreck and he felt her pain and wished he could do something to ease her worries. She was crying uncontrollably and it broke his heart. He tried to comfort her but she was too distraught. The paramedic informed him what hospital they were going to and suggested he follow behind them since they would have the sirens blaring.

He followed behind them closely hoping her son's health would be ok. The ambulance pulled into the parking bay and Junior pulled over on the street and parked quickly. He jumped out the vehicle and ran over the paramedics as they wheeled the baby into the hospital's emergency room. Shondra stayed close asking a plethora of question as they took him off the ambulance gurney and put him on a hospital bed. There were three doctors who immediately came and checked his vitals and questioned Shondra so they could be up to speed about his condition. She was being as helpful as possible answering all questions thoroughly but she had a dejected look. After the doctors finished questioning her they ran a series of test.

Shondra stood at the head of the bed rubbing his little hand and Junior stood at the foot of the bed helpless. Fifteen minutes later two of the doctors came back to Shondra.

"Mommy." One of them said. "We're gonna have to give him a blood transfusion to replace his platelets. We have blood but we usually ask the parents would they prefer their own blood."

"Well I'm anemic too." Shondra said quickly.

The doctor looked at Junior and asked. "Maybe daddy will give blood, is he anemic?"

"Oh I'm not the pops." Junior replied.

"Oh I'm sorry." The doctor said.

"Not a problem." Shondra spoke up. "I can call the father and see if he'll come down. Do we have time?"

"How long?" The doctor questioned.

"If he's home it shouldn't be no longer than fifteen minutes." Shondra assured him.

"Ok, that's fine. I'll come back in about twenty minutes to check." The doctor said then walked off.

"I hope you don't mind Junior but I'm only doing this for my son." Shondra explained.

"Come on Mooka. I know that don't worry about it. This about your son, I ain't gon' act up. Matter fact I'm gon' go in the waiting room when he get here."

"I'm glad you understand. I still love you I'm just worried about my son, that's all."

"I know and I love you too, more than anything. That's why I'm here, nothing's changed." Junior said seriously.

He hugged her tightly and smiled. She went and made the phone call while Junior waited by the foot of the bed until she came back. She returned five minutes later and said he was on his way then took her position back at the head of the bed.

Twenty five minutes passed and Chico walked into the hospital talking loudly asking for his son. Shondra waved him over and when he saw Junior he screwed his face up but didn't say anything to him, instead he took it out on Shondra.

"I told you y'all not gon' play house with my son."

Junior got up from the chair he was sitting on.

"Ain't nobody playing house faggot but watch your mouth when you talking to her. I ain't gon' warn you again." Junior whispered to him so no one else could hear then directed his attention to Shondra. "I'll be in the waiting room, let me know how everything works out."

Junior walked out the emergency room and went to the waiting room. While in there he had time to think about a lot of things. There was no way he could kill Chico or not allow him around his son because he needed to be in his life. He thought about the offer Craig extended him, it was really a sweet deal and he and Shondra could start off somewhere new like he promised her before he went down south. If he was going to be in NY then he definitely needed to handle the charges he had hanging over his head, he would get one of Craig's high powered lawyers and with no witnesses the most he would have to pay is a fine or do a couple of months for missing court. Then there was his beef with KB. As long as he didn't go back down south and he didn't bump into him in NY, it would eventually

fizzle out but at the moment it was touch and go. Changing his life was on the forefront of his mind and Shondra was the best part; his motivation.

Junior looked up and Shondra was standing in the entrance of the waiting room like she was in a trance. Junior thought the worse and shook his head and she shook hers slowly too. He bit his bottom lip and rushed over to her, pain in his eyes.

"What happened?" He asked softly.

"His blood..." She couldn't finish because she sounded like she was hyperventilating.

"Fuck! I'm sorry Mooka." He held her close.

"His blood...it doesn't match!"

Junior didn't know if he understood what she was saying. Shondra grabbed his hand and lead him to the doctor. He followed the doctor off to another room.

"We'll need your I.D. sir." The doctor said.

"I don't have my I.D. on me but my name is Lionel Chambers." Junior told him.

"Ok, you have to fill this out Mr. Chambers." The doctor produced a document of consent.

"No problem but please call me Junior." Junior told him.

"Ok." He chuckled as a nurse walked in and he instructed her on what to do.

After they drew his blood he was taken back to where Shondra and the baby were.

"You did it?" She asked when she saw him.

"Of course." He smiled wide. "What that faggot ass nigga say or do when he found out his blood didn't match?"

"He was hurt and he just left. He didn't say much." Shondra replied.

"Fuck him!" Junior said walking up and looking at the baby. "What you feeling like?" He asked her.

"If he not Chico's, I know he's yours! I'm so excited!" Shondra was smiling ear to ear.

The doctor came over to where they were standing.

"Ok we have a match so we're going start the transfusion. Mommy it's going to take anywhere from one to three hours ok? You can be right here while it's being done and once it's done, he'll be able to go home after we check everything to make sure he's fine."

"He's my son! I'm his father!" Junior screamed out so loud everyone looked at him. "Aww man this is the best thing that could ever happen!" He and Shondra celebrated briefly until the doctors came over to do the procedure.

After two and a half hours the transfusion was completed. Junior and Shondra were awaken by the doctor.

"Mommy, Daddy." He said addressing them both. "Everything was successful. We've checked his vitals and he'll be able to go home as soon as one of you sign the discharge papers."

"You go 'head and sign it daddy." Shondra said yawning and smiling at the same time.

"I like how that sounds." Junior smirked as he stretched when he stood up and walked over to the desk.

The nurse finished printing the paper work out and passed it to Junior. He was about to sign and saw something that confused him.

"I think y'all made a mistake and put my name instead of his."

The nurse took the papers and looked it over and pushed it back to him.

"No it's right. His name is Lionel Brown."

"Oh shit!" Junior signed the discharge papers and rushed over to Shondra. "You named him after me?"

"He's your son. I felt it in my heart."

They dressed Lionel and prepared to take him home.

***

The cab pulled up in front of Shondra's house and she exited then Junior came out holding his son, Lionel. Junior dug into his pocket and passed Shondra some bills to pay the fare. Another cab pulled up behind the one they were in and when the door opened Gloria and KB stepped out. By the time each couple noticed on another it was too late, they all stood frozen. It was reminiscent to the barbershop standoff. Junior eyed KB dangerously while Shondra and Gloria stared at each other. After thirty seconds or more Gloria spoke.

"You had a baby?" She asked Shondra.

"Yea girl, a boy." Shondra replied, her eyes welling up. "I missed you Glo'."

"I missed you too!" They walked then ran to each other and embraced, tears of a broken friendship bursting from their eyes.

Junior and KB never moved, they stood like soldiers waiting for someone to make a funny move. Gloria and Shondra was crying so hard they forgot about the tension between their men. They stopped and looked at each other then Shondra walked over to Junior to take Lionel out of his hand and he hurriedly gave him to her. Gloria looked at Junior and remembered him shooting the barbershop up. Then she looked back at KB and grabbed his hand and looked at Shondra.

"Please, can we end the beef between y'all right now? Please?"

Shondra added her plea. "Junior we have a beautiful son that needs you."

KB and Junior still didn't. Gloria looked up at KB.

"I wanted to leave from down there because I'm pregnant! You're going to be a father Keith." Gloria said.

Shondra walked over to KB slowly and held Lionel out to him. KB looked at him then took him in his arms. Junior slowly walked over to him and held his hand out. They shook hands ending the beef that started over three years ago. They all hugged each other then walked into the building.

FOUR  SHADOUGH
PUBLISHING

"I'm glad I grew up!" Junior said. "I have a son, I'm a father, I have a reason to live. From now on I ain't playin'...NO MORE GAMES!"

Other Titles by JUNE powered by FourShadough Publishing

Victimized - Buchanan's Secret
Paperback and Ebook

Ebooks

Frankie Blanco
The Council
The Council II - Death Sentence
Money Can't Buy Love
Red Sunday

Young Adult Fiction
Lil Mz. Understood by Harmony Miller
Mass Paperback and Ebook

Contact FourShadough Publishing
fourshadoughpublishing@gmail.com

Website
www.fourshadoughpublishing.com

Twitter
Jun4Shadough

Instagram
4shadough

Facebook Page
www.facebook.com/FourShadoughPublishing
www.facebook.com/june.miller.10

CPSIA information can be obtained
at www.ICGtesting.com
Printed in the USA
LVOW10s1752120517
534313LV00009B/419/P